d
d

man. "That's the man I stabbed that...," she insisted indignantly.

"Excuse me, ma'am. Step back please," the officer requested.

"That's my aunt," Helma told the officer.

"Could you get her out of the way?" the bristly little policeman asked.

"Excuse me," Helma said, "but if my aunt says she recognizes the dead man, wouldn't it be wiser to investigate her claim than to disparage her? . . . Aunt Em, could you tell the officer about the man who tried to steal your purse at the airport?"

"I already did. There he is on the ground, flat out." She shook her head and made *tsk-tsk*ing sounds. "I wonder what he tried to do this time that somebody killed him."

"You said you stabbed him?" the officer asked.

"But not like *that*," Aunt Em, said pointing to the body. "With a hat pin."

Helma was on her knees beside the dead man again. Just perceptibly, in the fleshy part of his arm, were three holes, one of them still flecked with blood.

*Other Miss Zukas Mysteries by*
**Jo Dereske**
*from Avon Twilight*

# FINAL NOTICE

## A MISS ZUKAS MYSTERY

# JO DERESKE

AVON

TWILIGHT

AVON BOOKS, INC.
1350 Avenue of the Americas
New York, New York 10019

Copyright © 1998 by Jo Dereske
Inside cover author photo © Teresa Salgado Photography
Published by arrangement with the author
Visit our website at http://www.AvonBooks.com/Twilight
Library of Congress Catalog Card Number: 98-93123
ISBN: 0-380-78245-6

First Avon Twilight Printing: November 1998

AVON TWILIGHT TRADEMARK REG. U.S. PAT. OFF. AND IN OTHER COUNTRIES, MARCA REGISTRADA, HECHO EN U.S.A.

Printed in the U.S.A.

WCD 10 9 8 7 6 5 4 3 2 1

*For the cousins*

# CONTENTS

vii

# CONTENTS

## ❦ chapter one ❦

# EMERGENCY
# PHONE CALLS

**O**n Thursday afternoon, when the phone call came, Miss Helma Zukas was refereeing an argument between two Bellehaven Public Library patrons who each accused the other of hogging the Internet.

"I'm almost finished," said the suited middle-aged man hulked in front of one of the six Internet computers in the busy reference area, scrolling through bright lines of text. "Besides, I started ten minutes late."

"But I signed up for two o'clock," said the young man in khaki shorts and a faded t-shirt shifting from Birkenstock to Birkenstock behind him. He tapped his watch, which had a strap repaired with duct tape. "It's four minutes after two."

"It is now time to end your session," Helma politely but firmly told the middle-aged man. "Internet periods are scheduled in half-hour increments. It's your responsibility to begin and end your session on time. Please relinquish the computer."

"It's not my fault," the man complained, still scrolling, eyes on the screen. "I couldn't find a parking place; there aren't enough spaces in front of the library. Otherwise, I would have been here on time. You owe me ten more minutes." He glanced at the t-shirted young man. "It won't hurt him to wait."

"I understand your frustration," Helma said, calling on verbal skills learned in the Confrontation Defusion refresher workshop the library staff had been forced to attend six weeks ago, "but your time is up." She glanced toward the reference desk and, not seeing Ms. Moon, the library director, in the vicinity, leaned closer to the man and added in a lower but much firmer voice, "Vacate the computer immediately or I'm turning it off."

The man stood abruptly, nearly knocking over his chair, and turned to glare at her. "I'm lodging a complaint," he said. "What's your name?"

"Wilhelmina Zukas," Helma told him, beckoning the young man forward. "It's Miss. You'll find forms at the circulation desk."

"Thanks," the young man told Helma as he sat down, his eyes already drawn hungrily to the screen.

Since the Bellehaven Public Library had initiated Internet access for the public a month earlier, the librarians had watched in dismay as their roles as information providers degenerated to settling quarrels, scheduling half-hour sessions as if they were receptionists in a busy dental office, replacing paper and dealing with computer glitches, not to mention fielding complaints from other patrons who were offended by what some Internet users were viewing on tax-funded computer screens.

"Helma," a voice said close to her ear. She turned to meet the long face of Harley Woodworth, the social sciences librarian.

"Yes?" she asked, glancing at the reference desk where three patrons awaited her attention, one of them balancing a toddler on her hip who was chewing the corner of a library book.

Harley worked his jaws and opened his mouth while holding his lips closed before he answered. "There's a phone call for you. I told him you were working the reference desk, but he said it was important."

"*Labas*, Helma," another voice interrupted.

Helma nodded to Bronus, a summer school graduate student at the college who'd appeared in the library after hearing Helma defend the library's overdue fine policies on a local radio show. Bronus had recognized her surname as being Lithuanian, too, and now went out of his way to greet Helma in Lithuanian whenever he spotted her.

Helma returned to the reference desk and reached for the phone but Harley shook his head. "You'd better take it at your desk." He sighed, his narrow chest heaving. "It's bad news."

"Who's calling?" she asked him.

"He didn't say," Harley told her, on his face an expression of dread curiosity.

"Then how do you know it's bad news?" Helma asked.

Harley Woodworth, who George Melville called Hardly Worthit, lived a life of gloomy expectation. No disaster or disease was too spectacular or too remote to contemplate. The worse the news, the brighter his eyes grew, the more sanguine his demeanor.

"He asked for 'Billie' first," Harley told her. "Anybody who'd call you Billie instead of Helma *must* be the bearer of bad news."

But Helma was already on her way to her cubicle in the crowded workroom, Harley and Internet users forgotten. Only two men still occasionally slipped and called her Billie, and they were both her brothers: Bruce in Michigan and John in Iowa.

The brother on the phone was Bruce. "What's happened?'' Helma asked. Around her in the workroom, voices stilled, their attention caught by her tone of voice.

''Nobody's dead,'' he hurriedly assured her.

''But . . .'' Helma began for him.

''It's Aunt Em,'' Bruce said.

Aunt Em was Helma's favorite aunt, her father's oldest sister, the eldest of six siblings, cruelly the last one left alive. Aunt Em was eighty-seven years old and still lived alone on her farm in Scoop River, Michigan, and this summer, after sixteen years of coaxing, she'd finally agreed to embark on her first airplane trip to visit Helma in Washington state. The visit was scheduled to begin next week during a period well researched by Helma, containing a July date on which it had rained only seven times in one hundred years.

''She had some kind of brain seizure,'' Bruce told her; he sounded weary, exhausted. ''The doctor called it a 'brain incident.' ''

''Is she all right?''

Bruce hesitated just long enough for Helma to feel a weighty ache in her heart. ''She's dazed,'' he told her. ''A passerby spotted her holding a wooden spoon and walking in circles in her front yard. Right now she doesn't remember any of it.''

''What is a 'brain incident'?'' Helma asked. ''A stroke?''

''I think the doc doesn't know exactly *what* happened so he gave it a catch-all label. He reminded us about five times that 'She is eighty-seven, after all.' ''

A page leaned into the cubicle and handed Helma her mail. Helma took it and distractedly dropped it on her desk.

''Is she in the hospital?'' she asked Bruce.

''For now,'' he said. Again Helma heard the hesitation.

''Bruce,'' she said, ''will you please just explain Aunt Em's condition?''

''Doctor Johnston won't release her to go home,'' Bruce

told her, his voice smoothing out as if he'd rehearsed these words. "She can't live alone any more. Not that she can't take care of herself, but she's a little . . . unstable. He claims it's a disaster in the making."

"Will she recover?" Helma asked. Aunt Em had been Helma's refuge during her formative years growing up with her untidy Lithuanian family. More reasonable than her boisterous, overemotional and oversensitive siblings, Aunt Em had offered Helma wise counsel, calm and orderly weekends. When Helma left Scoop River to attend college and library school Aunt Em had mailed her comfort foods: *kugelis* and *suris*, the Lithuanian white cheese, along with "little ear" cookies, everything packaged in brown paper and neatly addressed.

"He doesn't know. He says there will be some improvement but beyond 'some,' he just can't predict." Bruce sighed and in the background Helma heard the clock that hung in her brother's studio chime quarter past the hour. "I wanted to talk to you first because you've always been closest to Aunt Em. You know how the hospitals push everybody through these days. Heart surgery one day, home the next. The doc recommended placing her in Maple Farm."

"No," Helma said without hesitation. Maple Farm was a retirement home, not a nursing home but a group home, one step prior.

"Helma," Bruce said patiently, "she can't live alone. We'd take her if we had the room."

It wasn't a lame excuse. Bruce and his wife and their two sons lived in a two-bedroom home. Even if there were room, it would be too chaotic for Aunt Em, who'd always sought out and lived a quiet life.

"Send her here," Helma said, again without hesitation. "I'll take care of her until she recovers."

"There's no guarantee she *will* recover," Bruce said, his

voice touched by panic. "You don't understand. Aunt Em's behavior is unpredictable right now. You can't . . ."

"She was scheduled to visit next week anyway," Helma said. She sat taller in her chair, picked up the mail on her desk and realigned the envelopes, edge to edge. "I'm prepared for her. I can do it."

# ❧ chapter two ❧

# DISRUPTED PLANS

"**B**ruce called to tell me about poor Emily," Helma's mother Lillian said, an hour after Helma hung up from making the final arrangements with her brother. "She should have had children."

Helma switched the phone to her other ear and rose to grab a pen that was precariously balanced on the edge of her desk. Across the bookshelves that separated her cubicle from Harley Woodworth's, she glimpsed the dour librarian comparing spots on his forearm against the full-color "Dangerous Moles" poster that hung beside his desk.

"Why do you say that?" Helma asked her mother. The reason Aunt Em was childless had never been alluded to in Helma's presence but now her mother spoke as if it had been an unfortunate career choice.

"To take care of her," Lillian said fervently. "It's what children do. There she was, all by herself on that farm. She should have moved out after Juozas died, closer to people who pay attention, who keep an eye out." Lillian sighed.

Lillian had moved to Bellehaven eight years ago, after Helma's father died. Helma's mother didn't intend ever to return to Michigan but she subscribed to the *Scoop River Herald* by mail and constantly clipped out articles for

Helma to read about people Helma couldn't remember. Lillian's first words when she phoned were often, "Oh dear, you won't believe who died."

The autumn before, after decades of secretive and closely held grudges, Aunt Em and Lillian had met in Michigan and finally forged an uneasy transcontinental peace.

"But, dear," Lillian said. "Are you *positive* about bringing Emily here? Rhonda said she visited her in the hospital right away and Em was acting very peculiar."

"What did she mean by 'peculiar'?" Helma asked. Aunt Rhonda was never without opinions. She enrolled in one mail-order course after another, "educating herself beyond her possibilities," Helma's father had once claimed.

"Unpredictable," Lillian said, using the same word Bruce had. "Rhonda said Em could move in with her but you know she only has those two bedrooms and with your cousin Ricky moving back home . . ."

As far as Helma knew, her cousin Ricky, who was a few weeks younger than she was, had never left home for more than two or three months at a time. "Just long enough for his mother to change the sheets," Helma's friend Ruth liked to say.

"It'll only be for a few weeks," Helma told Lillian, "until Aunt Em recovers. Bruce is flying out with her on Sunday."

"I wish he'd bring the grandsons," Helma's mother said, her voice thick with longing.

"He will at Christmas," Helma assured her.

"This is July," Lillian said. "Christmas is years away. I suppose it gives me time to finish the train set I'm making in woodworking class, but . . . Well, you have a nice day, dear."

After Helma hung up, Harley Woodworth leaned across the bookcase that separated their cubicles and set a thick blue book on her desk, tapping it once with a long forefinger. "You can borrow this," he said solemnly. "Use it when your aunt arrives."

Across the front cover, engraved in heavy Roman type, the title read, *Diseases of the Elderly.*

"It's illustrated," Harley assured her. "That helps, you know, with identification. A lot of diseases begin with rashes." He rubbed his neck as if one were beginning there even as he spoke.

"Thank you," Helma said, not touching the thick tome. "This isn't a library book. I didn't know you had elderly relatives."

"I don't," Harley told her, his sloping eyes brightening. "At least not here. There's my Uncle Howard in Phoenix: prostate cancer, the slow kind. And my Aunt Lily in Denver suffers from sciatica. This is from my personal collection." He hesitated. "You can borrow any of them you want. I made my own catalog on cards like the library used to have."

"Thank you, but I hope it won't be necessary."

"I can give you my home phone number in case you have an emergency," Harley offered. "I made cross references by symptoms, too."

"If I have that desperate of an emergency, I'll call an ambulance," Helma assured him.

Unaccountably, Harley's long face grew more morose. He opened his jaws without parting his lips, then said, "Oh," and disappeared into his cubicle.

"But thank you," Helma repeated. Only a grunt came from the opposite side of the partition. Harley Woodworth was sometimes surprisingly moody.

A screech sounded through the open window and Helma glanced outside to see three preteen girls standing in the library fountain splashing water at each other. It was warm for Bellehaven, in the high seventies, the best that summer got.

Ms. Moon, the library director, emerged from her office holding a sheet of paper. She wore a dress of many colors that flowed and rippled with each step, transforming the individual bulges of her body into more symmetrical, if expanded, contours. Since her gradual but steady weight gain had become noticeable two years ago, she'd quit tucking, belting, exposing her knees, or baring her arms. Her frosted hair fluffed and tendriled around her rosy face.

"Helma," she said, stepping into Helma's small cubicle, effectively pinning Helma at her desk, "of course you may take vacation time next week." With a flourish, she placed the paper that was Helma's request for emergency vacation time on her desk and clasped her hands together. Helma's nose twitched at the earthy odor of Ms. Moon's perfume. "Your aunt's visit is so organic: generations harmonizing. Continuity and fluidity. What we learn from one life to the next creates a path, a road of experience, if we're lucky, a freeway." She smiled, her cheeks dimpling.

"Thank you," Helma told her as she double checked the vacation request form for Ms. Moon's signature.

"Oh no, this will be a sacred journey for you. Travel it with your aunt for as long as you feel the pull of the path." She laughed gaily and shook her finger playfully at Helma. "I don't want you to step inside the building for at least a week. Don't even think about us, not once."

After she returned to her office, laughter still fading on the air, George Melville rose from his desk in the cataloging corner of the workroom and stopped beside Helma's cubicle.

"She's up to something," the bearded cataloger said in a low voice, leaning into Helma's space. "She's been happy-lolly-ga-ga for a couple of days now."

"Perhaps her personal life is going well," Helma suggested, thinking even as she said it that Ms. Moon *was* unusually cheerful. Life in the library had been uncharacteristically benign the past week.

"No, something else is going on, I'd bet my new mechanical pencil on it. Watch your back."

"Your Aunt Em?" Helma's friend Ruth asked. "Your Aunt Em is coming *tomorrow*?"

"Bruce is bringing her," Helma said as she shook a clean topsheet over the double bed in her second bedroom, her "back bedroom," which she decorated with gifts from people she cared for but whose tastes didn't quite suit her own. "You already knew she was vacationing with me this summer, Ruth."

"Yeah but not that she'd need a nursing attendant and round-the-clock care."

"Only temporarily," Helma said.

"What's wrong with her again?"

"The doctor called it a 'brain incident,' " Helma told her.

"Weird." Ruth stood in the doorway, leaning against the jamb, her bushy hair brushing the top of the door frame. She wore red pants that were purposely too short and a Navy sweatshirt that hung to her knees, blotches of paint from her latest project smearing the sleeves. She watched the sheet billow and settle over the bed and said, "You do that like a TV commercial."

Ruth had recently converted to a new diet of carrots, celery, and peanut butter and she held a peanut-butter–packed stalk of celery she'd pulled from a plastic bag, nibbling at it with little enthusiasm. "And what in hell is everybody talking about when they say Em's 'unpredictable'? What does 'unpredictable' mean? Dingy? Suicidal? Homicidal? Should we go shopping for nice little bars for your windows?"

Helma tucked and smoothed the sheet at the foot of the

bed, curious herself what "unpredictable" meant. She hadn't spoken to Aunt Em. Bruce was handling the arrangements and Aunt Em was still in the tiny Scoop River hospital, in a room without a telephone, "raging to be free," Bruce had said, certainly in exaggeration. Aunt Em never *raged*.

"I spoke to her doctor," Helma told Ruth as she fluffed the pillows and set them side by side at the head, their seamed edges facing outward, folds even with the edges of the mattress. "He said she *will* improve but he can't predict how completely or how soon. Don't forget, she *is* eighty-seven years old."

Ruth deliberately chewed her celery, her throat working as she swallowed. "You're the one who's forgetting. Dragging a confused old lady across the country."

"Aunt Em's never been confused," Helma said.

"Last you knew," Ruth warned. "What time are they getting here?"

"Two-oh-seven. Bruce is flying with her from Muskegon to Detroit and then into Bellehaven on the commuter flight from Seattle."

"So what's your chief of police think of this?"

Helma dusted the bedside table and set out a coaster in case Aunt Em liked a glass of water beside her bed at night. "I haven't told him."

Ruth stopped chewing, shoving the wad of cellulose into her cheek. Her dark eyes narrowed. "Uh oh, trouble on the romance scene?"

"He's been busy," Helma said, resmoothing the pillow-cases and pulling the spread taut.

"Like little Bellehaven is experiencing a crime wave? I hadn't noticed. C'mon, Helm. What's going on?"

"Helma," she corrected. "I'm not sure," she told Ruth, going still, voicing it for the first time.

"You're not sure or you don't know?" Ruth demanded.

Helma didn't answer, then finally admitted, "I don't know."

"I'll find out for you," Ruth said, stepping away from the doorjamb, her eyes sparkling. She shoved her uneaten celery into the plastic bag and zip-locked it closed.

"I'd appreciate it if you didn't," Helma warned.

"Is that panic I hear in your voice? Afraid I'm going to be indiscreet?"

That was exactly what Helma feared; in fact, indiscretion was exactly what she'd *expect* from Ruth. Chief of Police Wayne Gallant and Miss Helma Zukas were not engaged in a romance, not at all, but through long association and mutual respect, they'd become . . . close. And there'd been that moment in the mountains the previous fall . . . So now, this sudden silence was uncharacteristic, troubling.

"Well?" Ruth demanded.

"I'm sorry," Helma apologized, arranging five throw pillows on the bed; odd numbers in life were strangely the most harmonious. "What were you saying?"

"Never mind. Okay, so if you require any geriatric babysitting, I'll be standing by. Dear old Aunt Em always struck me as the pliable type. I'm up for it." She glanced down the hall, a smile suddenly widening her face.

"Is Boy Cat Zukas in the hallway?" Helma asked.

The smile disappeared. Ruth raised her head, blinked her eyes, and said, "No," but Helma heard the irritated hiss receding toward the living room.

"So why can't he have the run of your apartment?" Ruth asked. "After the last couple of years, he's earned it."

"Because we each inhabit our own environment," Helma told her. She surveyed the room and declared it ready: the bed was made, closet and bureau space had been cleared, loose rugs removed from the floor.

"No kidding," Ruth said. "So anyway, let me know when your aunt recovers from jet lag and we'll do one of those old lady things: have tea or something. I'll wear a hat.''

After Ruth left, Helma checked her refrigerator one more time, standing at the door and mentally ticking off the foods she knew her Aunt Em preferred: fresh orange juice—not frozen, nonfat milk, white bread and applesauce, chicken breast and green beans, all healthful choices for the aged. Boy Cat Zukas, his tail switching, watched her from his wicker bed beside the door as she wiped away a spot on the refrigerator handle.

Beyond Helma's balcony, the waters of Washington Bay shone steel gray, occasionally glittering silver blue when the sun peeked through the clouds, striking the water like a beam. Two sailboats crossed the bay side by side, their sails taut, and beyond them, a black and white tugboat chugged back to port after having escorted a freighter from the bay into the wider waters that led across the world. Helma imagined the view through Aunt Em's Midwest eyes. What was it Ruth said sometimes: it'll knock your socks off.

She unlocked and slid open the glass door onto her balcony and said to Boy Cat Zukas, ''I'd prefer it if you left now.''

The black cat continued staring at her, then bared his teeth and made an irritable noise that sounded like, ''ack-ack-ack,'' flicking his tail but not moving and finally she reclosed the balcony door. She'd never touched the former alley cat and even though he was an animal, she suspected he was aware that she never intended to and considered his life immune from serious interference.

Fifteen minutes later Helma's phone rang.

''Here's the scoop,'' Ruth said in Helma's ear, her voice low and throaty, like a conspirator's. ''You're not going to like it.'' She paused for breath and dramatic effect and rushed on, ''Remember the divorce from hell? How our valiant chief of police slipped into a seemingly terminal decline until you stepped in and offered him a reason to live?''

"Ruth, who have you been talking to?" Helma demanded.

"Well," Ruth paused and then ominously singsonged, "she's baa-ack."

Helma reached behind her and without looking, pulled out a chair from her dining table and sat down. "His ex-wife?" she asked.

"The very one. Twenty pounds thinner, a whole lot richer, and gunning for bear."

"What does that term mean?"

"She wants him back, that's what. The campaign has begun."

"They're divorced," Helma reminded Ruth.

"Divorce means nothing to a woman with a mission. Trust me. What are you going to do about it?"

"It doesn't have anything to do with me," Helma told her. Without realizing it, she'd uncoiled the curly phone cord and reshaped it into a hangman's noose. She released it and it coiled itself again.

"Of course it does. Are you going to simply hand him over? You need a plan, a defense strategy. I'll help. I'm good at this kind of stuff. Inspired, even."

"Ruth," Helma said patiently. "This is none of my business. It's between Wayne Gallant and his ex-wife. I'm not interested in battle plans or defenses."

"You may not be now but you will be," Ruth grumpily predicted. "Good-bye." And the phone clicked in Helma's ear.

For a long time, Helma sat at her dining room table, gazing through her balcony doors toward the shifting light on Washington Bay, her mind far from Aunt Em's imminent visit.

* * *

The phone rang at 7:50 in the morning, as Helma washed her breakfast dishes. Her day was filled with last-minute preparations for Aunt Em's arrival, including dropping off a budget-shorn list of periodicals at the library for consideration at Monday's staff meeting. The library was closed but she had her own key.

She pulled off her rubber gloves and answered. "Hello?"

"Billie, it's Bruce. Change of plans."

She reached for the pencil and paper she kept beside her phone, ready to jot down a new arrival time. "Yes?" she said, pencil poised. Behind Bruce, she heard muted voices, as if he were in a pay phone.

"Dan broke his leg last night at a sleepover, trying to skateboard down concrete steps in the dark. I'm calling from the hospital."

"Will he be all right?" She glanced at the clock over her stove. It was nearly ten o'clock in Michigan. Bruce and Aunt Em should have already been in the air.

"He'll be living in a cast for a few weeks. But Aunt Em's on her way."

"Not alone?"

"Alone. She insisted. Ricky drove her to Detroit so she wouldn't have to change planes. It's a nonstop flight to Seattle but I'm worried about her making the connection to the commuter plane for Bellehaven. Can you pick her up in Seattle?"

"Cousin Ricky drove her to Detroit?" Helma asked, realizing her side of the conversation was nothing but questions and none of them sufficiently answered.

"Don't worry. Ricky's an ass . . . idiot, but he's a good driver."

"Don't you usually say Ricky drives like a bat out of hell?"

"Well, yeah, a little fast maybe but that's what today called for. What can happen? She gets on in Michigan and she gets off in Seattle. It's not like she'll wander off the plane and get lost. The flight lands at eleven-oh-three. Can you make it?"

"Sea-Tac airport's over a hundred miles away," Helma explained to her brother. "and she's arriving three hours from now."

"Great. Then you have plenty of time. I'll call you tonight. Somebody's waiting for the phone. Gotta go. Oh. You might have to buy her a few things. I took her by the house to pack a suitcase and she chose quite a mix. Not too many clothes."

Helma hung up. Two hours. It was two hours to Sea-Tac airport south of Seattle. And that was when the traffic was light. How often did that happen anymore? She'd been planning on driving five miles to the Bellehaven airport. There wasn't enough gas in her Buick. Her car was due for an oil change. She needed to change clothes.

The phone rang again and she snatched up the receiver, expecting to hear Bruce's deep laughter. It was all a joke; he loved playing the trickster.

"I have news and I can't paint," Ruth complained into Helma's ear. "And I can't paint because of the news. Do you want to take one of your predawn walks or something so I can tell you?"

"It's long past dawn," Helma told her. "But I have another plan. If you'll be out front in twenty-five minutes, I'll pick you up."

"Okay," Ruth agreed, not even inquiring about their destination. "I'll be ready."

Boy Cat Zukas was already outside, off on his feline rounds. Helma checked locks, drew the drapes even though the sky was heavy with low gray clouds, and grabbed the periodicals list to drop off at the library, feeling in the air a disturbance of plans gone awry.

Too late after Helma let herself into the library workroom she realized that she wasn't alone. From the sounds of recorded whale song, she realized that Ms. Moon was spending Sunday in her office.

Helma didn't *sneak*, she never snuck, but she did try not to disturb Ms. Moon as she tucked the periodicals list beneath the frog paperweight on Eve's desk. One slow step at a time she departed the workroom, hearing just before she opened the door the whale song being joined by Ms. Moon's rhythmic humming.

One lane of the street in front of the library was barricaded. City trucks were parked near an open manhole that was tented and had exhaust hoses running from it; the air smelled of diesel fuel. "Sewer line problems," the woman flagger told Helma through her open window. "Be a minute."

Helma tapped her fingers on the steering wheel, waiting for the flagger to motion her forward. She was running late.

The woman flagger had just beckoned Helma through the single lane when the traffic light in front of her turned yellow. She was already to the intersection; she was making a right turn; no traffic came from the left. The way was clear.

Helma Zukas did the sensible thing: she turned right on the yellow light. And five seconds later she glanced in her rearview mirror to spot a motorcycle policeman behind her, his blue lights flashing, waving one black-gloved hand for her to pull over.

She did, parking in front of a busy coffee shop, whispering, "Oh Faulkner." He pulled up beside her Buick, a chubby mustachioed man wearing dark sunglasses, needing to tip his bike to the side before he could dismount. Helma knew several of the Bellehaven policemen but she hadn't seen this small man before.

He leaned down and stared in at her, his moustache twitching. "I'd like to see your driver's license, please," he said.

"May I ask why you pulled me over?" Helma inquired.

"Your driver's license, ma'am."

"May I see some identification?" she asked.

He sputtered, then handed her a picture I.D. Helma studied it, matching the picture to his face. He was bald without his helmet. "The light was yellow," she said, returning his identification.

"It turned red while you were in the intersection," he said. "Your driver's license, ma'am. And your registration, please."

"It didn't turn red in my view," Helma told him.

"You sailed right through it without even looking."

"I always look and I resent your using the word 'sail' to describe a safe and prudent turn." Helma finally handed him her driver's license and registration and he returned to his motorcycle to write out a ticket while she remained in the driver's seat, not even turning when she heard a young voice say, "Look Mom, there's the librarian!"

When the policeman returned, he passed the ticket through her window for her to sign. She glanced at it and gave it back. "I can't sign this," she told him.

"It's not an admission of guilt, ma'am." His voice grew louder, higher pitched. "You're only acknowledging receipt of the ticket."

"Then you'll have to make it readable. You've spelled Wilhelmina incorrectly. I believe the time noted here is three minutes into the future. I can see your badge number is 087 but I'm unable to read your name: Olsen? Carolson? Camden? This document is too illegible for me to sign my name to. I'd appreciate a rewritten ticket, please.''

The policeman stood beside her car and stared at her, his eyes behind his sunglasses invisible, his mouth working.

"I'm in a hurry, please," Helma told him.

He spun on his shiny black boots and returned to his motorcycle where he wrote a new ticket in tight jerking motions. Helma Zukas had never received a traffic ticket in her life, not even a parking ticket.

But she would deal with the matter later. Since thanking the policeman was clearly inappropriate, she took the ticket without a word and tucked her frustration to the back of her mind and the traffic ticket into her wallet and drove with her usual precise diligence to the alley that served as Ruth's front street, her house being a converted carriage house behind a once grand home in the older section of Bellehaven.

Ruth sat on a granite rock in the alley, dressed more conventionally than usual: in magenta straight pants and a long white sweater, the sleeves pushed up to her elbows.

Ruth rose without using her hands; she'd been exercising again, and waved at Helma's approaching Buick as if Helma might drive right on past.

"What's up? Where are we going?" she asked as she opened the passenger door and ducked inside.

"Seattle. Sea-Tac to be precise. Bruce's son broke his leg so Aunt Em's flying here alone."

"He put a dotty old lady on a plane by *herself*? Geez, he's the one who's lost his marbles. How's she going to manage the flight change in Detroit?"

"Ricky drove her to Detroit so she wouldn't have to," Helma explained.

Ruth raised her hands to her cheeks. "Ricky? Your cousin Ricky? She probably didn't make it then. If Ricky's involved, something's bound to go to hell. At the very least, the plane will crash."

"Ruth," Helma cried, turning to Ruth so sharply she accidentally swerved her car, causing the driver behind her to honk his horn.

"Sorry. Really. Very sorry," Ruth hastily told her. "I'm sure she's fine, just fine. On in Detroit, off in Seattle. No problem. Now watch the road."

With her traffic ticket in mind, Helma drove at exactly the speed limit, and was passed by every vehicle on the freeway except for a pickup loaded with jostling calves.

"To market, to market," Ruth murmured, gazing at the calves. She turned the rearview mirror toward herself and checked her considerable eye makeup. "So do you want to hear my news?"

Actually, Helma didn't. Her mind was in turmoil with thoughts of Aunt Em. What if Ricky hadn't made it to Detroit on time? Or worse, what if at the last minute, Ricky decided to accompany Aunt Em?

"What is your news?" Helma asked Ruth.

"Voices from the past," Ruth said. She slumped into her seat. "Remember Paul?"

Unaccountably, three years ago, Ruth had fallen hard for Paul from Minnesota, a man with whom, even Ruth realized, she shared nothing in common. A man shorter than she was, usually the first and worst flaw Ruth couldn't tolerate and since Ruth was over six feet tall herself, a widely shared imperfection among the male population. They'd waged a long-distance affair until it became clear that neither of them was prepared to move across country for the other. Paul was the only man Helma had ever seen Ruth cry over.

"He's coming to Bellehaven in two weeks," Ruth said. "What am I going to do?"

"Did you invite him?" Helma asked, repositioning the mirror.

"No."

"Do you want to see him?"

"No. Yes. Hell, I don't know. It's like having your hari kari scars reopened."

"Hari kari, when properly executed, is a nonrepairable condition," Helma explained.

"Then you get the idea." Ruth hunkered even lower in the passenger seat, her knees against the dashboard and her head against the seat back. "I told you my story. Do you want to talk about the chief and his ex now?"

"No," Helma told her.

"Your loss. I could give you foolproof advice."

"Based on your own experience?" Helma asked.

"Ooh," Ruth said, raising her eyebrows. "Not nice." She raised her arm. "Have you ever seen your elbows?"

Helma took her eyes from a van full of children—their heads and mouths moving in unison—that was passing them. "Ruth, what are you talking about?"

"I saw mine in the mirror last week, *really* saw them. No more short sleeves. Melancholy. After a certain age, elbows get melancholy."

They settled into their private thoughts until they reached Seattle. A light drizzle began as they passed through the city, turning the pavement glossy and highlighting the tall buildings against the gray sky.

"Here it comes again," Ruth said, leaning forward and glancing up at the rain, "the reason all us famous artists live in the Northwest. The light," she intoned. "It's the light. It's so damn wet we're forced to stay inside and do *something*, anything. Mix time and frustration and you get art."

"What are you working on now?" Helma asked.

Ruth waved her hand. "Representational stuff."

"Vegetables still?"

"Mm-hmm. I hope your aunt hasn't forgotten how to cook," she said as she gazed with longing at the passing bustle and towering cityscape. Bellehaven's tallest building, twelve stories high, had been erected in a burst of optimism in the 1940's. Nothing since had risen higher than four stories. "You could try cooking therapy," Ruth continued. "You know that Lithuanian food she sends you? Maybe whipping up all those goodies again would bring her mind back. You'd both benefit."

"No one's claimed she's lost her mind," Helma said.

"I think that's what 'unpredictable' means. What's she like?"

"Who?"

"Your Aunt Em. I remember her but I was a kid. What's she *really* like? What are her vices?"

"I don't know of any," Helma told her.

Ruth harrumphed. "Then you weren't paying attention."

The traffic slowed to a crawl just before the airport exit and Helma glanced at her watch: fifteen minutes until the plane was scheduled to land.

"What's the holdup here?" Ruth asked. She rolled down her window and leaned out, glancing up and down the shoulder. "You can pass on the right," she said. "It's clear."

"That's illegal," Helma told her. "I'll wait."

Just then a red pickup zipped past on the right and Ruth looked smugly at Helma. "So be late," she said, motioning toward the disappearing red truck. "Keep Aunt Em waiting, wandering like a lost soul through the airport."

A moment later a second vehicle passed them on the right: a state police car with whirling lights. A hundred yards farther and they passed the red pickup parked on the shoulder in front of the police car. Despite herself, Helma felt a comradely stab of sympathy for the driver.

"Don't say it," Ruth warned.

They arrived at the airport parking garage with five

minutes to spare. The car tires squealed as Helma made the tight turns in the spiral tower.

"Where are you going?" Ruth asked as she exited onto the first available floor. "If you go up we'll be on the sky bridge floor. No elevators, no steps, lots quicker."

"I always park on the lowest level," Helma explained. "The stairs will be good for both of us."

In the shadowy garage, Ruth pointed to an empty slot. "There's a spot."

"There's one farther up," Helma told her. "To the left of the elevator." She passed two more empty spaces, then pulled into the first slot past the elevator tower.

Ruth turned on the seat and regarded Helma. "Hold on. There's a method at work here. I detect a pattern."

"We have to hurry, Ruth," Helma said, unbuckling her seatbelt and removing her purse from beneath her seat. "Aunt Em's plane is landing right now."

But Ruth continued. "You 'always' park on the lowest level, you say, to the left of the elevator. Is this one of those mnemonic things you talk about? All L's, so you don't lose your car? Lowest level, left of elevator."

"Lock the door when you get out," Helma reminded Ruth.

Ruth followed Helma toward the stairs. "L, L, L, L," she repeated. "I mean, Elevator's almost an L." Her voice rose. "I get it," she called. "Lowest level left of the elevator because you're a *Librarian*?"

## *chapter three*

# PINS AND NEEDLES

When Ruth and Helma, out of breath and their faces flushed, reached the gate, passengers were already emerging from the loading bridge and being drawn into the waiting crowd with hugs, laughter, and welcome signs. Business travelers, distinguished by their sleek good grooming, passed through the waiting area, eyes trained beyond the crowd.

"I knew it. She missed her flight," Ruth said as the flow of passengers dwindled. "Didn't I say something would go wrong? Ricky didn't come through, as if that would shock the universe."

"We'll wait until every passenger has left the plane," Helma told her, pressing forward and peering into the tunnel-like bridge. "And then I'll inquire." A young couple, rapt in each other, strolled arm in arm toward them, oblivious to an impatient businessman behind them.

"Something bad happened," Ruth whispered. "I mean, she's *old*. Things do. I had a friend who was flying to Ireland and this old guy in the seat in front of her dropped . . . never mind."

Finally, when it looked as if the plane had indeed emptied, a wheelchair appeared, accompanied by two flight attendants, one of them, a redhead, was pushing; the other, dark-haired and tall, walked beside the chair, her face solemn.

"Uh-oh," Ruth said. "This is not a joyful group."

Aunt Em sat slumped in the chair, her gray head sunk forward, her hands folded over the purse in her lap. A red umbrella lay across her knees. Upright, fastidious, always alert Aunt Em; now she appeared asleep, frail, and defeated. Helma swallowed and stepped forward.

"Are you the niece?" the solemn-faced attendant, obviously the superior in rank of the two women, asked Ruth. "Wilhelmina Zukas?"

"Not me," Ruth said, vigorously shaking her head.

"I am," Helma told her, keeping her voice low. "Was she ill on the flight?"

The redheaded attendant's eyes twinkled. "We wish," she said.

"I beg your pardon?" Helma asked. The attendant raised her finger to her lips. "Don't wake her up," she whispered. "She's been asleep the past hour. A little too much to drink."

"Aunt Em doesn't drink," Helma told her.

"I didn't think she was used to it," the attendant said.

The solemn, dark-haired attendant held Aunt Em's airline tickets. "I see she has an open-ended return flight," she said.

"Yes, she does."

"I suggest that a family member accompany your aunt on her return trip."

Never offer explanations or excuses, Helma's father had once told her. Nobody cares.

"Thank you," Helma said. "Would you tell me what happened on the flight, please."

The redheaded attendant leaned forward and said, "I think she was nervous about flying and if she wasn't used to drinking, either . . ." She shrugged and patted the air fondly above Aunt Em's shoulder. "It happens."

"But preferably not on our airline," the somber attendant said. She glanced at her watch and handed Helma Aunt Em's tickets. "We'll leave her in your hands now."

Before she followed her superior, the red-haired attendant said to Helma, "Your aunt's a riot; she can fly with me anytime."

Helma stared at her. Aunt Em a *riot*?

"Curiouser and curiouser," Ruth said, gazing after the retreating women.

Helma leaned down and straightened the collar of Aunt Em's blue cardigan sweater. She wore her amber earrings as usual, and probably beneath her blouse's collar, her amber necklace, the choice of jewelry closest to the Lithuanian woman's heart. Her thick gray hair was cut short and straight, with one natural wave over her forehead. "Aunt Em," Helma said in a firm low voice she'd developed to awaken dozing library patrons at closing time without startling them.

Aunt Em's eyes shot open; her head jerked upward. "Wilhelmina," she said in a strong voice, her eyes zeroing in on Helma with such intensity that Helma involuntarily leaned away before she hugged Aunt Em, smelling the familiar lavender talc.

"Am I in Seattle?"

"You are," Helma told her, now catching a whiff of alcohol that overpowered the lavender. "Were you ill on the flight?"

The creases on Aunt Em's forehead wrinkled even deeper. "Ill? I'm fine. Flying is easy. I don't know why I worried about it." She spoke in her lingering Lithuanian accent, its most prominent features the turning of the "g" in "ing" to "k," and "th" into sharp, tongue-to-teeth "t's." "I did fly, didn't I?"

"You did," Helma said, pointing through the window at the 767 parked on the tarmac.

"I thought so." She lifted the red umbrella and tapped its silver tip on the floor. "I brought my umbrella for your rain. Is it raining?"

"Not at the moment," Helma told her.

"A shame." She squinted up at Ruth. "Ruth Winthrop. I wish I'd grown up to be as tall as you."

"I love you," Ruth said, grinning and leaning down to kiss the top of Aunt Em's head while Helma unlocked the wheelchair brake.

"Don't do that," Aunt Em told Helma. "I can walk. The doctor said it's my head that's mixed up, not my legs." And she rose from the wheelchair, tucking her blouse into her navy pants, stamping her feet as if boosting her blood circulation. Aunt Em, who herself had once been considered a tall woman, was now Helma's height, her condensing spine held straight through sheer willpower. "That was a long sit. Where do we go now for the suitcases?"

As they made their way by tram, escalator, and long hallways to the baggage claim, Helma kept a wary eye on Aunt Em, who walked between her and Ruth, her eyes snapping from faces in the crowd to the airport shops, her lips moving as she read the signs. Aunt Em didn't dawdle; her stride was slow but strong. Helma began to relax. Despite her initial confusion, this was the old Aunt Em, no doubt about it.

"How's Ricky?" Ruth asked as they passed a display of plastic slugs outside a gift shop.

"I haven't seen him in a while," Aunt Em said, frowning at the lifelike slimy creatures.

"Didn't he drive you to the airport in Detroit?" Helma asked.

Aunt Em's frown deepened. Then she smiled. "Silly, I live in Scoop River, not Detroit."

In the cavernous baggage area, luggage spewed from a conveyor belt onto the carousel, suitcases tumbling and piling onto one another while an attendant madly tried to separate them.

"How many suitcases did you bring?" Helma asked Aunt Em.

"One," she said. "That old leather one that Lukas used to carry the . . ." Suddenly she clapped a hand over her mouth like a naughty girl telling secrets.

"Who's Lukas?" Helma asked. She'd never heard Aunt Em mention anyone named Lukas.

"Dead and gone," Aunt Em said. "At least I hope so," and she broke into a chortly little laugh. Ruth raised her eyebrows at Helma over Aunt Em's head.

"Well, tell us when you spot it," Ruth told her.

Aunt Em frowned at the carousel, watching bags rotate past and be hauled from the conveyor by the gathered travelers. A thick man in jeans and a flannel shirt jostled them and Aunt Em raised her red umbrella and gently nudged his arm. "A gentleman apologizes for bumping into ladies."

The man whirled around, his eyes narrowed. Ruth shook her head, raised her hands in innocence, and then pointed down at Aunt Em.

"Oh," he said. "Sorry, ma'am."

"I forgive you," Aunt Em said. "Oh," she said to Ruth, touching her arm. "There goes my suitcase."

"Around the loop again?" Ruth asked.

"No. With the flamingo on the side. That man is carrying it."

Helma spotted it first, a battered leather suitcase, once expensive, the kind secured by two leather straps. The flamingo was a decal that covered a third of one side: faded pink and jaunty. The case was in the hands of a man heading toward the doors that led out of the airport.

"I'll get it," Helma said. She ran after the man, switching her purse to her left hand and reaching out with her right. "Sir?" she called out. Where were the security guards?

A couple pushing a stroller crossed between Helma and the man and she nearly bumped into the very pregnant mother. "Sorry," she said and dodged around them in time to see Ruth grab the suitcase by one of its leather straps. The crowd parted around them, surprisingly few turning to watch.

When Helma reached the man, he was apologizing, his face flushed pink. He was tall and bearded, wearing thick glasses and a Mariners baseball cap. "I thought it was my uncle's," he said, gesturing to an older man and woman sitting on plastic chairs near the glass doors. "He said it was pretty old, no offense. Let me carry it back for you."

"That's okay," Ruth told him. "I've got it. You'd better find the right bag."

"Thanks. Sorry again."

"Geesh," Ruth said to Helma as she hefted the leather suitcase. "This is heavy; what did she do, bring her pots and pans?"

"Bruce said she packed a 'mix,' but not many clothes."

"That's about as informative as saying she's acting 'unpredictable.' Well, let's go get her and begin our merry journey north."

But Aunt Em was gone. The space where she'd been standing beside the baggage carousel was occupied by an East Indian family pulling case after case from the conveyor.

"She has to be here," Ruth murmured. They slowly turned in every direction, scanning the dwindling crowd in their corner of the baggage claim. Aunt Em was nowhere in sight.

"I'll check the women's restrooms," Helma told Ruth. "You stand over there in the open so she'll see you."

"You mean like a beacon, a lighthouse, a foghorn?" Ruth asked.

"Ruth, please."

"Yeah, yeah," Ruth grumbled as she walked toward the wide hallway, lugging Aunt Em's suitcase and mumbling, "You know Ruth, the tall one. You can't miss her."

Helma checked the first women's restroom. The stalls were full and Helma surveyed the feet beneath the doors. Aunt Em had been wearing beige crepe-soled shoes.

"You're out of turn," a woman standing fourth in line by the sinks informed Helma.

"I'm sorry. This is an emergency," Helma told her.

The young woman at the head of the line offered sympathetically, "You can go ahead of me."

"Thank you. No. I'm looking for my aunt. She's eighty-seven years old, short steel-gray hair, wearing navy pants and a light blue cardigan sweater. Amber earrings."

"You left an eighty-seven-year-old woman alone in this airport?" the first woman asked with a terse shake of her head.

"She could be anywhere," said another woman. "I heard about an old man who was lost in here for two days."

"I'd call security," the young woman offered.

"I will," Helma said and hurried from the restroom, hesitating outside the men's room. No, not even in her most confused moments would Aunt Em enter a men's restroom.

She checked the areas near the coin lockers, the car rental desks, and beneath the open escalators. Behind her, Ruth still stood alone, turning in slow circles and Helma thought that, yes, with her height, her wild hair, and her piercing eyes, Ruth did resemble a beacon. But it was as if Aunt Em had vanished.

Helma turned, searching for a courtesy phone to call security, and spotted Aunt Em emerging from a narrow hallway, her purse and umbrella clutched to her bosom, her cheeks flushed.

Helma hurried to her side, noting that the hallway ended at a door bearing a large "Employees Only" sign.

"Where have you been?" Helma asked her.

Aunt Em smoothed back her hair and said matter-of-factly, "I was looking for the restroom when a nice young man tried to steal my purse."

Helma gasped but Aunt Em calmly pulled at a round bead attached to her sweater lapel and unsheathed a gleaming hat pin three inches long. "I stabbed him with this. Isn't it clever? Stasys, you remember him, he does odd jobs for me and he used to take care of your canoe that Tony built. He gave it to me. 'The city is a dangerous place,' he said to me. 'You watch out.' " She smiled. "I think Stasys is sweet on me. He's always coming over, sometimes every day."

"Are you all right? Did he touch you?" Helma asked, glancing up and down the hall. She saw families, a group of teenage girls, a man in a suit, but no "nice young man" who looked like a purse snatcher.

"I'm fine. He didn't try to touch me after I stabbed him. That cooked his goose."

Helma was still trying to absorb the scene that Aunt Em was so calmly describing. She held up her hand. "You stabbed a man who tried to steal your purse?" she repeated. "A purse snatcher?"

"Three times," Aunt Em said. She demonstrated, plunging the wicked pin into the air in front of her three times. "Right in the arm. *Then* he let go of my purse." She thought for a moment. "But he made me drop my umbrella. It's not so easy to bend over anymore."

Helma examined the pin. "It's not bloody," she said.

"Of course it isn't. I washed it clean." She nodded toward the door with the "Employees Only" sign.

"Show me," Helma insisted.

The door wasn't locked as Helma expected, and indeed, when she pushed it open, she found a single restroom with a toilet and sink. No paper towels, only an electric hand dryer. She checked the sink and didn't find a trace of blood, nor on the chrome handles or floor, nothing out of order or even soiled. "Did you get any on your hands?" Helma asked Aunt Em.

"Any what?" Aunt Em asked, reinserting the hat pin into her sweater lapel.

"Any blood."

"I'm not bleeding," Aunt Em said, showing Helma her hands, front and back.

Helma reluctantly let the conversation go. Aunt Em had her purse and her umbrella and the security of her lethal hat pin. Who knew what, if anything, had actually transpired. Seeing her suitcase being whisked away might have activated a worried portion of her mind.

Ruth stood near a bank of telephones in animated conversation with a tall security guard. As Helma and Aunt Em approached, Helma heard snatches of conversation, not about missing Aunt Em but where to find the best smoked salmon.

"The market," the dark-haired guard was saying. "Definitely the market."

"Exactly which . . ." Ruth began, batting her eyes and then she turned and spotted Helma and Aunt Em. "Oh, here they are," she told the guard. "You won't have to go searching, after all. Where've you been?" she asked Aunt Em. "You scared Helma to jelly."

"To the powder room," Aunt Em told her.

"My aunt wishes to report an attempted purse snatching," Helma informed the security guard.

He straightened and mentally tidied up, the smile replaced by an alert coolness. "Ma'am," he said to Aunt Em. "Can you describe the man?"

"Oh yes, he told me where the restrooms were. He was very polite," and she smiled as if recalling a pleasant encounter.

"But what did he look like?" Ruth asked.

"Like a nice boy. Clean."

"Did he take anything from your purse?" the guard asked.

"I didn't let him have it," Aunt Em said indignantly, holding her purse closer. "It's mine."

"Would you like to fill out a report?" the guard asked her.

"Yes," Helma said.

"No," Aunt Em replied.

The guard turned to Helma. "Did you witness the incident, ma'am?"

"No, but . . ."

"Your aunt's the person who has to decide whether to submit a report." He glanced over their heads, his waning attention caught by two quarreling children.

"I don't want to make any trouble," Aunt Em told him. "And I'm sure he learned his lesson."

"All right, then," he said, touching his hat. "Everything okay?" he asked Helma.

"Will you at least make a note that this incident may have happened?"

"May have?" he repeated. "Then you doubt it did?"

Aunt Em looked from the guard to Ruth and Helma. "Is anybody under arrest?"

"Nobody's under arrest," Ruth said, looking regretfully at the handsome guard.

"Then let's move out of here like Billy Bejesus," Aunt Em said.

"John Wayne?" Ruth, who knew of Aunt Em's love of the actor and his movies, asked.

"In his movies," Aunt Em told her. "Ward Bond said it in *The Searchers*."

## ❧ chapter four ❧

# SETTLING IN

**"D**o you remember *how* you got sick back in Michigan?" Ruth turned in the passenger seat and asked Aunt Em, who'd stretched out in the back, her legs up on the seat, "so my ankles don't swell any bigger."

They were on the northern edge of Seattle, driving north in dusky light, the gray drizzle replaced by cauliflower clouds glowing as the sun set. Instead of heading directly home after picking up Aunt Em at the airport as Helma had anticipated, Aunt Em had requested a drive through Pioneer Square, "where I read the bums hang out," and a ride up the Space Needle. Helma, who only rode elevators in life-and-death situations, had sat on a bench and averted her eyes while Ruth and Aunt Em gaily joined a group of tourists boarding the glass-fronted cars that zipped up and down the side of the Space Needle as if it were the sanest venture in the world.

"Bruce's boy called it a brain fart," Aunt Em said, a bemused note in her voice. "That day is gone to me." In her mirror Helma saw Aunt Em tap her forehead. "It's unbelievable to forget a whole day."

"Not to me," Ruth said.

"But that's what happened," Aunt Em went on. "I woke

35

up in the hospital and a woman was bragging on the TV about her abdomen muscles. 'Abs,' she said. Abs like a washboard. Who cares?''

She drifted into a silent musing that in turn drifted into a doze by the time they'd left the city behind, punctuated by an occasional snore.

''More than a whole day is gone,'' Ruth said softly, glancing over her shoulder to be sure Aunt Em was asleep. ''Do you believe there really was a purse snatcher?''

''A week ago I would have believed her totally,'' Helma said. ''but her purse was intact and there weren't any signs she'd been accosted. I believe she *did* have an exchange with a man in the hallway but her imagination may have been stimulated when her suitcase was taken from the carousel.''

''Yeah, and don't forget she got looped on the plane.''

''She needs a good night's rest,'' Helma told Ruth. Behind her, a driver flashed his lights at Helma, signaling her to move from the middle lane into the slower lane, but she was driving the speed limit and held her place in traffic.

''At least,'' Ruth agreed. ''Why do you think he's coming?''

''Who?'' Helma asked, glancing in her mirror, wondering briefly if Ruth was warning her about traffic approaching too fast.

''Paul, who else? I mean, what's the point? We went through all that already. It ended like bad news, did he forget?''

Helma didn't answer, knowing none was expected, keeping her eyes on the road ahead of her and her hands lightly on the wheel at the ten o'clock and two o'clock positions.

A little while later, Aunt Em's voice came clearly from the back seat. ''Your father bought you this car when you graduated from high school ten years ago.''

''Twenty-two,'' Helma said.

"I remember," Aunt Em went on. "I told him to buy a solid car, a good heavy one, to protect you. It's a good thing."

"I've never had an accident," Helma told her.

"But we didn't expect you to keep it all of your life," Aunt Em said.

Ruth guffawed and Aunt Em said, "Buy a new car, something bright. Red is nice."


It was dark when Helma dropped off Ruth at her house.

"I'm getting in my little car and coming over," Ruth said as she reached for her door handle.

"Aunt Em's tired, Ruth," Helma began. Helma was tired herself; it had been a stressful day of unanticipated events. "Maybe . . ."

"That's a good idea," Aunt Em interrupted. "We'll have a drink."

"Only if I bring something," Ruth said and laughed her big laugh.

"Ruth . . ." Helma tried again.

In the dusky lights of the dashboard, Ruth made an impatient face. "I'm not up to sitting in my empty house, being forced to think. Have a heart. I'm a woman confused by love."

Aunt Em sighed. "Oh how romantic."

"Okay, good," Ruth said. "I'll do a few essentials and see you in twenty minutes, tops." And she slammed the car door overloud.

"Love," Aunt Em whispered.

In the parking lot of the Bayside Arms, Helma maneuvered Aunt Em's suitcase out of the trunk; it rattled and clunked, as heavy as if it really were packed with a collection of pots and pans.

"There's an elevator," Helma told Aunt Em, who was gazing into the starless sky, her umbrella poised to be unfurled. "You and your suitcase can ride it and I'll meet you on the third floor."

"Why don't you ride with me?" Aunt Em asked.

"I'm not comfortable in elevators," Helma told her.

"Ah, you're afraid. When you're afraid, don't torture yourself. If a horse threw me, *I* wouldn't be stupid enough to get back on it."

Helma waited until the doors closed on Aunt Em and the small outside elevator rose upward. She was four steps up the outside staircase when a voice stopped her.

"Helma?"

Walter David, the chubby building manager, stood at the bottom of the steps holding Moggy, his white Persian cat, in his arms. The well-groomed cat stared at Helma with its disturbing blue eyes, as blank as a stuffed animal's.

Helma glanced up the steps, hearing the clank and grind of the rising elevator. Walter David had been the manager of the Bayside Arms for four years. He drove a Harley Davidson with a specially made seat for Moggy and took his managership seriously, evincing an interest in every aspect of his tenants' lives, especially, it occasionally seemed, in Helma's. It wasn't unusual for him to sit in a lawn chair outside his apartment door and eye whoever approached the building, behaving like a suspicious French concierge.

"I wanted to warn you there's a stray cat hanging around." He glanced toward the rising elevator, absently scratching Moggy's ears. "Is that your aunt?"

"She'll be visiting for a few weeks. What does the cat look like?"

"What cat? Oh, the stray? It's gray and white, long-haired, matted around the neck. You know Mrs. Todd in 2B? It ate her Yorkie's dog food, the canned kind. Expensive." The elevator stopped and Helma heard the doors open.

"Thank you," Helma told Walter, taking a step upward. "I'll watch for it."

"Could I take you and your aunt for a picnic next week? To the park?"

"She might enjoy that. You could ask her. Excuse me now."

"You bet," he said, standing at the bottom of the steps and watching Helma climb the stairs to the third floor.

By the lights that shone over each apartment door, it was apparent that Aunt Em wasn't on the landing that stretched across the front of the Bayside Arms. Helma checked the elevator, pushing the down button to open the doors. Only the leather suitcase stood inside the boxy enclosure, the flamingo decal facing Helma. With feet firmly planted on the landing outside the elevator, Helma reached inside and pulled out Aunt Em's suitcase. Where could she have gone?

Aunt Em didn't have a key to 3F, Helma's apartment, but Helma tried the door anyway. It was still locked.

Beside Helma's doormat sat a vase of mixed daisies and baby's breath. Even in her concern for Aunt Em, she stopped and checked the arrangement for a card, wondering briefly if Wayne Gallant was attempting to make amends for his silence. There was no card.

Just then, the door to apartment 3E opened and Mrs. Whitney leaned out, her silvery hair glowing in the light from above her door. "Helma, come in. Your aunt is here."

Stepping into Mrs. Whitney's apartment was like entering a gift shop run by apple-pie grandmothers in a retirement home: doilies and afghans, crocheted hotpads and doll clothes, all done up in bright colors at odds with the softer—some said drabber—colors favored by northwesterners.

Aunt Em stood before a wall of shelves, each shelf packed with brightly dressed dolls nodding and grinning into the room. "My oh my, isn't this *something*?" Aunt Em was saying.

"That's Dolly Dingle," Mrs. Whitney told her, pointing to a doll with an especially vacant smile.

"I remember the ads," Aunt Em said. "Was that last year?"

"Oh, longer ago than that," Mrs. Whitney said, patting Aunt Em's arm.

Helma waited patiently while the two women discussed the dolls they'd owned as children, briefly trying to remember the dolls of her own childhood. She recalled a ballerina doll her cousin Ricky had buried alive after he watched a horror film, but mostly she remembered books.

"I'd like to show you your room, Aunt Em," Helma finally interrupted.

"I have some nice fresh peach cobbler for you to take home," said Mrs. Whitney, who always baked more than she could eat. To Aunt Em she said, "Your niece could use a little plumping up, don't you think?"

Aunt Em eyed Helma critically, tipping her head. "A few pounds would be good. What can a man hang on to?"

Mrs. Whitney brightened. "Oh yes, that nice young policeman . . ."

"Excuse me," Helma said. "I'll get your suitcase, Aunt Em. It's standing out in the weather."

Aunt Em struggled with her red umbrella. "Oh, do I need this?" she asked hopefully. "I know all about your rain."

"Don't open it in here," Mrs. Whitney warned, shaking her finger. "Bad luck, they say."

"I've already had that," Aunt Em told her.

Helma finally maneuvered Aunt Em the twelve feet from Mrs. Whitney's door to her own, picking up the suitcase on the way inside.

"Flowers," Aunt Em said, pointing her umbrella at the vase. "From your policeman?"

"There's no card," Helma told her.

Aunt Em gasped and clutched Helma's arm. "Then don't touch it. It could be booby trapped."

"It's not a trick," Helma assured her. "The card probably blew off."

"I've seen that before, when it's a bomb."

"Where?" Helma asked.

Aunt Em looked away, out over the parking lot. "Maybe in a movie," she finally said. "A John Wayne movie."

Aunt Em had learned to operate a VCR so she could watch John Wayne films on video. Her love for the actor had answered the question of what to buy her for Christmas for many relatives for many years, since he'd made more than a hundred movies.

"My my," Aunt Em said, gazing around Helma's tastefully maintained apartment. "I hope you have somewhere to kick off your shoes and scratch your . . . nose."

Boy Cat Zukas yowled at the balcony door the instant the kitchen lights flicked on and Helma opened her drapes and slid the door open for him. "You have a cat," Aunt Em said, watching Boy Cat Zukas watching her as he sidled to his wicker bed, his golden eyes unblinking. "That's a surprise. But cats get to be like people. I've had Morris since 1947."

If Morris the cat had lived with Aunt Em since 1947, that would make him over fifty years old.

Helma brought the flowers inside and set them in the middle of the table, repositioning one of the sprigs of baby's breath more symmetrically, then she lugged the suitcase to her second bedroom where Aunt Em sighed when she crossed the threshold and said, "This is a little better," gazing around the room at the gifts and furnishings Helma preferred to keep in a less public room.

"I'll help you unpack," Helma told her as she set the heavy suitcase on the bed and undid the straps.

The suitcase was unlocked and when Helma lifted the lid, she stared at the contents. "Where are your clothes?" she asked Aunt Em.

Aunt Em peered over Helma's shoulder. "I didn't bring any, did I?" she said, shaking her head as if she found the omission very curious. She pointed to her black purse. "I have underwear in there."

"Didn't Bruce help you pack?"

" 'Bring what's important,' he said. So I did that."

The suitcase was filled with a hodgepodge of possessions, the closest to wearable being a beautiful woven linen table scarf the color of a winter moon. "My mother made that as a girl in Lithuania," Aunt Em said, pronouncing it "Lit-wania." In its center was wrapped an antique green glass bowl. Helma was surprised it had survived the trip intact.

"And this is for you," she said, choosing a small handmade book with an embossed rose on the cover and giving it to Helma.

"It's lovely, thank you," Helma told her, feeling the clothlike pages.

"For your lists," Aunt Em said.

Helma reached into the suitcase and held up a pair of men's black suspenders.

Aunt Em actually appeared to blush. "A memento," she said.

Three videos, all John Wayne movies, were held together by a rubber band: *The Searchers*, *Hondo*, and *The Quiet Man*. There were matchbooks printed with names that sounded like nightclubs: Blue Beauty, Ricky's, The Flame, a tiny purse made of slinky silver mesh, a dried corsage, old seed packets, a book of John Greenleaf Whittier's poetry, a pair of worn black high heels too small and too dangerous for Aunt Em. Photographs were scattered at the bottom of the suitcase: some of them yellowed, all of them old. People Helma didn't recognize but who looked vaguely familiar, all of them young and similarly bold-eyed.

And then Helma realized what this suitcase held. "Pack what's important," Bruce had told Aunt Em, and Aunt Em had packed her life, bits and pieces of her past, each seemingly insignificant item weighted by memory of events and people long gone. Helma gently closed the suitcase lid.

"I'll find you a nightgown," she told Aunt Em. "And tomorrow we'll go shopping."

When Helma returned with a gown, slippers, and robe, Aunt Em stood in front of a seascape hanging on the wall. She turned and regarded Helma. Her eyes sagged in exhaustion. "Do you think I'm acting like a Dumb Dora?"

"No, I don't," Helma assured her.

"Sometimes I do," Aunt Em said. "I hate it." She gave a small shake of her head and fingered the nightgown Helma held. "This is very plain."

"You sent it to me for Christmas," Helma told her.

"Shame on me. A young woman like you needs something pretty, something . . ." She made motions across her bosom to indicate a low neckline.

The doorbell jangled in Ruth's impatient ring and Aunt Em stiffened, raising her hands to her cheeks. "Who's that? What do they want?"

"It's just Ruth, Aunt Em," Helma assured her. "I'll let her in."

Ruth had changed to a plaid outfit that resembled a pair of men's pajamas. In her arms she cradled two bottles: whiskey and red wine.

"Come in, come in," Aunt Em invited. "Now all we need are glasses."

"That can be arranged," Ruth intoned, setting the bottles on Helma's counter and reaching toward a cupboard.

"Are you sure you want to drink alcohol after your experience on the plane?" Helma asked Aunt Em.

Aunt Em frowned. "What happened on the plane?"

Ruth winked and shrugged and pulled three glasses from the cupboard. "Single malt or burgundy?" she asked.

"Liquor's quicker," Aunt Em said and Ruth poured whiskey into two glasses.

Helma put the kettle on for tea for herself but Aunt Em stopped her, "You have a glass of wine and we'll toast my visit." So Helma did, joining Aunt Em when she raised her glass, saying, "*Sveikata*." To your health.

After two sips of wine, Helma asked, "Who's Lukas?"

Aunt Em set her glass down so hard, whiskey sloshed onto the counter. Helma wiped it up with her napkin. "I don't know any Lukas."

"You said that was his suitcase, with the flamingo."

"Did I?"

Helma nodded.

"Long ago," she said slowly, as if she were forcing up memories, "he was a good friend, the best of friends." She clasped her hands together and tightened them once to illustrate. "Like you and Ruth, only he was a man, but we didn't . . . you know." She made incomprehensible motions with her fingers.

"In Michigan?" Helma asked. "A friend of yours and Uncle Juozas's?"

"No," she said, picking up her glass again. "Before that. Before Michigan."

Aunt Em had lived her entire life in Michigan; how could there possibly be a "before Michigan"?

"But . . ." Helma began.

"So enough with the interrogation," Ruth said as she poured more whiskey. "We—"

"My fingers are tired," Aunt Em interrupted. "Will you unclasp my necklace?" She turned her back so Helma could reach the filigreed clasp of the amber necklace. The necklace, strung with chunky, larger than usual beads, had come from Lithuania with Helma's grandmother, passed from mother to daughter. Since Aunt Em had no children, the necklace was next intended to pass to Helma.

All the Lithuanian women Helma knew owned amber: pendants and earrings and necklaces. They were laden with it at events, rivaling each other for size and purity of color. Not that amber was so very valuable but because it had fetched up on the shores of the Baltic Sea, a place so many still clung to as their homeland even if they'd never laid eyes on its sandy shores. Helma appreciated the way the amber resembled the flowing waters of the rivers and creeks of Michigan but she rarely wore necklaces of any kind, and when she did, she chose jewelry more . . . subtle.

"What's that?" Aunt Em suddenly asked, freezing.

Helma froze, too, her fingers still on the clasp of Aunt Em's necklace. Ruth gulped the rest of her whiskey and set down her glass, her head tipped. A man's voice penetrated the walls from outside. No, two men, quarreling, intermingling and shouting over one another, argument escalating to pure rage. Then a shout and a crash.

Helma hurried to the telephone in the kitchen, tapping out 911.

"A quarrel is taking place outside the Bayside Arms," Helma told the operator. "Two men. I believe it has become a physical confrontation. Send the authorities at once."

She hung up to the sound of a prolonged scream that sent chills up her arms. In his basket, Boy Cat Zukas hissed, his eyes piercing toward the walls.

"We've got trouble," Ruth said, heading toward the door.

Someone was in danger, mortal danger. "Stay here, Aunt Em," Helma warned. "We'll be right back."

With Ruth behind her, Helma ran down the stairs of the

Bayside Arms, her feet pounding on the steps, passing windows where the tenants safely stood with faces pressed to the glass. A light rain fell, as fine as mist. Another door slammed and Helma saw Walter David's heavy figure race ponderously across the parking lot toward the dumpster.

"Walt," Ruth called but he paid no attention.

Helma followed him, already hearing sirens in the distance. Suddenly Walter came to a halt, stopping so quickly his forward momentum nearly pitched him on his face. "Oh sweet mercy," she heard him say.

Sprawled on the ground at Walter's feet was a man, lying on his back. By the light of the street lamp, Helma could see he was probably in his thirties, fair of skin and hair, dressed in jeans and a dark t-shirt. A bruise, or maybe a birthmark, darkened the right side of his neck. Blood shone damply in the center of his shirt and pooled on the ground around him, black in the artificial light cast from the lamp above the dumpster.

"Oh, shit," Ruth swore softly, the words catching like a sob.

Walter David cleared his throat. "Do you think he's . . ." he asked Helma.

But Helma had already dropped to her knees beside the man. She leaned forward and lightly touched her fingers to the carotid artery in his neck, searching for his pulse.

There was nothing, no little leap beneath her fingertips, no breath when she leaned close to his face. She looked into his still face, feeling a surge of grief and sorrow for his loss, his diminishment as he lay lifeless on the pavement in the lightly falling rain.

She sat back and a police car, its lights flashing and siren wailing into the quiet night, careened into the parking lot, the headlights sweeping across the tableau formed by Helma, Ruth, Walter David, and the dead man.

She recognized Officer Sidney Lehman. He glanced at

her, then at Ruth, and raised his eyebrows; they'd met before under similar circumstances. The other officer she recognized as number 087, the motorcycle policeman who'd given her a ticket that very morning.

The officers went to work and Helma stayed out of the way, standing silently beside Ruth and Walter David, watching as the misty rain clung to her hair and clothing. Radios crackled, another police car arrived, followed by an ambulance, three more police cars, and a police van. Temporary lights were set up, brightening the scene like a movie shot, hardening everyone's features. Barricades appeared, strung with yellow tape: Police Line Do Not Cross. Traffic slowed on the street; a crowd, dotted with open umbrellas, gathered beyond the circle of lights. Voices were hushed, awed.

Officer Lehman stepped close to Helma and Ruth. Before he could speak, Ruth raised her hands as if she were surrendering and said, "Okay, so here we are again. It's a coincidence, purely a coincidence. I swear it. This is how we found him, right Walter?"

"That's right," Walter David told the policeman. "Just like he is now."

"Do you recognize him?" the policeman asked.

"No," Helma said.

"He doesn't live in *my* apartments," Walter told him.

"Not a clue," Ruth said.

"I'm giving the chief a call," he said. "He'd want to know about this right away." He slid into his car and began speaking on the radio.

"Oh geez, Helm," Ruth said. "Why does this stuff happen to us? I lead a full life; I don't *need* it."

"Step back, ma'am," Officer 087 said, stepping close to Helma.

"I'm well behind the taped area," she informed him without moving.

He stared at her and Helma recognized in his eyes the instant he identified her as the woman he'd ticketed that morning and she also recognized by the tightening of his face that it wasn't a pleasant memory.

"You've been on duty since eight this morning?" she asked. "Recent research has proven that such long shifts impair judgment."

"I worked a split shift," he said, then spun around with as much precision as if he still wore his black motorcycle boots and walked away as if he'd revealed too much.

"What was that about?" Ruth asked.

Suddenly a voice sounded clearly above the murmuring and conjecture of the crowd. "Why, that's the man who tried to steal my purse."

Helma turned to see Aunt Em who'd slipped through the barricades and milling policemen and now stood beside the dead man, holding her umbrella over his body.

"Excuse me, ma'am. Step back please," Officer 087 requested.

"He is," Aunt Em insisted indignantly. "I stabbed him."

"That's my aunt," Helma told the officer.

"She's confessing to this crime?" he asked, staring coldly at Helma as if she and Aunt Em were making jokes at his expense.

"No, she just flew in this afternoon. She . . ."

"Could you get her out of our way?" the bristly little policeman asked.

"Excuse me," Helma said. "But if my aunt says she recognizes the dead man, wouldn't it be wiser to investigate her claim than to disparage her?"

His moustache twitched and in the harsh artificial lights, his face darkened. He opened his mouth but Officer Lehman raised his hand to silence him. "She's right," he said. "There may be something to this. I'll do it."

He stepped up to Aunt Em with Helma right beside him and Ruth peering over her shoulder. "Excuse me, ma'am."

Aunt Em squinted up at him, then at Helma. "Oh, is this your young man?"

"No, Aunt Em. Could you tell the officer about the man who tried to steal your purse at the airport?"

"I already did. There he is on the ground, flat out." She shook her head and made tsk-tsking sounds. "I wonder what he tried to do this time that somebody killed him."

"You said you stabbed him?" the officer asked.

"But not like *that*," Aunt Em said, pointing to the body. She jabbed her left index finger into her right forearm three times. "With a hat pin."

"Wow," Ruth said. "Good job."

Helma knelt beside the dead man again, peering at the man's right forearm, which lay across his bloody chest. Just perceptibly in the fleshy part of his arm were three holes, one of them still flecked with blood.

## 🌷 chapter five 🌷

# THE OPEN DOOR

**C**hief of Police Wayne Gallant arrived while Helma, Ruth, and Aunt Em stood beside the body talking to Officer Lehman. Around them, the crowd had grown to such proportions that one policeman had been delegated to restrain the curious from disturbing the crime scene.

Officer Lehman met the chief at the edge of the crowd where the bright light turned to shadow, passing him a clipboard which Wayne Gallant studied before he joined Helma and Aunt Em. He was casually dressed, his big body clothed in slacks and a green polo shirt. Wayne Gallant was tall, with slightly cool, piercing blue eyes edged with fine lines that made him appear as if he were holding back a wink and a grin. His graying dark hair grew into a sharp widow's peak he usually combed over to conceal.

"On TV, they cover the body," Aunt Em said. She still held her umbrella over the dead man and seemed unable to take her eyes from him. Helma found her own eyes being drawn again and again to the three puncture marks on the man's arm, pondering other possibilities besides Aunt Em's hat pin.

"They'll cover him when they've finished investigating," Helma told her. "Maybe this isn't the same man who tried to steal your purse. The light here isn't very good and your . . ." She closed her mouth, realizing she'd been about to remind Aunt Em of her uncertain memory.

Aunt Em considered Helma, her expression thoughtful, then said. "You don't believe me, Wilhelmina?"

A policeman jostled Aunt Em and hastily apologized but she didn't notice, her Baltic blue eyes focused on Helma's, eyes like Helma's father, like all of them.

Helma touched her arm. "I believe you. Let's go upstairs now. The police can come up to talk to you. This must be upsetting."

"The older I am the less death is my enemy." She looked back at the body. "Have you seen somebody killed before?"

"I have," Helma told her, ignoring Ruth's quiet, "Habitually."

"It's sad, even for a purse snatcher."

Wayne Gallant nodded briefly to Helma, maintaining his professional demeanor, and Helma returned the nod, stepping away from Ruth, who'd nudged her in the ribs as if Helma could have missed his arrival. Aunt Em gazed up at Wayne Gallant and then at Helma. "Ah," she whispered. "*He's* the one."

The chief frowned, glancing between the body and Aunt Em as he listened to Officer Lehman explain Aunt Em's assertion that she'd stabbed the dead man when he attempted to steal her purse. He leaned over the victim and examined the man's forearm, using a small flashlight with an intense beam.

After a long moment he rose and asked Aunt Em, "Do you still have the hat pin?"

"Of course," she said, handing him her umbrella and removing the long pin from the lapel of her sweater. She held it out to him. "But I washed it."

"Glen," he said to one of the men near the body who immediately held out a plastic bag.

While he placed the pin inside the bag he said to Helma, his voice distracted, "If you want to get out of this rain, I'll be up in a few minutes to talk to your aunt."

Helma glanced up toward her apartment. Her door stood wide open, a bright rectangle of light spilling into the night. "Did you leave the door open, Aunt Em?" she asked.

"I suppose so," Aunt Em conceded. "I was in a hurry to see what the fussing was about."

Helma never left her apartment without locking her door and taking her keys, even to discard the trash. The sight of her door standing open with a clear view into her kitchen was disturbing.

"Don't worry about it," Ruth said, glancing up at the open door. "This place is crawling with cops. You could leave the crown jewels on your doormat and nobody would dare touch them."

"We'll be waiting," she told Wayne Gallant and walked Aunt Em to the elevator. "Don't go inside until I arrive," Helma warned her.

"You take this," Aunt Em said, offering the red umbrella, then she pulled it back. "No, I might need it to . . ." and she made parrying motions as if defending herself against an attacker.

"I'll keep an eye on the investigation," Ruth called after Helma as she threaded her way through the throng standing near the apartment building and up the stairs to the third level. She passed Mrs. Whitney's window and was grateful to see Mrs. Whitney sitting in her overstuffed chair crocheting purple yarn, her hands flashing, totally unaware of the tragedy in the parking lot below.

Aunt Em stood in Helma's doorway, leaning on her umbrella and peering inside. She turned at the sound of

Helma's footsteps and said, shaking her head, "It is not good, Wilhelmina."

Helma gazed over Aunt Em's shoulder. Somehow, with the crowd and all the policemen and authorities tending to tragedy in the Bayside Arms parking lot, an unscrupulous person had taken advantage of their averted attention to trespass her apartment and do who knew what kind of damage.

"*Zyltas*," Aunt Em said. Grass snake. There were no curse words in Lithuanian and the terms for snake and toad were as strong as the language got.

Helma's cupboard doors stood open; the lids were off her canister set, the alignment of her sofa pillows interrupted, magazines disturbed. The intruder had been in a hurry, not bothering to conceal his search.

Standing in the doorway, Helma took five breaths: in for a count of four, hold for four, exhale to the count of eight, concentrating only on her breath. When she was finished, she nodded once to herself and without stepping inside, turned back to the railing and looked down at the flurry of police activity beneath her. She spotted Ruth standing close to a tall policeman, drinking from a styrofoam cup.

Helma Zukas did not shout in public—or private— places, no matter the circumstances. She raised her hand in an attempt to catch someone's attention but it was immediately apparent that the crowd was focused on the scene near the dumpster, not more minor tragedies above their heads. She wasn't about to leave her apartment or Aunt Em alone again.

"Wait, Aunt Em," she said and took one step inside, saying in a loud voice, "If anyone is in this apartment, leave this moment because the police are coming up the steps to investigate."

Aunt Em frowned and squinted toward the empty stairs. After waiting a few moments with no response, Helma asked Aunt Em, "Would you like to stay with Mrs. Whitney for a while?"

"I'm not missing this for anything," Aunt Em told her.

"Then come inside but don't touch anything."

Aunt Em sat gingerly on the edge of a dining room chair, her hands gripping her umbrella handle, while she watched Helma dial a number on her telephone.

"Bellehaven Police," a woman answered Helma's call.

"Please dispatch a message to Chief of Police Wayne Gallant and inform him Miss Helma Zukas's apartment has been ransacked," she said. "He's currently in the parking lot of the Bayside Arms investigating a homicide."

"I'll send someone else, ma'am," the receptionist said in a soothing voice.

"No thank you. I believe they're already here. Simply notify the chief, please. That's all that's necessary."

There was a pause and the voice asked, "Oh, are you the librarian?"

"I'm a professional librarian at the Bellehaven Public Library, yes," Helma told her. "Is that pertinent?"

"Well . . . I . . . I'll make the call."

"Thank you," Helma said and hung up.

"I could go down and tell him myself," Aunt Em said, struggling to rise. "Or whistle. I can still whistle." And she pursed her lips, letting out a piercing blast.

Helma stared at her. She'd never known Aunt Em to whistle, hadn't even known she was capable. Within moments she heard the sound of heavy footsteps and in through her still-open door stepped Chief of Police Wayne Gallant, his forehead creased, a lock of dark hair falling across his brow. He looked from Helma to Aunt Em. "What's wrong?"

Aunt Em smiled smugly at Helma, for an uncomfortable instant reminding Helma of her cousin Ricky. "I told you," she said.

"My apartment's been ransacked," Helma told him.

"I did not close the door," Aunt Em confessed in a conspirator's whisper, as if she were responsible. "And they walked right in, free as the birds."

"You must have whistled," Wayne Gallant said to Aunt Em, saying it with such admiration that Helma was shocked to hear herself say, "I can whistle," wondering if she still could.

"I'd like to hear that sometime," Wayne Gallant said, a grin flashing across his face.

"We haven't checked yet to see what's missing," Helma told him.

"Wait a minute," he warned them. He walked through the apartment, down the hall toward the bedrooms, his cool eyes scanning Helma's life. Aunt Em rose partway from her chair, watching him. And now the expression on her face reminded Helma of Ruth.

"All right," Wayne Gallant said when he returned. "It looks like our man did a quick sweep through your apartment. I'll send up Sid to go through it with you. Tell him whatever's missing. I'll talk to you after I've finished downstairs."

"I'm sorry, Wilhelmina," Aunt Em told Helma after the chief left. "Everything is my fault."

"None of this is your fault, Aunt Em. How could it be?"

"I left the door open so the robbers could come in. I stabbed the purse snatcher and he chased me to Bellehaven." She looked at Helma, her tired eyes tearing up. "Are the police going to arrest me? Did I kill him?"

"Oh, Aunt Em, definitely not," Helma told her, placing both hands on Aunt Em's shoulders. "He was stabbed with an instrument far more lethal than a hat pin."

"Then I'm innocent?"

"Completely."

"At least I am this time," she said inexplicably.

Helma continued to gaze around her apartment, spotting further evidence of the intruder. Two paintings had been removed and now leaned against the wall beneath their accustomed places; three more were askew. Had the thief been searching for a wall safe? She stood, aching to remove the chaos from her apartment, to erase every vestige of the intruder's visit, then sat down again. Robbery and murder. Murder and robbery.

Aunt Em had nothing to do with the death of the purse snatcher in the parking lot but Helma was beginning to wonder if he had something to do with *her*. The prick marks in his forearm *might* be attributed to another cause besides Aunt Em, but that seemed too coincidental. It had been at least eight hours between the airport incident and his death, time enough for him to drive to Bellehaven and lie in wait for their return, but he would have had to know where Aunt Em was going. And then to be killed himself?

Her thoughts were interrupted by the arrival of Officer Sidney Lehman. When Helma had first met him five years ago he'd been a pink-cheeked young officer unsure of his authority. Now he had a touch of cool aloofness; even his movements had an unconscious self-assurance.

"Busy night," Sidney Lehman commented, flipping his notebook to a clean page and jotting a line at the top.

Helma explained again about the open door, pausing while Aunt Em said, "I did it," as if glad to have *that* off her conscience. He nodded, scribbling notes and then saying, "Let's see what else we've got here."

The doors concealing the washer and dryer off the hallway were open. In Helma's bedroom her closet doors gaped and empty boxes she kept in anticipation of Christmas were pulled from the top shelf and jumbled on the floor. Her dresser appeared untouched but again paintings had been removed from the walls. She shuddered at the image of an ıntruder prodding and poking her belongings, passing judgment on her possessions.

Her purse lay on the bed, its contents scattered beside it. There was no cash left in her wallet.

"Credit cards?" Officer Lehman asked, pointing his pencil at her wallet. Aunt Em stood in the doorway watching, her hands over her mouth.

"I don't carry credit cards," Helma told him, "or ATM cards." Her driver's license, library card, and AAA cards were still in their allotted slots. She noticed the officer gazing quizzically at the traffic ticket lying beside her purse, open as if the thief had read it. She picked it up, refolded it, and returned it to her purse without comment.

Aunt Em gave a soft cry when they stepped into the guest bedroom. Both her suitcase and purse had been dumped on the bed and the contents jumbled together. Her wallet too was empty but Aunt Em was more concerned about the hodgepodge of belongings she'd brought with her from Michigan than her missing cash. She sat on the bed and began sorting through her mementos, sighing and whispering.

"Is anything missing, Aunt Em?" Helma asked. She wouldn't have known. The black suspenders were tangled in the straps of the high-heeled black shoes, the matchbooks scattered among the photos.

"The medal," Aunt Em said. "Lukas's medal from the Great War. Oh," she said with such sorrow that Helma reached out and touched her shoulder. "The silver bag. Pansy's silver bag."

Pansy had been Aunt Em's sister. Helma barely remembered her: flamboyant, beautiful, dead in a train-car miscalculation. "A high roller," Helma's father had said once. "Liked the sauce."

Helma searched the floor and beneath the bed but the silver mesh bag was definitely gone. "Do these things belong to your brothers and sisters?'' Helma asked. She remembered her aunts and uncles as raucous, opinionated, crazily generous and like many oversensitive people, insensitive to the feelings of others. Always quarreling and ''at odds'' with one another but as fiercely loyal as members of the Mafia.

''Some do,'' Aunt Em said vaguely. ''Some don't.''

They finished listing missing items and then Helma fixed Aunt Em a cup of tea while Officer Lehman performed his police duties. She'd been fortunate. The crowd that had allowed the thief to step in and out of her apartment undetected had also kept him from leaving with anything sizable. The robber had made off only with objects he could slip into his pockets: cash, the silver bag, a World War I medal, perhaps a few other antique possessions that had struck his fancy in Aunt Em's suitcase.

Ruth barged in through the unlocked door. ''I just heard,'' she said, gazing around the disheveled apartment. ''What'd they take?''

''Cash, a couple of items of Aunt Em's. That's all we've discovered so far.''

Ruth dropped onto the sofa. ''Double whammy, maybe triple.'' She turned to Aunt Em. ''Welcome to Washington.''

''Thank you,'' Aunt Em said seriously, ''it's a lovely state.''

''State of chaos, you mean.'' Ruth frowned. ''Funny though, how all of this began when you . . .''

''It's too soon for conjecture,'' Helma said hastily, glancing toward Aunt Em.

''Right,'' Ruth agreed. ''Sorry.''

When Wayne Gallant returned, Aunt Em was beginning to wilt. It *was* three hours later in Michigan, but as the chief stepped inside, unconsciously ducking through the door the way tall men often did, she briefly revived, her eyes sparkling with interest. "Grill me now," Aunt Em told him, "before I fall asleep."

"Thank you, ma'am. Tell me about the man who tried to steal your purse."

Aunt Em frowned at the chief. "He's dead, downstairs on the ground."

"I mean while he was alive. Had you ever seen him before?"

Aunt Em thought, frowning and pursing her lips. She shook her head. "Not until he told me where the restrooms were."

"Did you approach him?"

"I asked him about the restrooms."

"You didn't wait for Ruth and Helma to return to ask them?"

"Not at my age."

Wayne Gallant bent toward her, his blue eyes warm, his smile apologetic, as if Aunt Em were the only person in the world. "Think carefully. Do you remember if he asked you if he could help you or did you ask him?"

"I think . . ." Aunt Em wrung her hands together. "I don't remember."

"But you thought he worked for the airport. Was he dressed like an employee?"

"He was wearing the same clothes he's wearing now." She raised her clasped hands to her mouth. "Maybe a jacket, too. Did he have a hat?"

"Not with him. Did he say anything to you after you stabbed him?"

"It wasn't suitable to repeat," Aunt Em said, glancing over at Helma as if she were protecting her sensitivities.

The chief's eyes twinkled. "I see."

Aunt Em yawned. "Is there more?"

"Any other questions can wait until tomorrow," the

chief told her. "Helma can bring you to the station. I'll give you a tour."

"My memory isn't so good the last few days," Aunt Em said, "but it's still better in the daylight. I'm getting old." She glanced from Helma to Wayne Gallant. "We're all growing older, all of us at the same time."

"I'll help you get the bed ready," Helma offered but Aunt Em shook her head, rising from the chair with the help of her umbrella. "I can do it myself. You two . . ." and she made motions between the two of them. "And Ruth, it's time for you to leave, too."

Ruth didn't stir from the couch. "I think I'll talk cops and robbers for a while."

"Ruth," Aunt Em said, dropping her voice as if Helma and the chief couldn't hear. "Helma and the policeman need to talk *alone*."

Wayne Gallant looked down at his shoes; Helma avoided Ruth's grinning face.

"Gotcha," Ruth said, rising under Aunt Em's stern gaze. "See ya, kids. Don't solve it all without me."

The door closed behind Ruth, and Wayne Gallant watched Aunt Em turn from the hallway into the bedroom. "Your aunt arrived earlier than you expected."

"She had an attack of some kind; the doctor's calling it a 'brain incident,' " Helma told him. "He doesn't want her to live alone again."

"A fall?"

"Maybe, she can't remember. Whatever it was, it's altered her personality. She's more . . . uninhibited, and her memory is uncertain."

"Something similar happened to my grandmother," the chief said, his pencil going lax in his hands. "She was in a car accident, a minor fender bender, totally unscathed, but afterward she quit gardening and baking, took up Bingo and smoking." He grinned. "We kids sure liked her better, but my mother . . ." He shook his head and made a motion with his hand, as if he were releasing a ball.

"Did your grandmother ever revert to her old self?" Helma asked hopefully.

"Not exactly. But she did quit smoking, at least we think she did." He held his pencil poised over his paper. "Are *you* all right?"

Helma rubbed her arms, suddenly chilled. "Fine." She nodded toward her disordered apartment. "This is . . . disturbing."

He nodded. "We have an opportunistic thief here. He hit two other apartments in the building under the same circumstances: the tenants rushed outside to investigate the disturbance and left their doors unlocked."

"What did he steal from them?" Helma asked.

"Cash mostly. A watch and a necklace. He didn't make as much of a mess in their apartments as he did yours."

"Mine is the end apartment, on the top floor," Helma said. "He had less chance of being interrupted." She paused, listening to Aunt Em cough in her bedroom, then said, "It's true that the murdered man is the purse snatcher my aunt stabbed at the airport, isn't it?"

"Right now, I'd say yes."

"I believed she imagined the incident," Helma told him. "I didn't press for an investigation."

"I've already called Sea-Tac. They're pulling the tape off their surveillance cameras so we can see if this guy was hanging around the airport all day and targeted anyone else, or if . . ." He stopped.

"Or if he specifically chose Aunt Em," Helma finished for him. "Have you identified him?"

"Not yet. No identification. No tattoos."

"I noticed a mark on his neck," Helma said. "Approximately two inches by four. Was it a birthmark?"

"A burn," the chief told her. "Not fresh but recent. What prompted you to call nine-one-one?"

Helma leaned back, replaying the evening carefully before she answered. "I heard two men quarreling. Shouting. Then the scream of a mortally wounded person. That's all."

"You couldn't make out any individual words?" He idly turned his mechanical pencil, end for end.

"No, but the tones indicated escalating rage."

"Was your aunt carrying anything of value?"

"Her suitcase contains mostly mementos from her past. I only glimpsed the contents before we were interrupted by the fight. And I didn't see what she carried in her purse. Money, certainly. But if that *is* the same man who attempted to snatch her purse, why follow us a hundred miles? Revenge for having thwarted his robbery attempt?"

"Never dismiss any motive," the chief advised. "Don't forget, if our investigation proves what your aunt says is true, she *did* stab him."

"But to *die* outside my apartment building? If he was planning to attack Aunt Em, then who attacked him?"

The mechanical pencil turned faster in the chief's hand, point and eraser stabbing his notepaper in a drumbeat. Helma had seen him make the same motions before. He was frustrated, without answers.

"The killer is still at large," Helma said. "If the purse snatcher was following Aunt Em, might *his* killer be interested in her, too?"

"The death could be a personal quarrel between two men, nothing to do with your aunt. We just don't know yet. I'd warn you to keep your doors locked and be careful, but I know you always do."

"Always," Helma said. They were silent, having said what needed to be said about the bad business at hand. She looked around at the disorderly room, knowing she had a long night ahead of her.

"Tell me," Helma said, her voice too loud in the quiet apartment. "Before you became chief of police, did you issue traffic tickets?"

"I still do sometimes."

"Did you give tickets to people for turning on yellow lights?"

"I heard about that," he said, clicking his mechanical pencil and sliding it into the spiral binder of his notebook.

"You heard about *my* traffic ticket?" Helma asked, rising from her chair. "Why?"

He shrugged. "I guess there are people who thought I'd be interested."

Helma sat down again. "I have no intention of paying the fine. I was within my legal rights."

A pained expression crossed Wayne Gallant's face. "Ignoring red lights is an epidemic in this city right now and we're cracking down on offenders. Zero tolerance."

"I wholeheartedly agree but a yellow light does not signify the same action as a red light."

"We'd be better off if it did," he said.

Helma smoothed the crease in her left pant leg; the chief rocked a little in his chair, slipped his notebook into his pants pocket, and rubbed his big hands together. Into the awkward silence came the sound of water running in the bathroom off the guest bedroom. Helma stood. "Thank you for responding to our crisis. Seeing you put Aunt Em's mind at ease."

"Yours too, I hope," he said, standing too. "Let me know if you find anything unusual when you clean up in here."

"I will. Oh," Helma said, motioning to the vase of flowers she'd discovered beside her door but there was no acknowledgement in the chief's eyes and Helma realized he wasn't the bestower and said no more about them.

He shifted his shoulders, rubbed his right hand through

his hair, then said, "I've been meaning to call you."

Helma had learned that silence usually elicited more response after a comment like that than all the questioning in the world so she remained silent, gazing at the chief as if he'd simply paused to take a breath between sentences.

"I've been busy," he said. "My children are visiting right now."

"How nice for you," Helma said. "And them."

"It is." He swallowed, then swallowed again. "It's an awkward situation and I'd like to talk to you about it this week sometime, maybe some evening after your aunt's asleep."

"You can phone me," she said. "In a few days I should be more familiar with Aunt Em's schedule."

"I will," he said and as Helma walked with him to the door of her apartment he lightly touched her shoulder and then pulled his hand away in the same manner he might have if he'd forgotten he was on duty and had absently taken a sip of an intoxicating beverage.

"Please call me if you have any more information about the murdered man or the robbery, as well," she told him as he stepped onto the landing.

"Will do," he nodded and left her, striding along the landing toward the steps and down into the parking lot where three police cars were still parked, lights shining on the darkly stained spot where the purse snatcher's body had lain.

## ❧ chapter six ❦

# FRIED POTATOES

**H**elma stayed up until two o'clock in the morning, returning her apartment to order, Lysol-spraying the hard surfaces and washing every bit of fabric the thief might have touched. Her washer and dryer hummed and thumped, its cycles a noisy comfort while she worked. Now that she knew the flowers hadn't come from Wayne Gallant, she removed them from the vase and placed them in a plastic bucket in the corner of her balcony, next to a pot of wildly successful geraniums. Boy Cat Zukas had disappeared through her open door during the disturbances and hadn't reappeared on her balcony to be let in but that wasn't unusual. The routines of his tomcatting days and nights still lingered, despite his altered state. Aunt Em slept on in the guest bedroom, peacefully unaware of Helma's labors.

Other than the money that had disappeared from her wallet, no other possessions of Helma's, in her purse or elsewhere, appeared to be missing. Under cover of the spin cycle, she slipped into Aunt Em's room and removed her black patent leather purse from the bureau, walking into the hall toward the living room with it held in both hands, glancing guiltily over her shoulder.

One by one she sorted through the items in the shiny

black bag, not snooping at all, but gathering information
for investigative purposes. Had Aunt Em opened her wallet
in the airport and the purse snatcher seen a tempting amount
of cash? Then had he followed Aunt Em, Helma, and Ruth
back to Bellehaven, thinking that despite Aunt Em's deadly
hat pin, they were easy marks?

The plastic picture holder held Aunt Em's expired
driver's license, a yellowed card printed in Lithuanian
which Helma couldn't read, but which might have been a
prayer, plus photos of Aunt Em's nieces and nephews,
mostly old school pictures with strangely unformed faces
rendered bland by their similarity of pose and smile.

The leather wallet was old, worn shiny and soft, more
of a man's billfold than a woman's, its corners devoid of
color or angle. Tucked in the empty bill holder, conforming
to the shape of the wallet as if it had rested there a very
long time, was a brittle envelope, half letter size, its edges
rust-colored.

With two fingers, Helma cautiously extracted the envelope. On the outside, written in faded and browned ink, a
note read, "Come home if it gets too hot. J." J. might be
Uncle Juozas, Aunt Em's husband who'd died ten years
ago, after fifty-eight years of marriage. "A congenial part-
nership," Aunt Em had called their union.

Helma gently opened the creased envelope. Inside was a
train ticket, valid for a one-way trip from Chicago to Scoop
River, Michigan on the Pere Marquette Railway. The date
of travel was open but the purchase date was November,
1928, almost seventy years ago. She held it in her hand,
studying its outdated print style. If she were to bend the
paper, it would surely crack like a dried autumn leaf.

"Too hot" in November? It didn't make sense. Aunt Em
would have been eighteen years old, and what was she doing in Chicago?

Helma carefully returned the ticket to the envelope and

tucked it back into the bill holder exactly as she'd found it, wondering if Aunt Em had been carrying the outdated ticket in her wallet for nearly seventy years; that was beyond sentiment.

The purse also held her underwear, the only clothing she'd brought with her, an embroidered handkerchief, comb and folded rain bonnet, magnifying glass, a mending kit, mints, and two dollars in loose change. Nothing else in her purse—not even the underwear—was as unusual as the train ticket.

Just before she went to bed, Helma heard a sound from outside the Bayside Arms that was familiar but which she couldn't place. She cautiously pulled the curtain aside and spotted a fireman standing in the light of his firetruck, hosing off the pavement near the dumpster site. Helma dropped the drapery and stepped away from the window.

Helma couldn't say if an actual noise had awakened her. It was more an awareness of another presence in her apartment. She sat upright in her bed, automatically noting the time on her digital clock: 5:43, and the weather through a gap in her curtains: partly cloudy, before she remembered there *was* another presence in her apartment: Aunt Em.

The second stage of awareness was her sudden recall of the night before. She lay back on her pillow, stunned by the rush of images: the dead purse snatcher lying on the wet parking lot pavement, her burgled apartment, Aunt Em's hat pin. And lastly, the flowers that hadn't been sent by Wayne Gallant.

She raised her head, sniffing. The odor wafting beneath her bedroom door was heavy, greasy like fried foods. She visualized the food stocking her refrigerator and couldn't recall a single item that would benefit from frying. She sniffed again, her nostrils delicately flaring: onions for certain. Coffee and potatoes. But she didn't have either item in her cupboards.

Then a burst of laughter brought her upright: Ruth. Helma sighed and swung her feet out of bed into the slippers she kept poised beside it. She'd slept so soundly during her brief night that she hadn't moved; her bed was unruffled. With one hand she pulled from her hair the single curler that held down the stubborn curl on the left side of her head, and with the other she reached for the robe lying across the foot of her bed.

In her living room, all the curtains stood open, the door onto her deck as well; not even the opaque screen was pulled and the sky to the west *did* look like possible sunshine. The smell of saltwater mingled with the food odors.

In the kitchen, outside the bounds of his allotted territory, Boy Cat Zukas sat washing his face in front of a meticulously clean saucer. Ruth sat on the counter, her legs swinging, a cup of coffee in her hand. "Whoops," she said, sliding off the counter. She saluted Helma with her cup. "Morning."

"Ah, Wilhelmina," Aunt Em said, waving a spatula toward the open door to the balcony and Washington Bay beyond. "I didn't know last night that it was so beautiful, like Lake Michigan."

"Only with islands and thousands of miles beyond," Helma pointed out.

"It doesn't smell as nice as Lake Michigan, though," she said, wrinkling her nose. "And no sand dunes."

"Did you sleep well?" Helma asked her, gazing at the pots and pans covering the stove top.

"I dreamed I stabbed a man and he died in your dumpster." She watched Helma's face closely for her reaction.

"No," Helma told her. "You defended yourself against a man who tried to steal your purse. He *was* killed later, but not by you. You were with me."

"It comes and goes," Aunt Em said. She shook her head as if scaring away something ugly that was buzzing around her.

"You're up early," Helma said to Ruth. Unless she stayed up all night, Ruth was rarely awake this time of morning. Ruth's eyes were bagged, overbright, and tinged with red. Helma guessed it had been one of the nights when Ruth hadn't met her bed. Actually, she felt the way Ruth looked.

"Couldn't sleep after all that excitement," Ruth told her, "so I came over to see if you and the chief had solved one mystery," she wiggled her eyebrows like Groucho Marx, "or another."

"Not yet," Helma said, and Ruth guffawed.

"I was just going to wake you up for a good breakfast," Aunt Em told Helma. She wore a blue skirt and pale blouse that Helma had left hanging in the spare bedroom closet, covered by an apron worn inside out that had been a gift from Ruth: bright red with cartoon characters Helma didn't recognize and which had also been consigned to the spare bedroom. The clothes were snug around Aunt Em's middle but otherwise they suited her surprisingly well.

"What are you cooking?" she asked, nodding to the pots and pans on the stove.

"Potatoes and eggs and ham." She tapped a small kettle with steam escaping between the rim and lid. "And prunes to give you good health. I stewed them with wine. After last night we need strong food."

"But I don't have any of those foods, except the eggs." Helma had planned soft poached eggs, warmed croissants, and fresh orange juice, tea with warm milk.

"I know," Aunt Em said sadly. "You must shop more often; you were out of everything. I went from neighbor to neighbor." She tsk-tsked. "Some of them weren't even up. When you're old you wake up early so you can be busy before the day notices you're still alive. Ethel gave me cinnamon rolls from her freezer."

"Ethel?" Helma asked. Who was Ethel?

"Next door," Aunt Em said as she lifted a lid and poked into a frying pan with the spatula. "Your Mrs. Whitney."

"Oh."

"Ah," Ruth said, "diet be damned: *real* food. I'm famished."

Aunt Em beamed. "Hurry," she said to Helma. "Get dressed."

"Yeah," Ruth said, waving Helma onward. "I want to hear what happened after I got thrown out last night."

Helma left them and performed an abbreviated toilet in her bathroom, all the time hearing Ruth and Aunt Em chattering in the kitchen, punctuated by occasional laughter, hurrying, aware of that uncomfortable sensation of being left out.

When she returned to the dining room, Aunt Em was dishing food onto three plates: crusty fried potatoes and onions, shiny with grease; thick slices of pink ham with translucent fat curling around the edges; eggs over easy fried in butter; dessert bowls of prunes; tall glasses of orange juice; and cups of coffee. Helma's stomach blanched. It was more food than she ate in two meals, more fat than she ate in a week.

"Don't look like that," Ruth said. "See, no coffee for you. You get tea." Under her breath, Ruth whispered, "Eat. Don't hurt her feelings."

A piece of potato fell from Aunt Em's spatula to the floor. She picked it up, mumbled a few words in Lithuanian, kissed it, and placed it on her plate.

And when all three were seated, their heaping plates in front of them, Ruth raised her glass of orange juice to Aunt Em and said, "Your first morning in Bellehaven. It can only get better . . . we hope."

Aunt Em raised her own juice and the three clicked glasses.

"Eat up," Aunt Em told them, dabbing her lips with her napkin. "And then we'll solve the murder."

"Good idea," Ruth said, spearing fried potatoes on her fork as if murder were a delectable dessert.

"Oh, and robbery," Aunt Em added. "Wasn't there a robbery?"

Ruth gazed around Helma's apartment. "You'd never know it."

"I cleaned," Helma told her.

"Oh, that's right," Aunt Em said, sagging in her chair. "Lukas's medal, Pansy's purse."

"This meal looks delicious, Aunt Em," Helma said to divert Aunt Em's attention from her loss.

"I'd better not drive God up a tree," Aunt Em said in Lithuanian, an adage Helma had often heard her father say when he was frustrated over what couldn't be changed, "or he won't come down when I need him."

Helma took a bite of one small piece of crispy potato, leaving half on her fork. She hadn't eaten fried potatoes since her last visit to Michigan before her father died.

"Tastes like home," Ruth said, exactly what Helma was thinking.

"This is farm cooking," Aunt Em told them. "Not like I ate in Chicago."

"When were you in Chicago?" Ruth asked.

"When I was too young to know any better."

Helma caught the glitter of curiosity in Ruth's eyes and was about to deflect any questions regarding Aunt Em's personal past when she thought, why not? Helma had always known Aunt Em as a very private person and now here she was, offering information that Helma herself was trying to puzzle out.

"Was that before you married Uncle Juozas?" Helma

asked, remembering the train ticket from 1928.

"Maybe," Aunt Em said cagily. "Who wants to know?"

"Nobody but us chickens," Ruth said as she chewed a bite of ham and Aunt Em laughed.

"Someday maybe I'll tell it all. Everybody from long ago will have a party and remember it together." She paused and frowned, then said, "Ah, they're all as dead as the purse snatcher, aren't they? I forget." She shrugged and speared more potatoes. "That's the way life is." And she snapped her fingers with as much verve as she'd whistled the night before.

Ruth snapped her own back. "Just like that. So speaking of . . . what have we got here: a dead purse snatcher who followed us from Seattle for more than our good looks."

"Or to revenge himself on me for stabbing him," Aunt Em offered, sitting a little straighter in her chair and savoring the word "revenge."

"It wouldn't have been easy to follow us," Helma said. "It was hours after we left the airport before we headed home."

"Maybe he tailed us all day long," Ruth suggested and then shuddered. "There's a creepy thought. Unless he knew you."

"I didn't recognize him," Helma said. "He may have used my license plate number to discover my address. The chief said not to discount the motive of revenge, but . . ."

"Yeah; it seems a little farfetched. But the criminal mind is a mysterious piece of work."

"I knew criminals," Aunt Em told them. "Lots of them. Murderers, blackmailers, robbers, car thieves, cattle rustlers. They think just like we do only they don't stop at thinking."

Ruth stopped chewing and stared at Aunt Em. "How'd you know criminals?"

Aunt Em shrugged. "It's like mushroom hunting."

"Funny I never thought of it that way," Ruth said.

"When you search through the woods," Aunt Em went on, "you look and look but you can't find any mushrooms. And then finally you find one. Just one, and suddenly your eyes change and you see mushrooms everywhere."

"Did you know criminals in Scoop River?" Helma asked.

"Everywhere," Aunt Em said. She waved toward the balcony and Washington Bay. "Even here in this beautiful country." She nodded sagely. "Like mushrooms."

"I don't believe it's a coincidence," Helma said. "The purse snatcher didn't just happen to end up murdered here in the parking lot."

"Coincidences happen," Aunt Em said. Her face brightened. "Oh, I just remembered your policeman last night. Did you spoon?"

Helma didn't answer and Ruth offered, "Probably not. His ex-wife came back to town last week. She's changed her mind about giving him up."

"With this ring I thee wed," Aunt Em recited. " 'Til I am bored or you are dead."

"Whether the purse snatcher followed us or not," Helma began, thinking it was wiser to discuss murder than romantic entanglements and disentanglements, "someone murdered *him*."

"Let's say that the murderer spotted the purse snatcher lurking around your apartment building," Ruth suggested, "and thought, 'Whoa, this guy looks like evil incarnate, I think I'll stab him dead.' Couldn't you just kiss him?" She sat back and tapped her fingernail on the edge of her empty plate. "Or is that too extreme?"

"Another extreme thought," Helma said, "is that this mysterious felon remains at large." She turned to Aunt Em. "Is this conversation upsetting you?"

Aunt Em vigorously shook her head. "No. It's interesting."

Ruth tapped her fork against her plate and said seriously, "Supposing the purse snatcher *did* follow us and suppose he *was* going to continue the job but he was killed, not by an acquaintance of *his*," she pointed to Helma, "but of *yours*? Somebody out there watching out for you, maybe hanging around in parking lots and sitting in dark bushes, or even in the library, just waiting and watching . . ."

"Ruth," Helma said, nodding toward Aunt Em who was listening to Ruth with held breath, her eyes sparkling.

"Nah," Ruth hastily said. "Too crazy."

"I like it," Aunt Em told her. "An angel, like on that TV show."

"Except angels don't usually go around stabbing people to death for the sake of their TV charges," Ruth said.

"Avenging angels do," Aunt Em told them. "John Wayne killed Geraldine Page's husband in *Hondo*. He claimed it was an accident, but . . ."

The phone rang and Ruth reached behind her toward the counter and handed the receiver to Helma, holding the stretched cord above the dirty plates.

"Helma, this is Wayne Gallant. It'll be on the news but I wanted you to know we've identified the victim."

"Was he local?" Helma asked.

"His name's Peter Binder, with a couple of aka's, although he's stuck to his own name the past couple of years. Thirty-seven. Originally from upstate New York but he's been a real rolling stone since he was twenty-two, not always successful at staying ahead of the law. Breaking and entering, assault, extortion, robbery, unpaid traffic tickets, etcetera. But here's the interesting part: in the past year he's lived briefly in East Lansing and Traverse City."

"Michigan cities," Helma said.

"That's right."

While Aunt Em and Ruth were engaged in a discussion of the John Wayne videos Aunt Em had brought with her, Helma asked, "Was he on the same flight as Aunt Em?"

She heard a sound through the telephone like the release of a breath. "Does she remember seeing him on the flight?"

"Not at all, but I can ask again."

"We're checking it. There were no effects on his body. Somewhere there's a motel room or rental car . . ."

"Or an airplane ticket," Helma finished.

"Right. Okay, well, I'll give you a call as soon as we verify it or come up with anything else. Don't mention it to your aunt yet. Oh, also no fingerprints from the robberies. It looks like our boy wore gloves but we're still working on it." He paused overlong and then said, "See ya."

"Good-bye," Helma told him as she replaced the receiver and met Aunt Em's and Ruth's expectant faces.

## ❧ chapter seven ❧

# BEARING GIFTS

"**E**ast Lansing and Traverse City?" Ruth asked. "He lived in Michigan?"

Helma nodded. "During the past year, so probably not long enough to make any real connections. His name was Peter Binder, his given name, that is; he had aliases although none he'd used lately."

"As far as the police know," Ruth said.

"Peter Binder," Aunt Em repeated in a slow voice. "I knew a Petras Bayless." They turned to her and she added, "But he's an old man who spits tobacco in his daughter's sink. He might be dead."

Ruth's mouth skewed to one side; her brows gathered, then rose as she looked at Helma. "He accompanied the goods from there to here," she said from the side of her mouth like a movie gangster.

"That's a possibility," Helma agreed. "It's being looked into." She turned her attention to Aunt Em, asking, "Did you talk to people on the airplane yesterday?"

"Was that only yesterday?" She dabbed at her mouth with her napkin and shook her head in disbelief. "There wasn't much else to do. All of us crammed together in those little seats, and the movie screens are too tiny to see."

"How about sitting next to you?" Ruth asked. "Anybody interesting?"

Aunt Em took a sip of coffee, then said, "A woman with three names who wrote mystery books. She said a lot of women of a certain age write mysteries." She frowned, then nodded as if she'd just puzzled something out. "Killing off men."

"Anyone else?" Helma asked. "Any men?"

"A rabbi sat across the aisle, but we mostly talked about which of us was the most guilty: Jews or Catholics."

"Now there's a prize worth winning," Ruth commented as she took another helping of fried potatoes.

"Can you remember what you were carrying in your purse?" Helma asked.

"When?"

"On the airplane trip from Michigan to Seattle."

"The usual. My tickets too, until that snippy stewardess took them away from me." Aunt Em poured herself a second glass of orange juice. Her plate was nearly empty.

"Did she open your purse?"

"I did, but it was bumpy and I spilled. We all scrambled to pick up everything. All of us except her."

"Were all the contents returned to you?" Helma continued to gently ask while they finished their breakfast, carefully making her questions nonchalant.

Aunt Em nodded. "Everything. Even my underwear. *That* was embarrassing. It isn't very fancy, not like you probably wear," she said, nodding to Ruth.

"I only wear the stuff when I have to," Ruth said.

Aunt Em nodded in approval. "It would last longer that way, wouldn't it?"

"Cheaper too," Ruth agreed.

"Think about everything that was in your purse," Helma told Aunt Em, bringing the conversation back to the flight. "What was valuable?"

"My money. There was a magnifying glass; my eyes are growing old now. I had one of those cute little bottles of Scotch from the plane but I drank it. Some old papers."

"What kind of papers?" Ruth asked.

"My father's naturalization papers. My birth certificate. All like that. They were papers from my 'important' drawer in the kitchen."

"But you don't have those papers now," Helma said.

"Ah, you snooped in my purse," Aunt Em said without any accusation in her voice. "You didn't see my papers?"

"No," Helma told her.

Aunt Em pushed back her chair and rose from the table. "I'll look in my suitcase."

As soon as she left the room, Ruth said, "What we have here is an unsavory character on a little plane trip who sees an old lady drop her purse and something so juicy rolls out of it that he tries to snatch her purse in the airport. Failing that he follows her here and winds up dead."

"There weren't any papers in her purse," Helma said. "Unless the person who burgled my apartment stole them."

"Or unless she never had them in the first place."

"The distant past does seem more relevant to her than the present." Helma reached for the phone. "I'll call Bruce."

"I tried to call you last night," Bruce told her as soon as Marcus, the nephew with no broken bones, called him to the phone. "No answer. You really should get an answering machine."

"We must have been outside. How's Daniel feeling?"

"Aggravated. There's no glory in wearing a cast in the middle of summer. Is Aunt Em okay? What do you think of her?"

"She's . . . enthusiastic."

Bruce laughed and Helma asked him, "Do you know

what was in Aunt Em's purse when she boarded the plane?''

"You mean her underwear?"

"Besides that? Did you see any legal papers? Her birth certificate? Our grandfather's naturalization papers?"

"I have Gramps's papers," Bruce told Helma. "She gave them to me for safekeeping before she left. Her birth certificate and some social security forms, too. Want me to get them for you?"

"No. Aunt Em thought she'd brought them with her."

"I told you she wasn't the same," Bruce said, sounding so much like the I-told-you-so brother of old that Helma said, "She's fine, just tired from her trip."

Ruth rolled her eyes and after Helma hung up, asked, "Why didn't you tell him about the murder?"

"I will after it's solved," Helma said and reached for Ruth's plate.

Ruth pulled her dish back. "Let me finish these potato scraps; then I plan to lick the plate clean. Are you afraid he'd come sweeping in and steal Aunt Em from under your nose?"

"Of course not. His son just broke his leg. There's no reason to compound his worries in the midst of his own family crisis."

"If you say so. So he has the papers she claims were in her purse?"

Helma nodded. Which statements of Aunt Em's could she trust? The spilled purse rang true. And the stabbing scene with the hat pin had almost been verified. Besides those two incidents, Helma was reluctant to believe anything unless she witnessed it with her own eyes. "The purse snatcher went to extreme lengths to find out where I lived so he either saw something of value in Aunt Em's purse on the plane or he wasn't on the flight and he was seeking revenge because she'd stabbed him."

"I'll buy that. What about *his* murderer?"

"They could have been partners, a team," Helma speculated. "They quarreled—I heard *that*."

"Probably about whether to break down your door or not." Ruth grimaced. "Let's hope the guy who *didn't* want to is the murderer and now he's sunk back into his swamp. End of case. Because if the *other* guy won, he's still out there waiting for the perfect moment to finish the job."

"But the man Aunt Em stabbed is dead, so there'd have to be another motive besides revenge," Helma pointed out. "We're back to a valuable object."

"Hell, I don't know." Ruth rubbed her temples. "I'm getting a headache. Let's talk about something simple."

Ruth chewed her thumbnail, thinking, and Helma looked away. Finally Ruth asked, "What about those flowers on your doorstep last night? Were they from the chief?"

"No. There was no card."

"Not even a florist's card?"

"Only a bouquet in a glass vase," Helma told her.

"Mystery man." Ruth gazed around the apartment. "So where are they?"

"The vase is in the recycle bin and the flowers are on the balcony, in a plastic bucket."

"There's a waste of good money," Ruth said. "If somebody sent *me* flowers, they'd be on display big time. On my table at least."

The last time Helma had seen Ruth's table it was so cluttered there hadn't been room to set a plate and fork.

"Maybe the murderer left them," Ruth suggested. " 'So sorry I'm going to make a mess in your parking lot.' Have you thought of that?"

"No, Ruth, I haven't," Helma said. "I'm sure the card just blew off." She stood. "I'll tell Aunt Em that Bruce has her papers."

"Oh jeez yes," Ruth said. "We're out here spinning

tales and she's in there frantically rummaging through her suitcase." Ruth followed Helma down the hall to Aunt Em's bedroom.

Aunt Em sat on her unmade bed, her suitcase open and its contents to either side of her. She wasn't frantic or even searching, only casually choosing an object, gazing at it, and setting it to one side or the other. "Oh, hello dears," she said, glancing up at Helma and Ruth. "Are you having a nice visit? Now have I been here one day or one week?"

"You got here yesterday." Ruth picked up a silver necklace tangled with a silver ring. "Were these in your purse?" she asked Aunt Em.

Aunt Em took the delicate silver in her wrinkled hands. "Jonukas brought me these from Paris, after the war, the second one. They were for Danute but she ran off with that marble layer from Ohio before he even came home. Broke his heart."

Jonukas was Helma's father, the name a diminutive form of John. "Who was Danute?" she asked.

"Ah, a beautiful girl." Aunt Em tapped her head. "Not too many lights on up here. But a Charlie Einstein of beauty."

"Albert," Helma corrected.

"Who's Albert?" Aunt Em asked.

"Albert Einstein."

"Yes?" Aunt Em waited expectantly.

"Never mind," Helma said. "What happened to my father and Danute?"

"She ran off," Aunt Em repeated. "I thought he'd cry his eyes out over her." She sniffed a little. "Your mother stepped right in and picked him off when his defenses were down."

Helma was ignorant of this story and she wondered if she should stop Aunt Em; this was bordering on gossip, but Ruth eagerly asked, "So that's why you and Helma's mother didn't get along?"

"Partly, and partly other things."

"But you and my mother reconciled your differences last fall," Helma reminded her.

"I don't remember that," Aunt Em said.

"Mother flew to Michigan," Helma prompted her. "You said you wanted to 'duke it out,' " and when Aunt Em continued to shake her head, Helma added, "She brought you a salmon."

"For a present?" Aunt Em asked. "A dead fish?"

"It was smoked."

"A dead fish," Aunt Em repeated. She was warming up, her memories poking and prickling, threatening to well up and devour hard-won goodwill.

"Why are you carrying a train ticket from 1928 in your wallet?" Helma asked to distract her. "Valid for a trip from Chicago to Scoop River."

Aunt Em froze. Her eyes narrowed and Helma asked, "Did Uncle Juozas send it to you? To come home for Christmas?"

Slowly, she shook her head. "In case of emergency."

"If someone in your family became ill and you had to return to Scoop River?"

"For *my* emergency. In case I had to leave in a hurry."

"But you must not have," Ruth said, "if you still have the ticket."

"My emergency was too big for a train," she said, gazing down at her hands, absently running the fine silver necklace across her lined palm.

"What do you mean, Aunt Em?" Helma gently asked. "What was the emergency?"

Aunt Em seemed to shrink. "Ah," she said in a small voice. "It doesn't matter now. The ticket reminds me of

Juozas. He was a good man. You should have a man like him, Wilhelmina, somebody . . . steady."

Helma's doorbell rang. When she looked through the peephole before she unlocked the double lock, she saw the bright-haired figure of her mother on the landing. Helma opened the door and, without waiting for a greeting, her mother stepped inside, jumping from one breathless sentence to the next, holding out a bouquet of snapdragons as she spoke. "I heard about *it* on the radio." She swept her hand down toward the parking lot where a new dumpster to replace the one the police had taken glowed green in the morning light, not a sign of last night's violence remaining.

"Stabbed, they said, and discovered right *here*. You think you're safe . . . Wouldn't *you* put barriers around the spot? At least for a couple of days so people wouldn't step on it. Where's Emily? Did she see it? I hope it wasn't too much for her; she's not well you know, not after that brain thingamajig. What a greeting for her: murder."

Helma took the flowers and closed the door while her mother glanced expectantly around her apartment, her eyebrows raising at the three place settings on the table, as curious that there were three, Helma was sure, as by the fact that dirty dishes still sat on Helma's table. Lillian wore a matching sweatpants outfit, both pieces in dusty purple. She'd lost eleven pounds over the winter and now favored clothing with more "cling" to it.

"Aunt Em's fine, Mother," Helma told her. "She's in the bedroom."

"Resting, poor thing," Lillian said. "Who had breakfast with you, dear?" she asked, nodding toward the table. She smiled, her teeth showing. "Was it the chief of police, here to discuss the murder with you? A man needs a woman's perspective, I always say."

"It was Ruth," Helma told her and Lillian's smile sagged.

Ruth and Aunt Em entered the living room from the hall-way, Aunt Em first. When she saw Lillian, she stopped, tip-ping her head while Lillian opened her arms and cried, "Emily dear," and rushed forward, happily embracing Aunt Em, who stood stiffly, not returning the hug. Helma's mother stepped back uncertainly, her penciled brows gathered.

"What's she up to?" Aunt Em asked Helma in a voice intended to be a whisper but reaching every corner of Helma's apartment.

"Up to?" Lillian asked. "I'm not up to anything. I'm happy to see you."

"Why?" Aunt Em demanded.

"Because you're my sister-in-law. I thought we worked out all those silly quarrels when I came to visit you last fall."

Aunt Em nodded toward Helma. "That's what she said, but I don't remember it."

"Mother brought you flowers," Helma said, offering the bouquet of snapdragons her mother had handed her.

"Oh no, dear," Lillian said. "Those are for you."

"You brought me flowers?" Helma asked.

"I didn't bring them. I found them on your doormat."

Behind Aunt Em, Ruth said, "Somebody dropped those off in the past forty-five minutes because they sure weren't there when I showed up."

Both Helma and Ruth headed for the door, intending to scan the street and parking lot, while behind her, Helma heard her mother croon, "A secret admirer. Isn't that nice?"

The usual Monday morning traffic passed the Bayside Arms. The air was warm, soft with humidity. A block away, Helma glimpsed a man in coveralls mowing a steep lawn. There was no movement among the cars in the build-ing's parking lot, no sign of anyone sitting behind the wheel of a parked car.

"It's not like a killer would hang around expecting you

to blow kisses from your landing, anyway," Ruth said, standing beside Helma at the railing and scanning the morning.

"I don't believe the murderer would come back to leave flowers," Helma said.

"Haven't you heard that saying about the criminal always returning to the scene of the crime? Who said that anyway?"

"It's one of our library stumpers," Helma told her, referring to the notebook at the reference desk where the librarians jotted questions they weren't able to satisfactorily answer. "But I'll mention it to the chief."

"Good idea. It might shake him up a little; kill two birds with one stone, as they say, remind him that other men find you attractive."

"According to your theory, this other man is a murderer. That hardly makes him a viable suitor."

"It's the *idea* that will occur to him, that's what we're aiming for, a reminder that he'd better get off his . . ."

"I'm not aiming for anything, Ruth. I already explained I'm not interested in a competition. Wayne Gallant's life is his own business, not mine."

"We're talking his *ex-wife*, Helma Zukas. Ex-wives hold a unique place in a man's heart. If she does a good enough job ripping it to shreds he starts to think she's the only one who can put it back together again."

"Ruth, I'm not listening to this," Helma said, turning and placing her hand on the doorknob. "My main concern is why a purse snatcher was so intent on robbing Aunt Em and why he's dead. Of far lesser concern is who's leaving me gifts." She stopped, frozen by a sudden thought.

"What is it?" Ruth asked.

"Suppose the flowers aren't intended for me?"

"So who else? Boy Cat Zukas?"

Helma slowly shook her head, still thinking. "Aunt Em," she said.

"Aunt Em," Ruth repeated. "That *is* creepy. Tell the chief."

"I already said I planned to." Helma turned her doorknob but the door had automatically locked when Ruth had closed it behind herself.

"I don't suppose you keep a spare key under the mat," Ruth said, watching Helma fruitlessly turn the knob.

"Research shows that's the first place a burglar checks."

"I never lock my door," Ruth said. "Saves everybody time. We'd better get back in there before they unsheath the claws."

Helma raised her hand to press the doorbell, but before she could touch it, the door opened and Aunt Em stood there, her lips pursed, her face deadly serious. "It's a call from the library," she told Helma. "It's very important."

Helma hurried to the phone, noting as she crossed the kitchen the stiff-backed way her mother sat on Helma's sofa, her lips a tight line.

"Helma, it's George Melville. We need you down here."

"What is your emergency?" Helma asked the library cataloger, sounding even to herself like a 911 operator.

"The Moonbeam," he said, referring to Ms. Moon, the library director. "She's called a meeting to launch one of her maniacal schemes. Didn't I tell you? Bet you ten bucks she was waiting until you walked out the door before she dropped this little bomb."

"What is it?"

"Too complicated to explain on the phone but trust me; it's a doozy. Can you make it? Ten o'clock."

"My aunt . . ."

"Yeah, I know. I heard about the murder in your parking lot, too. And now *this*. Not your day, is it? So can we count on you?"

George Melville was irreverent, cynical, a natural parodier and a frequent juvenile trickster. But no matter how hard he tried he couldn't hide the fact that he was good at his job and possibly even, to his chagrin, enjoyed it, so a request like this was too unusual for Helma to ignore. She glanced at her mother and Aunt Em sitting across from each other, their eyes not meeting. And Ruth, who sat in the rocker, absently rocking it with one foot, a dreamy smile on her face, doubtlessly caught in a fantasy about her upcoming visit from Paul in Minnesota. Certainly Aunt Em would be safe with either or both of them.

"I'll be there in twenty minutes," she told George.

"I can hold her off until then," George said. He hesitated, then added, "Thanks, Helma," before he hung up.

"There's an emergency at the library," Helma told the three silent women. "I must attend a meeting."

"Did somebody steal a book?" Aunt Em asked, ignoring Lillian who said, with a touch of disdain, "People do *that* all the time."

"I'll explain when I return," Helma said.

"I have to pick up some groceries," Lillian began and then when she saw the expression on Helma's face, amended it to, "but I can do that later."

"We can watch one of my John Wayne movies," Aunt Em offered eagerly. "*The Searchers.* It's my favorite."

"I guess this calls for me to hang out and play Mills Lane," Ruth said.

"I didn't know you played music," Aunt Em told her.

Because it was an event still in the news, Helma knew Ruth was referring to the referee in a famous ear-biting boxing match.

"I'll be home as soon as I can," Helma told them. The last thing she did before she left her apartment was to place the bouquet of snapdragons in the plastic bucket on her balcony with the other flowers from the unknown donor.

## ❧ chapter eight ❧

# INNOVATIONS

**H**elma left Ruth, Aunt Em, and her mother behind in her apartment and hurried down the steps, curious about the library's emergency and doubting Ms. Moon's latest idea was any more peculiar than others she'd launched in the past three years. There were the children's camp-outs in the library, the adopt-a-librarian program, her plan for a meditation room behind the biography section, which was abandoned the third time Jack the janitor disposed of used condoms, and a hiring policy which had replaced the retiring Mrs. Carmon at the circulation desk with a man called "Dutch," a policy George Melville dubbed, "Hire-the-Unfit."

After the events of the past twenty-four hours, Helma welcomed the respite of a library crisis. In fact, she experienced a ripple of excitement along the back of her neck, similar to the arousal of a good soldier contemplating a tactical opportunity.

"Excuse me, Helma."

Helma started; she hadn't noticed Walter David, the building manager, standing outside his first-floor apartment. His face was glum. "Yes?"

"The police told me about the robberies in the building last night. I'm damn sorry."

Helma believed him. It was uncharacteristic for Walter to use profanity, at least in her presence.

"It wasn't your fault," Helma told him. "We accidentally left our door open. The thief took advantage of the moment."

"I try to keep an eye out for trouble," he said, gazing lovingly across the front of the building. "But with both crimes happening at once: murder and robbery . . ."

"I've always felt very secure in my apartment," Helma assured him. "Tell me, did you notice anyone delivering flowers to my apartment last night or this morning?"

He shook his head, an even glummer expression crossing his face.

"That's all right. I only wondered," Helma told him. She turned to leave when Walter said, "Somebody *did* deliver flowers yesterday afternoon though, between two and three."

Helma halted. The flowers could have been delivered any time since she'd spent the entire day in Seattle. They'd been left in a vase of water and wouldn't have wilted. "Can you describe the person who delivered them?"

Walter bit his lip and removed his Seattle Mariners cap as if that would help him remember. "It was a man. He acted like he knew what he was doing. No hesitation, you know what I mean? Typical delivery person so I didn't pay much attention. Nothing unusual, no weird hair or clothes or tattoos." He shrugged and apologized again. "Sorry."

"If you see anyone delivering flowers again, will you try to remember his features?"

"Sure," Walter said eagerly. "Does it have anything to do with the murder last night? Are you working with the police again?"

"No, it's an entirely different matter," Helma said, adding "I hope," beneath her breath. "Thank you, Walter. Good-bye."

" 'Bye. The police did a good job of cleaning up, though. You can't tell anything happened out there."

Helma's parking spot in the tiny lot beside the library was empty. She'd often wondered if another employee parked there on her days off. Either they didn't or the warning had gone out that Helma was on her way.

As was her custom, she lined up the Buick's hood ornament with the flagpole on the library lawn, causing her to park equidistant from either white line that demarked her territory.

Eve, the fiction librarian, was the first to spot Helma entering the workroom. She stood beside the door to the staff lounge, wearing a short pink skirt and sleeveless top, twisting a yellow curl around her finger. "Am I ever glad to see you," she said, meeting Helma halfway. "George said you were coming." Eve spoke in quick sharp bursts, each sentence ending on the upbeat as if to frame a question.

"He said Ms. Moon had called a special meeting."

"Yeah. Wait 'til . . ." Eve gasped and raised her hand to her mouth. "Oh. That dead man in your dumpster. I forgot. That was so creepy."

"He wasn't actually *in* the dumpster," Helma began but at that moment Ms. Moon emerged from her office carrying a stack of papers. "Helma," she said, her eyes widening and her usual benign smile faltering. "I thought you were taking today off, the entire week, actually."

"I only dropped by. Is there a meeting?"

Ms. Moon licked her lips and held her sheaf of papers closer to her bosom. "We don't want to interrupt your reunion with your aunt. I'm sure you want to comfort her after that terrible crime right under your nose."

"It happened in the parking lot."

"Don't concern yourself with us. You can hear all the details when you come back to work."

"After it's a *fait accompli*?" Helma asked.

"If you'd *prefer* to abandon this precious and fleeting visit with your very elderly aunt," Ms. Moon said with a tiny sad shake of her head as if she couldn't imagine herself doing anything so absurd.

"An hour is manageable," Helma told her.

Ms. Moon's smile bravely flickered on again. "Join us, then," she invited generously, motioning Helma into the staff lounge as if a fine feast awaited her.

The other five librarians already sat at the round table, anxiously eyeing Helma and Ms. Moon's entrance, library matters currently more compelling than the murder at the Bayside Arms. Helma placed her hand on the back of one of the two empty chairs.

"Oh, Helma," Ms. Moon said. "Would you mind sitting here instead? This is where I sat last time and it's advantageous for the group dynamic if I take a different position for this meeting."

"We can only hope," George Melville mumbled from beside Helma. The bearded cataloger was staring at a round object on the table in front of him with as much enthusiasm as if it were a freshly squashed insect.

Helma looked more closely. The object was a round pin-on button, red with yellow lettering. "I Love Myself," the button declared. An identical button sat in front of each librarian.

Ms. Moon followed Helma's glance and brightly said, "Oh, I have one for you, too, Helma," and began rummaging through her stack of papers.

"Why?" Helma asked.

"To wear at the reference desk so our patrons will realize we're all complete beings, with no greater need than to serve the public." Her smile went over their heads. "Our aura of completeness will be sensed and shared by our public.''

''Then maybe we should pass these things out to the public,'' Roger Barnhard, the children's librarian suggested, not touching his own red and yellow button. ''I know a few patrons whose auras I'd like to complete.''

''I'll offer mine up for the cause,'' George told her.

''What a *wonderful* idea,'' Ms. Moon crooned. ''We could keep them at the reference desk. I have the perfect wicker basket at home and I'm sure the library board would approve the purchase of a few thousand of these buttons.''

''For the sake of harmony,'' George deadpanned.

''I do not intend to wear this button,'' Helma said. ''Nor will I pass out favors at the reference desk.''

''Neither will I,'' Harley Woodworth joined in hastily, lightly hitting his fist against the table. ''It's unhealthy.''

''Why isn't it healthy?'' Eve asked him.

''Who cares?'' George asked. ''That's a good enough reason for me.'' He raised his hand. ''Count me out.''

''Me too,'' added Roger.

''Ditto,'' joined in Roberta, the history and genealogy librarian.

Ms. Moon flushed; she pursed her lips and tucked her golden hair behind her ears. ''In that case,'' she announced coolly, ''you may all return your buttons to me. No one gets to wear one.'' She sniffed and raised her chin: a nonverbal ''So there.''

Wordlessly, all except Eve pushed their ''I Love Myself'' buttons across the table toward Ms. Moon.

''Can I give mine to my boyfriend?'' Eve asked. ''I think it's kind of cute.''

''That's inappropriate,'' Ms. Moon told her, holding out her hand until Eve relinquished it.

''Are the buttons the topic of this special meeting?''

Helma asked, glancing at George, who gave a single shake of his head.

Ms. Moon took a deep breath, shivering her billowy dress, and launched into a well-rehearsed, golden-toned speech.

"Each of us is uniquely different," Ms. Moon began, and Helma watched her co-workers' eyes go distant before Ms. Moon paused to take her first breath. Helma's own attention wandered to the dead Peter Binder as words like "full potential," "embracing our uniqueness," and "understanding and accepting ourselves" resounded in the staff lounge.

If Peter Binder had followed them from Sea-Tac, had his murderer followed *him*? She imagined three different vehicles traveling north on I-5, switching lanes together, stopping at the same rest areas, pulling off the same exit in tandem. But if Peter Binder had flown on the same plane as Aunt Em, he'd only arrived in Seattle yesterday. What had he done to make enemies so quickly? Unless his killer had accompanied him from Michigan: partners in crime.

Suddenly Helma was aware of George Melville sitting upright to her left, and to her right, Eve leaned forward on her elbows. Helma looked up at Ms. Moon.

"You're all familiar with the Myers-Briggs personality test," Ms. Moon was saying, "which categorizes each person as one of sixteen personality types. Some organizations, including libraries, have administered this test to their staff to promote understanding and a more efficient organization."

Ms. Moon paused while her words sunk in, making eye contact with each librarian at the table. Then she gave a musical little laugh and said, "Well, we're *not* going to do that." And just as everyone was beginning to relax she added, "I have a gentler, more pertinent test. It's called the Bert and Lamb. After taking it you'll learn to view yourself not as a thinker or a feeler, not a judger or a perceiver, not even an extrovert or introvert, but as a color. We'll be reds or blues or greens, lavenders, yellows, or whites, and so on. A rainbow.''

"I don't believe white exists in the rainbow," Helma said. "But the point of taking this test is?"

"Why, for the good of the library," Ms. Moon told her, blinking her eyes as if she were shocked by the question. "We may discover that some color classifications will naturally be more useful assuming different library responsibilities than the ones now held."

"Oh, naturally," George said.

Roger Barnhard tore a sheet of paper from his tablet and folded it in half. "You're planning to use this test to reorganize the library?"

"By color," Ms. Moon affirmed. "A palette of harmony."

"Oh goody," George mumbled. "A new way to library."

Ms. Moon sat down in rosy-cheeked triumph. The staff of the Bellehaven Public Library silently stared at her for several long seconds. Then, one by one, they each turned to stare just as silently at Helma, entreaty on each and every face, even George Melville's.

Helma cleared her throat. "I believe this test to be an invasion of my privacy and a threat to the otherwise efficient operation of this library."

"Helma, Helma, there's no need to fear self-analyzation. We must be open to new opportunities for greater cohesiveness," Ms Moon implored, opening her arms to Helma. "Visualize it: after taking the Bert and Lamb test, each librarian will occupy the niche best suited to his or her personality, like, like . . . a glove, yes, fingers in a kid glove functioning as one, beckoning our public into the library."

"Massaging their demands," George said.

"*Touching* them?" Harley asked.

"Of course not," Ms. Moon snapped. "He's speaking metaphorically."

"Doesn't Bert and Lamb make paint?" Eve asked.

"Is there a problem with the way the library staff is currently functioning?" Helma asked Ms. Moon.

"If it ain't broke . . ." Roger said, folding his piece of paper into a credible crane.

"Every group can function more efficiently," Ms. Moon said, her voice rising, then breaking. "More in accord. And now we have that opportunity. It could be glorious, a library renaissance. We'll be a shining example to the library community nationwide." She rose from her seat, shoulders back, eyes to the middle distance, as if hearing a stirring library anthem.

"I'm sorry," Helma said, interrupting her reverie, "but I don't see this endeavor as productive use of library time at all. We're in the midst of budget cuts, new shelving installation, restroom remodels . . ."

"Miss Zukas," Ms. Moon said, her hands forming fists she pressed against the table top until her knuckles turned white. "You are forgetting yourself. I am the director of this library and I intend to implement this project."

They all stared in disbelief as Ms. Moon's face reddened and she stamped her foot, not once but twice, repeating in a desperate cry, "I *am* the director."

## ❧ chapter nine ❧

# COLORS OF
# THE RAINBOW

The staff meeting abruptly ended when Ms. Moon gathered up her papers and "I Love Myself" buttons and left the staff lounge without her usual admonishment to, "Remember, today is a day like no other." For a few moments the six librarians sat silently staring at the empty doorway.

"I think she got the point," Roger said, launching his paper crane as if it were an airplane toward the wastebasket, where it fell short.

"Yeah, but do you think it'll stop her?" George asked.

"Not on your life. We're doomed to be colors."

"Not if we refuse to take the test," Helma told them.

"You're *really* not going to take it?" Eve asked her.

"Of course not," Helma said, surprised Eve had even asked. "I informed Ms. Moon I wouldn't."

"If we all refuse," Harley added, "what can she do?"

"Fire us," George told him, drawing his finger across his throat.

Roberta stood and looked out the door of the staff lounge. "She's closed her door," she said in a hushed voice as

96

she returned to her chair. "She must really be upset."

"I'll make those chocolate chip brownies tonight," Eve volunteered. "She loves those."

"A nice arrangement of carrots and celery would be more appropriate," George suggested.

"Don't be mean," Roberta told him.

"So Helma," George said. "What's the scoop on the dumpster murder?"

All faces turned toward Helma.

"If you're referring to the man found beside the dumpster at the Bayside Arms, it's too soon for the police to have determined means and motive."

"Who was he?" George asked.

"His name was Peter Binder," she said, glancing from face to face and seeing not a glimmer of recognition. "He may have just arrived from back east."

"I heard he was stabbed," Roger said.

"A man did it," Eve said with certainty. "Men stab but unless they're stuck in the kitchen, women use nicer weapons. A gun maybe."

"A gun is *nicer*?" Roger asked.

Eve nodded gravely. "That's what I'd use. You don't get dirty. You know, blood all over you."

"Have you been reading true crime magazines, Evie?" George asked.

"I don't have to read anything to know that."

"Excuse me," Helma said. "I'll go home now but I'm postponing my vacation and returning to work tomorrow, at least until we're through this crisis."

In her cubicle, Helma first checked the library's circulation records on her computer. No library card had been issued to a Peter Binder. Then she opened the Bellingham phone book to the yellow pages. Five florists were listed within the city limits, and she called all of them.

"Do you make deliveries?" she asked. All of them did.

"Did you deliver a mixed bouquet—mostly daisies—to the Bayside Arms Sunday afternoon?" None of them had.

None of them had delivered a loose bouquet of snapdragons to the Bayside Arms that morning, either.

"The flowers probably came from a grocery store," the last florist suggested with a touch of disdain. "Bouquets *we* deliver are kept fresh in water. Always."

Helma hung up, lightly penciling a tic beside the last florist's telephone number. It was a waste of time to phone the grocery stores but if that's where the flowers came from, their purchases might have been last-minute acts. Bought by a man who'd just arrived in town, perhaps?

The day had begun in the public area of the library. Patrons waited beside the reference desk for Eve to begin her duties, every computer was already in use and every newspaper—rigidly attached to a stick—was in a reader's hands. The building pulsed with the digestion of information.

Helma found a photograph-packed biography of John Wayne for Aunt Em and was heading for the circulation desk to check it out to herself when she heard, "*Labas*, Helma."

Bronus sat near the microfilm readers, his long legs extending into the seating area, beside a stylish young woman holding a copy of *Elle*. Helma's Lithuanian was long lost and when she did use it for simple greetings, it was with those she was closest to, like Aunt Em. Otherwise it felt too personal, like using *du* instead of *sie* to address a stranger in German. "Hello, Bronus," she told him. The young dark-haired woman, dramatically made up, gazed speculatively at Helma, then as if realizing Helma was no threat, smiled.

"Is your aunt enjoying herself?" Bronus asked.

Helma stopped. "How did you know my aunt was visiting?" she asked him.

Bronus was blond and broad shouldered, tall, with prominent cheekbones and a well-defined mouth. If his hair had been darker he might have passed for one of Helma's cousins.

He nodded toward Eve, who was taking her place at the reference desk, removing blue chewing gum from her mouth and wrapping it neatly in a piece of note paper as if it were a packet she intended to reopen. "She told me on Saturday that you were going on vacation because your aunt was visiting."

It was time to schedule another meeting about staff privacy.

"Got it," another man, slightly older, but also with the clear-eyed intensity of the student about him, joined them, holding a reel of microfilm that Helma recognized as past issues of the *Bellehaven Daily News*, and Helma took the moment to smile politely and excuse herself.

At the circulation desk, she reached for the scanner to check out the John Wayne book when another, larger, hand slipped in front of hers and held the scanner in place.

"I'll do that," Dutch, Mrs. Carmon's replacement told her. Dutch was a retired army sergeant who Ms. Moon had hired to "diversify the staff intellectually." Dutch understood duty, detail, and the chain of command, recognizing Ms. Moon—and no one else—as his leader.

"I'm perfectly capable of checking out library material," Helma told Dutch, her hand hovering above his. "I've been a librarian here for eighteen years."

The burly man's hand remained on the scanner. A tattoo, the red and green tip of a dragon's tail, peeked from beneath his shirt cuff.

"And I'm responsible if the transaction is handled unsuccessfully," he said.

"You can watch," she told him, not moving.

A middle-aged woman in shorts approached the desk, her arms full of books.

"Ma'am," Dutch said to Helma quietly, nodding his thumb-shaped head toward the woman.

Helma hesitated, debating priorities, when Dutch said, his voice irritable with unaccustomed compromise, "If you'll do it fast so I can help this patron."

Helma swiftly and successfully completed the transaction and left the library.


"There's an emergency situation at the library," Helma told Ruth, Aunt Em, and her mother. "I've canceled my vacation time this week."

Ruth warily narrowed her eyes and Helma's mother began fussing with the hem of her lavender top. The whir of the video tape rewinder buzzed in the corner of the room.

"You're worried about what I'll do, aren't you?" Aunt Em asked. "You don't have to. I've already decided."

"What would that be?" Lillian asked cautiously. "I'm . . ."

"I'll go to the library with Wilhelmina," she announced, and both Ruth and Lillian relaxed. "I want to see a librarian at work."

"It ain't always a pretty sight," Ruth told her and Aunt Em laughed in a comfortable way, as if she and Ruth had spent the morning gossiping.

"It might not be very interesting for you," Helma tried. "There's the mall. Maybe you and Mother . . ."

"Oh," Lillian breathed, smiling. "I think going to the library is a *lovely* idea, just lovely. You can see all those . . . books, shelves and shelves of them, all through the library. And computers; libraries all are run by computers now. The way those librarians help people," she shook her head in admiration, "they're an inspiration to the service industry everywhere."

"A regular theme park," Ruth added.

Aunt Em beamed, eagerly nodding, and Helma gave up.

Aunt Em's eyes were still good; she could read a book or watch a video; there was always plenty of entertainment in a library.

The phone rang and Helma reached for it.

"Wayne Gallant here," the familiar voice said. "There's no doubt; Peter Binder was on the same flight as your aunt. He even traveled under his own name."

"Was he alone?" Helma asked.

"As far as we know. He didn't check any baggage through but that's not unusual. The airport sent up their surveillance tapes and we've pinpointed him talking to your aunt with a carry-on bag over his shoulder. Can you bring her down to take a look? It might jog her memory if she sees him again—alive."

"What time would be convenient?" Helma asked.

"Right now?"

"We'll be there in twenty minutes," Helma told him.

"I'll come with you," Ruth said when Helma explained the phone call, "since I was on the scene, a witness almost."

"I'd love to join you," Helma's mother said, patting her hair and making little ready-to-leave motions, "but there's a building meeting and I'm the program chair." She stood and kissed the air toward Aunt Em. "I'll see you again soon, Emily."

"That'll be the day," Aunt Em said, not mimicking John Wayne's voice but matching his inflections perfectly.

"You can leave your umbrella in the car," Helma told Aunt Em as she opened her car door in front of the police station. The clouds were too high and light for rain.

"I'm always prepared," Aunt Em said, getting out with her umbrella in hand, "like a Girl Scout."

"But . . ." Helma began.

"Take a closer look," Ruth said in a low voice next to Helma's ear. "She uses her umbrella instead of a cane."

As they walked up the sidewalk, Helma watched Aunt Em. She carried the red umbrella by the handle and, not constantly, but every little while, she steadied herself by pushing the tip against the sidewalk.

Wayne Gallant led them down a hallway in the busy police station to a small room that held a video player and electronic equipment. Posters of bright sunshiny places hung on the pale walls. "Have a seat here," he said, pointing to two chairs and pulling up two more from against the wall. A manila folder sat on the small table.

"Binder's only on camera a few seconds, as if he had a pretty good idea of the camera's range."

He clicked on the machine and a pulsing black and white picture came to life, shot from an overhead angle: travelers milling around a baggage carousel. The chief touched one dark figure with the end of a pencil. "Here's the first glimpse we have of him. Notice how he keeps his face turned away from the camera?"

"That's Peter Binder?" Ruth asked. "How can you tell? If you ask me it could be anybody, maybe even a woman."

"We've had the tape analyzed, comparing this image to later, clearer images." The chief backed up the tape and replayed it. The man was only on screen for two seconds, passing the baggage claim, a carry-on bag slung over his shoulder. Even in the jerky frames, he moved quickly, purposefully.

"Have you found his carry-on?" Helma asked.

"Not yet, nor his car, either. We will though," he added grimly.

"Unless his murderer scrammed with them," Aunt Em suggested.

"That's a definite possibility," the chief said. He fast-forwarded the tape, then stopped it. "And here's the only other time we caught him."

"That's me," Aunt Em exclaimed, pointing to the black and white figures.

There on the screen Aunt Em spoke to the man with the carry-on, a view of the side of his face, and Helma recognized the profile of the man who'd died beside the Bayside Arms's dumpster.

"He's not very tall, even standing up," Ruth commented.

They watched silently, mesmerized, as the living Peter Binder pointed behind him and Aunt Em nodded, also pointing in the same direction with her umbrella, before they both moved out of the camera's range.

Aunt Em leaned forward, staring at the screen. "He's telling me where to find the restroom. And then he tried to take my purse."

"There wasn't a camera in the hallway he lured her into?" Helma asked.

"No."

"But there's not a picture of him fleeing the airport in terror, blood dripping down his arm?" Ruth asked.

"We have a group of men passing through the claim area shortly afterward," the chief told her. "He might be with them but there's not enough of an image to be certain."

"I'll bet they were all tall men, right?" Ruth asked.

"Right."

"Clever boy," Ruth said.

"Did my hat pin match the stab marks on his arm?" Aunt Em asked.

Wayne Gallant nodded and absently opened the manila folder. "They did. There's no doubt it's the same man."

"Have you discovered the reason he was on the flight to Seattle?" Helma asked.

The chief glanced at a page in the folder. "His roommate in Traverse City, the last place he lived, said it was a sudden decision, but sudden decisions weren't unusual for Binder.''

Helma leaned forward but she was still too far away to read the printing on the page. "So Binder and his roommate weren't close?" she asked.

"They kept different hours, different habits. He said Binder was in and out, gone a few days at a time, sometimes longer. But he always paid the rent on time."

"So he wouldn't call attention to himself," Helma said. "Binder was after something Aunt Em owned or he believed she owned." She turned to Aunt Em. "Can I see your purse?"

"Didn't you already peek?" Aunt Em asked, but she handed over the patent leather purse and Helma unsnapped the gold clasp and spread the contents on the table beside the video machine. They all gazed at the various items Aunt Em carried: her worn wallet, the magnifying glass, plastic rain bonnet, comb. None of it appeared worth an arrest.

Ruth chose the folded plastic rain bonnet in its tiny plastic case and held it up, considering it. "At what age is every woman issued one of these things?"

"It comes in your first social security check," Aunt Em promptly replied.

Ruth guffawed. "Thought so." She set the bonnet back on the table and skewed her eyes. "I think we need to squint. Maybe Binder *thought* he spotted a valuable object."

All but Helma dutifully squinted at the arrangement of belongings. If she couldn't spot anything valuable straight on, what sense did it make to obscure her vision?

"You might mistake that key holder for a gold band," Ruth suggested.

"Or maybe the wallet was stuffed with money," Aunt Em said, her face still puckered in a squint.

"Was it?" Helma asked her.

"I think so. I put most of my cash in it. You can't always trust the banks, you know."

"Like how *much* cash?" Ruth asked.

"Fifty dollars," Aunt Em replied, drawing the number from an amount that long ago, perhaps during the Depression, meant a fortune. The low voice in which she said the words, with respect, caused Helma to believe that the actual number was much higher.

Ruth looked disappointed but Helma could see Wayne Gallant had come to the same conclusion as Helma. Fifty dollars, in this case, didn't actually mean fifty dollars. But how could they ever know how much it *did* mean? It was common knowledge that Aunt Em mistrusted banks. She'd tucked cash in flower vases, empty metal Band-Aid boxes, old pickle jars, and cardboard candy boxes, usually leaving them in plain sight around her house. "If a robber comes," she'd said, "he'd look too hard to find it."

Helma began returning the items to Aunt Em's purse one by one. Clumsily, she knocked the plastic bonnet to the floor and as Wayne Gallant leaned to pick it up, she stood and pushed back her chair so he wouldn't have to reach beneath it and naturally, she was better able to read the words on the page in the open folder he'd left on the table, grateful that some policemen were so conscientious at labeling their notes.

*Phone interview with Joseph Gobowski*, the heading at the top of the page read. A common enough name in western Michigan. Helma said it twice to herself, then sat down, smiling as Wayne Gallant handed her the rain bonnet.

"Thank you very much," she told him.

"Tell him," Ruth said to Helma.

"Tell him what?"

"About the gifts. I'll show your Aunt Em where the big brave policemen hang their uniforms while you two discuss current events."

The two women left Helma and the chief in the room by themselves. The video player hummed. From beyond the walls came the wordless rise and fall of conversation. Helma absently realigned her chair with the others.

Wayne Gallant rocked back in his chair and asked, "What gifts do you want to tell me about?"

"I'm uncertain of their significance but I've received two anonymous gifts."

The rocking stopped. "What kind of gifts?"

"Flowers. I found an attractive mixed bouquet in a glass vase on my doormat last night. A loose bouquet of snapdragons appeared this morning."

He resumed rocking, thinking, his hands behind his neck. Helma waited.

"Flowers," he murmured, gazing at the ceiling. "No cards?"

"No, I did phone the local florists and none had delivered bouquets to my apartment."

He brought the chair flat to the floor with a thump. "Have you sensed any danger?"

"No, but Ruth has a theory . . ."

"That you're being watched by an admirer? An admirer who might even commit murder if he believed you were in danger?"

"That's correct, but the idea seems improbable to me."

"Which? That you have an admirer or that he'd kill for you?" The corners of his eyes crinkled as he smiled.

"Killing does seem the more farfetched of the two options," Helma said. "Another possibility is that the flowers were intended for Aunt Em. Their appearance coincide with her arrival."

The chief frowned and tipped back in his chair again. He folded his hands together and turned his thumbs around one another, his gaze blank. Finally, he gently brought down the front feet of the chair and asked, "Any ideas who'd leave flowers for your aunt? Any idea at all, no matter how remote?''

"No. This is her first visit to Washington."

He nodded. "If you find any more 'gifts,' call me before you touch them."

"I will."

"Did you discover anything else missing from your apartment?"

"No, and I thoroughly cleaned last night."

"I counted on that."

"Are you any closer to finding the thief?" Helma asked.

"Not yet, aside from the fact that he wore gloves."

"It's unusual for anyone to be carrying gloves in the summer, " Helma pointed out.

"He could have kept them in his car," the chief said, "stopped to view the commotion, and taken advantage of the moment. If we come up with anything more I'll let you know."

Helma noted how he'd used the word, "if," and suspected that Wayne Gallant believed the robbery might go unsolved. "Is there a connection between the robbery and the murder? If the two men were partners, could the murderer have then tried to finish the purse snatcher's job by ransacking my apartment?"

"Two other apartments were also robbed," the chief reminded her.

"As a cover, perhaps?"

"We're not ruling out any possibility right now," he told her. "We'll follow every lead we have." His voice had gone impersonal, slightly indulgent, and Helma rose from her chair.

"If there's nothing more, I'll rejoin Ruth and my aunt."

"No, that's all for now." He rose, too, pushing in his chair. "Your aunt's memory's uncertain. You might continue to gently prod her about her plane trip and the purse-snatching incident.''

''Have you found the murder weapon?'' Helma asked.

''We did. Keep this under your hat for now. We brought the dumpster to the station and sorted through it piece by piece; it was the night before garbage pickup so it was full—pity the guys who did *that*—but we found the murder weapon.''

''Was it a knife?'' Helma asked.

''It was a telephone.''

Helma stepped back, certain Wayne Gallant was teasing her. ''Binder was stabbed,'' she reminded him, ''not choked or hit over the head.''

''This was an altered cellular telephone. One end of it was cut to a sharpened point, a shard basically, about five inches long, as lethal as any knife.''

''So it was a lengthwise half of a telephone? Did you find the other half?''

He gave her a grin of approval. ''We did. It had been thrown into the dumpster after the killing. The sharpened portion had been cut off and then fit back together to conceal that it was actually a sophisticated and concealable weapon, one of those brands they advertise will survive a toss from a thirty-story building. The guts of the phone were gone. Plastic is far stronger than people give it credit for.''

Helma nodded distractedly. ''The B-2 is made almost entirely of composites,'' she told him. ''So this wasn't a crime of passion because the murderer had to consciously take the phone apart before he killed Binder, yet if he'd thought through his plot more carefully, he wouldn't have left the murder weapon near the scene. That was very neglectful.''

She was aware of the chief's eyes on her, smiling *that* smile, but she ignored it and went on anyway. ''If you consider that act as a sign of panic or a lack of proper planning, then this murder was most likely his first serious crime. He probably isn't a known felon.''

''As I said, we're following every lead.'' The chief's face was still pleasant but Helma realized from the set of his mouth and his cool eyes, that he'd shared all he intended with her.

He opened the door for her and said, ''Would you care to have lunch with me tomorrow? There's something I'd like to discuss with you. A personal matter.'' Helma felt her own expression turn just as serious as his, although she felt a curious desire to shift from foot to foot.

''I'd like to,'' she told him. ''I can meet you at noon.''

''At Saul's?'' he asked, mentioning the deli two blocks from the library.

''Saul's,'' she agreed.

As Helma drove Ruth and Aunt Em home, her thoughts shifting between murder and lunch with the chief, wondering if the ''personal matter'' had anything to do with his ex-wife, Ruth asked Aunt Em, ''What happened to Danute, the woman Helma's father was madly in love with before Lillian snagged him?''

''Ruth,'' Helma warned, but Aunt Em turned eagerly in her seat and spoke to Ruth.

''Ah, Danute. She left the marble layer and came back for Jonukas. I knew she would. I told him so.''

''She came back?'' Ruth asked.

''Full of fire and desire,'' Aunt Em said.

''What happened?'' Helma couldn't help asking.

''You'll have to ask your mother,'' Aunt Em said stiffly. ''It was her doing.''

## ❧ chapter ten ❧

# TALK ON THE WATER

"**D**id you tell anyone on the airplane that you were traveling to visit me?" Helma asked Aunt Em as they drove down the hillside after dropping off Ruth. Beneath them, the bay and islands formed a panorama Helma had never lost her awe of and couldn't imagine ever taking for granted. The humpy islands receded to the horizon, one after the other, always holding a touch of mist that gave them a smoky blue cast. The high morning clouds had given way to broken sunshine and the waters of Washington Bay faded and sparkled with the changing light.

"I told everybody who would listen," Aunt Em said, leaning over and patting Helma's leg.

"Did you mention my name?"

"Maybe, probably."

"Did you meet anyone who wanted to visit you in Bellehaven? An admirer, perhaps?" Helma stopped, waiting for traffic to clear so she could turn onto the wider street. A man in an electric wheelchair whizzed past.

"A man, you mean?" Aunt Em asked. Her eyes sparkled.

Helma nodded. "Someone who might send you flowers?"

Aunt Em sighed and looked out the window. "No, no. I've never liked cut flowers. You have to kill them before you put them in a vase, you know." She made snipping motions with her fingers, then shivered in distaste. "It upsets me if somebody sends me flowers."

Helma hadn't known that. She wondered what Aunt Em had done with all the arrangements Helma had sent her over the years.

"I'll show you Boardwalk Park," she told Aunt Em.

"Will there be whales?" Aunt Em asked for the third time.

"Not in Washington Bay," Helma explained for the third time. "They're farther out to sea, in the islands. I could make reservations at a nice resort on San Juan Island for the weekend."

"You like *knowing* what you're going to find better than stumbling on it?" Aunt Em asked.

"I've never found stumbling very efficient."

"I don't think living is supposed to be very efficient," Aunt Em said, shrinking down into the passenger seat and folding her hands together on her lap. "It's a messy, juicy business."

Helma turned into the city park that stretched along the eastern curve of the bay, where she normally walked in swift, well-paced circles every day. The tide was in and water lapped against the rocky shore. The bay was too small, the islands too many and the day too still for there to be waves, only the gentle movement of water sliding over water.

Because the day had turned sunny, Boardwalk Park was busy, occupied by Bellehavenites who viewed a sunny day with a sense of responsibility as potent as their pleasure. Helma pulled into a space beside a station wagon cluttered with toys and stepped out of her car to open the door for

Aunt Em. In front of the car, a line of blue hydrangeas were in full bloom, bluer than the water.

Aunt Em straightened herself, placing one hand at her back, and gazed past Helma, her face softening. Helma turned to see two young girls struggling past on rollerblades, wearing helmets and knee and elbow pads, clutching at one another and giggling, their feet slewing in every direction.

"Let's sit close to the water," Aunt Em said, her eyes still on the children, "as close as we can."

So they did, on a wooden bench that faced the bay, smelling salt water and the always present odor of decaying sea life, breathing to the rhythm of the day, letting murder, robbery, and purse snatchers wash from their thoughts.

"You and Ruth have been friends a long time," Aunt Em said.

"Since we were ten," Helma told her. They'd made their separate ways from Scoop River west, Helma's journey more direct than Ruth's, who'd spent years in the Southwest and Seattle before moving to the less expensive and, some said, more beautiful, Bellehaven.

"Who was your best friend?" Helma asked her. Two kayaks skimmed by fifty feet from shore, two people in each one, their conversation magnified over water.

"Best friends," Aunt Em repeated. "I was best by myself." She laughed. "Like John Wayne in *The Searchers*. In the end, when he stands outside on the porch alone and the door closes while everybody else is happy inside. That was me."

"You were an outsider?" Helma asked.

"In eighty-seven years," Aunt Em said, answering Helma's previous question, not her last. "Two men were my best friends. Juozas, but maybe he doesn't count because he was my husband. And Lukas."

Lukas again. "In Chicago," Helma said. "Did you know him in Michigan, too?"

"Only Chicago."

"How long did you live in Chicago that he became your best friend?" Farther out in the bay, Helma glimpsed the gleaming head of a sea otter. If their conversation hadn't become so interesting she would have pointed it out to Aunt Em.

"Time isn't what makes you best friends," Aunt Em said. "Why is it that now I remember what happened so long ago better than what I ate for breakfast? It's a bad trick." She shifted on the seat, uncomfortable, Helma was aware of that, but her own curiosity was too compelling.

"Why did Lukas give you his medal from World War I?" she asked, remembering the medal that had been stolen from Aunt Em's suitcase.

"He just did," Aunt Em said, turning her head away, closing the subject.

In all her life, no one had mentioned in Helma's presence that Aunt Em had lived in Chicago. True, it had been seventy years ago but still, in Helma's father's family, they'd thrashed around stories of each other's lives as if they each owned their brothers' and sisters' experiences, too, and couldn't hear enough of the details.

Suddenly, Helma was struck by a thought, a reason why a Lithuanian girl in her teens might leave the rural area for Chicago. "Aunt Em, did you move to Chicago to become a nun?"

Aunt Em's mouth fell open and Helma rushed on, "To join the Sisters of St. Casimir order, the Lithuanian nuns?"

She closed her mouth, leaned over, and patted Helma's hand as if she were delusional. "No, dear. Definitely not." She was silent as the two children on rollerblades giggled past, then said, "I do remember those nuns, though. Tough as brass."

Helma remembered them, too.

"I hated going to confession," Aunt Em said.

It had been a weekly ritual at St. Alphonse School, no excuses. Helma recalled herself at eight, marching into the church with the rest of her class, the nuns clicking their clickers, waiting her turn and racking her brain for sins she'd committed that week so she'd have something to offer the priest, and finally, in despair, under cover of the dark confessional, confessing to "stealing a pencil and telling a lie," her lie being the stolen pencil.

"*Labas*," a man's voice suddenly said behind them. Hello. Helma turned sharply on the bench, startled.

It was Bronus, grinning, wearing tight black and green cycling clothes and straddling a bicycle that was as oversized as he was. With him was the same dramatic-looking young woman Helma had seen in the library, nearly as tall as Bronus, her cycling suit a single piece of purple spandex. A black helmet covered her sleek hair but her dark eyes seemed to burn from her face.

Aunt Em turned, on her face a welcoming smile, and immediately launched into a happy tirade of Lithuanian, speaking too fast for Helma to understand, catching a word here and there and gathering the gist of the conversation. Aunt Em was asking him who, what, where, when, and why.

Bronus laughed and said in his perfect English, without accent but which retained the cadence of Lithuanian. "My name's Bronus Muszkaviczas. I'm from Pennsylvania and I'm here doing summer graduate work at the college *and* testing out the Northwest."

"You come from the coal mining country?" Aunt Em asked.

Bronus nodded. "My grandfather was a timber man, shoring up timbers in the mines." He smiled at Aunt Em. "I know Helma from the library."

Aunt Em beamed at Helma and told Bronus, "She has an important job there, but I don't think she looks like a librarian, do you? Not like they make librarians look on TV and in the movies."

"I agree," Bronus said, humoring Aunt Em and beckoning to the young woman. "This is Celine."

"You are certainly beautiful," Aunt Em told the girl, "like a dancer."

Celine smiled and inclined her head, her exotic face turning hesitant, almost shy.

"Close," Bronus said. "She's a drama student."

"But not Lithuanian?" Aunt Em asked.

"No, I'm sorry," Celine said in a perfectly modulated voice.

"Do you like Bellehaven better than Seattle?" Bronus asked Aunt Em.

"You knew she was in Seattle?" Helma asked.

Bronus shrugged. "If *my* aunt came to visit, *I'd* pick her up in Seattle and not let her ride that little commuter flight up here."

"I almost remember Seattle," Aunt Em said. "There were bums on the street, like in the Depression." She turned to Bronus and invited, "Can you both come home with us for coffee?"

"Thanks," Bronus said, "but we've still got six miles to put in on this bike ride. I'm in the library a lot; maybe we'll run into each other." He shook Aunt Em's hand, bending low over her until she blushed and then took Helma's, smiling at her, his blue eyes narrowing the same way Helma's brothers' did.

"Ahh," Aunt Em sighed, watching them pedal away. "A beautiful couple. He would be a good man for you, Wilhelmina. Strong. A man who has kept his lugan roots."

Aunt Em used the derogatory term for Lithuanians which

made Lithuanians so hot to hear that they could only safely say it to each other.

"Our roots aren't so important after a few generations, Aunt Em," Helma said. "We're melted together."

"Never," Aunt Em said, raising her chin. "Roots is all we have when we're all thrown together like we are in America. Three hundred million people and we all eat the same breakfast cereal and watch the same TV."

"Two hundred sixty-eight million," Helma corrected.

"That's what I said. Almost three hundred million people with everything the same unless we dig around to find the differences, the good differences."

They stood, planning to take a short walk close to the water when Helma spotted a stylish blonde woman in a pastel suit who appeared out of place in the park, walking straight toward them across the grass, her high heels sinking into the turf. She was slender, her oval face tastefully made up. A set of keys jangled in her right hand as if she'd just stepped from her car. She stopped five feet from them.

"Are you Helma Zukas?" she asked in an impersonal voice, not smiling. She stood ramrod straight, her arms at her sides.

"May I ask why you wish to know?" More than once Helma had been recognized in public and found herself fielding pleas for dispensation of library fines or a request to place a bestseller on hold. This woman looked all business.

"Yes, she is," Aunt Em answered, "from the library."

"That's what I thought," the woman said. And with that, she abruptly turned and walked back across the park the way she'd come.

Helma and Aunt Em watched her retreating figure striding away, her shoulders stiff and head high.

"What's eating her?" Aunt Em asked.

Helma wondered the same thing. "Maybe she's unhappy with the library's service," she told Aunt Em.

Helma had once overheard a woman in the library with her elderly mother and two toddlers, say, "At both ends of the age spectrum you just try to wear them out and hope they'll take a long nap so you can catch your breath."

And that was exactly what she did, walking with Aunt Em around the park, shopping for new clothes in the slowly reviving downtown, buying her movie magazines, until Aunt Em herself suggested they return to Helma's apartment.

As they carried their packages up the steps and passed Mrs. Whitney's apartment, Mrs. Whitney tapped on her window. Helma and Aunt Em waited in front of her door until she opened it.

"This is for you, I think," Mrs. Whitney said, and handed Helma a foil packet of kitty treats. The package was battered and Helma held it at the corner by two fingers.

"Where did you find it?" she asked. She rarely bought treats for Boy Cat Zukas, certain they contained either addictive or tooth-rotting ingredients. And when she did buy them, this wasn't his brand.

"That stray cat was on the landing trying to chew it open. I thought you'd bought the package for Boy Cat and accidentally dropped it." She shook her head. "That cat did *not* want to give it up."

"Thank you, Mrs. Whitney," Helma said, still holding the package by two fingers, doubting any fingerprints remained on the packet.

"You run along, Wilhelmina," Aunt Em said, giving her packages to Helma. "You must be tired after such a busy day. You go home and watch *The Searchers*. I think I'll visit with Ethel for a while."

"Oh, come in, come in," Mrs. Whitney said, her pink

cheeks dimpling. "I have the cutest thing to show you."

"Call me before you leave Mrs. Whitney's," Helma told her. "I'll meet you at the door."

"Yes, yes," Aunt Em said, waving her hand. "So the murderer won't kill me from here to there." And the two older women went inside, closing the door on Helma and her carefully held kitty treats.

Joseph Gobowski answered on the first ring.

"Gobowski," he snapped into the phone.

"Hello?" Helma responded. She held a pencil, ready to jot notes on the pad of paper in front of her.

"Yeah?" he asked.

"Mr. Gobowski," Helma said in her best official library voice. "This is Miss Wilhelmina Zukas calling from Bellehaven, Washington. I'm sorry to call so late but we've been discussing your roommate's death and I have a few more questions."

"Who's we?" he asked.

Helma paused for the briefest moment, turning her pencil in the same manner she'd seen Wayne Gallant turn his: end over end, eraser, then lead tapping against her paper. "I'm speaking of the Bellehaven chief of police, of course."

"Oh. *Him*," Gobowski said, resignation slowing his voice.

"This'll only take five minutes of your time," Helma assured him.

"That depends on how long my answers are, doesn't it?" There was a clink against the phone, as if he were taking a drink from a glass.

"That's correct so let's get started. You said that Peter Binder's decision to fly to Seattle was a surprise to you, is that right?"

"Sorta. He was always taking off, but the Seattle thing came out of the blue."

"He didn't give you a reason?"

"Said he wanted to see why everybody went ape over the place, that's all."

"When you say 'he was always taking off,' what do you mean?"

Joseph Gobowski paused before answering. Helma noted that on her page. "He'd go wherever anybody paid him. Quick jobs, you know. No paperwork. Cash on the barrel."

"That's illegal," Helma pointed out. "In cash transactions, no contributions are made to taxes or social security."

Gobowski laughed. "So turn him into the IRS. A guy takes his chances. Sometimes the pay's good, sometimes it isn't. Sometimes he doesn't get paid at all."

"Did Mr. Binder always get paid?" Helma asked.

"Pity any guy who tried to fink out on a debt to Pete."

"What kind of work did he do?"

"He liked to brag he was a private dick but no way, Jose."

"A detective?" Helma repeated. "A private detective?"

"Yeah, but it wasn't so, just a lot of big talk. Once he said he was following some guy but all he did was deliver a car downstate for him."

"Could he have been on his way to a job in Seattle?" Helma asked.

"Maybe. Didn't I tell you cops all this before? Don't you read each other's notes?"

"Thank you very much," Helma said. "You've been very helpful. We'll be in touch if we need further information," and she gently replaced the receiver even as she heard Joseph Gobowski say, "Hey!"

At nine o'clock, Helma's phone rang but when she answered it, the line went dead. Positive it was Aunt Em, Helma phoned Mrs. Whitney's apartment.

"Not us, dear," Mrs. Whitney said. "Why don't you come over and have a little nip with us?"

"No thank you," Helma told her. "I have some work to do here."

But instead, Helma inserted *The Searchers* video into her VCR, curious about Aunt Em's favorite movie. She'd never been a fan of John Wayne's and watching the actor play a bitter, lonely man relentlessly searching for his captured niece, Helma wondered why this was Aunt Em's best-liked movie. Yet, when the credits rolled, she discovered certain images wouldn't let her go. It was disturbing, yet somehow satisfying.

When Aunt Em finally did phone, it was nearly eleven o'clock, just as Helma was preparing to fetch her as if she were an errant child. Helma opened her door for her and Aunt Em entered holding an eight-inch-tall doll in a blue gingham dress, its yarn hair in yellow braids and hands angelically folded. She set it on the table.

"What do you think this is?" she asked Helma, stepping back to gaze at the doll. Helma caught a whiff of a sweet alcoholic beverage.

"A doll," she guessed.

Aunt Em shook her head. "But that's what you're *supposed* to think." She reached out and lifted the doll's skirts over her head. "Look at this," she said, a sound like a giggle passing her lips.

The doll's dress hid its form: a plastic cone-shaped bathroom deodorizer. Helma had once seen a similar type of doll concealing a roll of bathroom tissue.

"It's a deodorizer cozy," Aunt Em announced. "Ethel makes them and sells them at craft bazaars."

"It's . . . clever," Helma said.

"Do you really think so? I think it's tacky. I bought this one as a gift for your mother."

"Aunt Em," Helma said cautiously. "I think Mother would really like to be friends with you. More than friends. You're sisters-in-law."

"When she apologizes," Aunt Em said as she made the doll decent again.

"What for?"

"For gossiping about the past."

"What did she say?" Helma asked.

"That I only married your Uncle Juozas to hide out. It hurt him and he's the last person in the world I wanted to see hurt."

"Hide out from what?"

Aunt Em turned from the table and pulled aside the drape, looking out toward the dark view of the bay. "Ah, Wilhelmina. Those days are long gone; rain into rivers. I talk about the past too much now because that's all I have left in my future. Everyone who shared it is dead and I soon will be, if there's any sense to this life."

"Tell me, Aunt Em," Helma pleaded.

"It's not fit for young peoples' ears."

"I'm not that young anymore," Helma told her.

"Age is a . . . relative thing, that's what smarter people than me say."

"Do you have a picture of Lukas?"

"Why?" Aunt Em asked, dropping the drapes and considering Helma, her arms crossed.

"I'm curious, that's all. It's easier to understand a story when you know what the people look like."

Aunt Em bit her lower lip and thought for a few moments. "I have one," she said. "I'll show it to you. Come with me."

Helma followed her into the bedroom where Aunt Em sat on the bed and pulled a handful of black and white snapshots with serrated edges from the bedside table. She shuffled through them, then separated out one smaller photograph and gave it to Helma.

The photo was smaller than the others because one of the three people in the shot had been scissored out. It had originally depicted a young Aunt Em standing between two men in front of a bank of rose bushes; now all that remained of one of the men was his hand on Aunt Em's waist and the cuff of a white shirt and suit jacket.

"Who was this?" Helma asked, touching the disembodied hand.

"Nobody. This is Lukas," she said, touching the other man who was tall and jaunty looking, a dark lock of hair falling beneath a rakishly perched cap. He wore a suit, too, unbuttoned, one arm casually over Aunt Em's shoulders. His face was in profile, smooth, too young for much character except youthful confidence. He gazed across Aunt Em's head at the missing man, as if they'd been sharing a joke.

"Is Lukas still alive?" Helma asked.

"We lost touch, but I doubt it. He'd be an old man now."

"He's handsome."

"He thought so," Aunt Em replied, but fondly.

In the photo, Aunt Em was slender, her hair bobbed, more arresting than beautiful.

"You were handsome, too," Helma told her.

"Ah," Aunt Em said, taking the snapshot from Helma. "That's when I was young and bold."

## ❧ chapter eleven ❧

# LIBRARY
# CONFRONTATIONS

**"L**ibraries should be filled with books,"
Aunt Em said, turning with the aid of her furled umbrella
and gazing around the library at the banks of computers.

"We have those, too," Helma told her. "It's all information, only in different guises."

The library was five minutes from opening to the public
and Helma was giving Aunt Em a tour. A group of patrons
waited on the front steps, peering in through the locked
glass doors, their arms laden with books.

Ms. Moon entered the public area from the workroom
and glided toward them, her bright smile aimed at Aunt Em
as if Helma had suddenly turned invisible.

"Ooh," Ms. Moon breathed. "You must be Miss Zukas's aunt. I'm so happy to meet you." She laid her hand
on top of Aunt Em's as if she were about to shake it but
then slid her palm across Aunt Em's in an intimate stroking
motion the same way Helma had seen some people stroke
a cat.

"You *must* be Ms. Moon," Aunt Em said, gazing down
at her stroked palm as if it had been slithered across.

"Are you here today to participate in VAP?"

"That wasn't my intent at all," Helma interrupted.

"What's VAP?" Aunt Em asked.

"Aunt Em's here to read and relax," Helma protested again. Ms. Moon didn't even glance in her direction.

"VAP," Ms. Moon said to Aunt Em, her eyes glistening with emotional fervor, "is a volunteer program I instituted in our library for the good of the community. It stands for Validate the Older American Program, reclaiming our country's greatest treasure: the elderly."

Aunt Em frowned, her lips moving. "Validate the older American Program," she repeated. "Shouldn't that be VOAP instead of VAP?"

"VAP is so much smoother to say," Ms. Moon went on. "It sounds freer, lighter . . . younger."

"So how are we validated?" Aunt Em asked.

"You assist the public—and the library—by being present, helpful, a force for age parity . . ." She glanced toward the workroom door. "Oh, look. Here come some of your contemporaries now."

Two elderly women and one man entered the public area. They wore red buttons and at first Helma feared they'd read, "I Love Myself," but when the group moved closer, she saw that the white letters spelled out, "Here for You."

"Are you new in town?" one of the women, who wore a dark wig cut in a bowl style, asked.

Aunt Em nodded. "I've been here one day. I stabbed a man, I was robbed, and I found a body in a dumpster."

The three older Americans gazed at Aunt Em skeptically. "Is that actually true?" the other woman, whose silver hair was cut short like a boy's, asked.

Aunt Em glanced up at Helma and confessed, "Well, actually, the body was *beside* the dumpster, not in it."

"Busy, dear, aren't you?" the wigged woman asked and she held out her hand. "I'm Janet Pomeroy."

"Oh," Aunt Em said. "One of my best friend's name was Petorri."

"Not Petorri, Pomeroy," the woman corrected, and they led Aunt Em away to begin her morning as a volunteer.

Petorri. Helma filed that away. Aunt Em had named two people as her best friends and Petorri wasn't Uncle Juozas's last name.

Ms. Moon smiled fondly after them, then finally turned to Helma, all pretense of good humor melting away. She straightened her shoulders and raised her chin. "Now that you've thought about the Bert and Lamb test overnight, I trust you've changed your mind."

"As I stated at the meeting, I won't be taking the test," Helma told her. "It's an invasion of my privacy and of no concern to management."

Ms. Moon's wide blue eyes tightened. "Then don't be surprised if someone else takes it *for* you."

Helma was too surprised not to ask, "How could they?"

"I work with you every day. I believe I could judge how you'd respond to the questions."

"I don't believe you could."

"I do."

"That's not possible."

"It is."

The conversation was threatening to develop into a childish back and forth which Helma had no interest in continuing. The library had opened to the public and around them swirled the populace, storming the new bookshelves, racing toward the sticks of morning papers, circling the Internet computers.

"Excuse me," Helma told Ms. Moon, "I believe I have a file to manage."

Ms. Moon said nothing and as Helma walked toward the workroom, she felt the director's eyes contemplating her back.

George Melville stood before the small mirror next to the workroom door, straightening his tie. He smoothed his beard, squared his shoulders, saluted himself, and said, "Prepared to do battle among the unsorted public, sir!" and marched through the workroom door toward the reference desk for his three-hour stint.

Harley Woodworth looked up as Helma passed his cubicle. "Have the police figured out who murdered the man in your parking lot?" he asked.

"Not yet," Helma told him, "but I'm sure they will soon."

"Probably," Harley said, his attention elsewhere. He held up the photocopied pages he was reading, several lines highlighted in yellow. "There's a question on this test about murder."

"What test?" Helma asked.

"The Bert and Lamb, Ms. Moon's personality test."

Helma knew better than to engage the morose librarian in conversation about depressing subjects but murder *was* on her mind. "What does it say?"

Harley brightened and flicked the papers with his finger. "According to this article, which was in one of my old *True Paranoia* magazines, there's a question that asks, 'Have you ever wanted to murder someone?' " Harley shook his head. "Who'd ever tell the truth to that one?"

"Perhaps it's a trick question," Helma told him.

"What do you mean?" Harley asked, his eyes narrowing as he rolled the pages into a lengthwise tube.

"If your response is no to that question but you answer yes to another specific question, it creates a contradiction that alerts the grader and skews your personality profile."

"So in all innocence, you could end up fitting the profile of a criminal, maybe a *murderer*?" Harley asked, his voice rising.

"Perhaps," Helma told him.

"I knew it," Harley said. "I wasn't so sure before but now I am." His voice dropped a sincere octave. "Thank you for refusing to participate in this test. You're an inspiration."

"You're welcome," Helma told him.

Helma's phone buzzed and when she answered it, she was greeted without preamble by Dutch's clipped military voice.

"A gentleman is on the telephone asking to speak to your aunt. We do not page patrons unless it's an emergency."

"I'll take the call," she told him.

She heard the abrupt click of the call being transferred and said, "This is Miss Wilhelmina Zukas. How may I help you?"

There was silence on the line.

"Hello?" Helma said and the line went dead. She immediately dialed the circulation desk and asked Dutch, "Did the man who called for my aunt give you his name?"

"No, ma'am," Dutch told her.

"How old was he?"

"He didn't say."

Helma silently counted to four and tried, "Did he *sound* like a young man or an older man?"

"Just a normal man. Is that all, ma'am?"

"Yes, it obviously is," Helma said. "Thank you."

Helma had volunteered to take thirty minutes of George's reference desk duty while he conducted a tour for reluctant summer school tenth graders. As she walked through the book stacks, her arms laden with unread library journals, she heard the unmistakable rise and fall of Lithuanian conversation being conducted in low voices.

She detoured toward the comfortable chairs arranged near the genealogy section and found Aunt Em deep in conversation with Bronus, Celine, and another man.

Bronus glanced up at Helma's approach and smiled. "*Labas*, Helma. You remember Celine. This is Douglas."

"Hello," Helma said. Douglas rose and shook hands with her. He was as tall as Bronus but softer, darker, with a cleft in his chin and long thick eyelashes. She recalled seeing him the day before with Bronus, holding a box of microfilm. "Great library," he said.

"Thank you," Helma acknowledged. It was common for college students to prefer the smaller, friendlier, yet, due to computers, completely adequate public library, to their own complex campus library.

"Can you take me home on your lunch hour?" Aunt Em asked Helma. "I'm going to make Bronus *kugelis* for tonight. And for you, too," she hastily added.

"That would be a treat for me," Bronus said.

And a treat for Helma too, which made it that much harder to protest. They didn't know Bronus or anything about him except that he spoke Lithuanian and he claimed to be from Pennsylvania. That didn't exactly insure his moral and ethical integrity despite Aunt Em's being smitten.

"I have a class in half an hour," Bronus said. "I'd better leave in a few minutes."

"What are you studying?" Helma asked.

"Environmental ethics."

Aunt Em tipped her head. "Is that like deciding whether to pollute a river or not?"

"Something like that," Bronus said.

"You have to go to school for that now? Curious."

And they slipped back into speaking Lithuanian, hardly noticing when Helma left.

Helma returned to her cubicle in the workroom, leaving George to hold off the tenth graders for a few minutes longer. She quickly phoned the police department and asked for Wayne Gallant.

"What can I do for you?" he asked.

"Could you check the background of a Bronus Musz-kaviczas? He's from Pennsylvania, about thirty years old, a grad student at the college."

"You'd better spell that one for me."

Helma did and he asked, "Any reason?"

"He's befriended Aunt Em and I'm curious, that's all."

"Can't be too careful," he said. "I'll see you at noon."

When she hurried back to the reference desk, George Melville had circled the students around himself and was giving a lecture explaining why panhandling wasn't allowed inside the library building. He waved gratefully at the sight of Helma and said to the students, "Okay, let's move 'em out."

Summers were slower, the library clientele older and less frantic than when public school was in full session and panicky students—or their parents—labored over class assignments.

"My article won't come up," a woman complained through tight lips before she'd even reached the reference desk, motioning to one of the computers.

Helma rose and followed her to the computer where, if the woman clicked the mouse on the correct icon the entire magazine article should appear on the screen. The system *was* being slow, the "waiting for reply" message blinking on the screen.

Glancing at the citation of the article the woman was anxiously awaiting, Helma said, "This is from last week's *Newsweek*. There's a copy right here in the periodicals department." She nodded toward the shelves of periodicals. "The older issues are filed beneath the newest, just raise the shelf."

"I don't have time for that," the woman told Helma indignantly and sat down cross-armed in front of the computer, regarding the screen with a challenging scowl while across the room, the article she waited for rested unread on the shelf.

Helma sat at one of the unused Internet computers and called up the Social Security Administration's website. In the Death Index, she typed in Lukas Pettori.

One near match appeared on the screen: Lucius Pettori, born in 1947 and died in 1966. Aunt Em's Lukas had been a World War I veteran; he'd given her his medal. She tried permutations of his name but none were successful. He might have died before 1937, when the Social Security Administration began their records, or it *was* possible he was still alive, in his nineties, so she tried one of the people-searcher engines.

"See you tonight, Helma."

Helma removed her hands from the keyboard and turned to face Bronus, Celine, and Douglas. Bronus glanced at the computer screen and Helma shifted slightly, blocking his view.

"Your aunt said not to bring anything," Bronus said, "but is a bottle of wine okay?"

"I'm sure she'd like that," Helma told him.

"Will do, then," he said and the three left while Helma went back to her search. There were no matches for Lukas Pettori, living or dead.

Helma began her lunch hour ten minutes early and found Aunt Em in the library foyer, deep in conversation about copper bracelets and arthritis with an elderly man dressed in jeans and a black t-shirt.

"Oh, Helma, this is Fred." Aunt Em blinked her eyes at the man, smiling widely. "Give him your phone number, dear," she told Helma.

"I don't think . . ." Helma began.

"But Em," the man named Fred said, "you already gave me your niece's phone number."

Aunt Em covered herself well. "See how eager I am? You call me and we'll have that cup of coffee."

Helma drew Aunt Em away from the man and asked her, "Why don't we postpone dinner tonight and you can spend the rest of the day here at the library with me?"

"Dinner?" Aunt Em looked blank for a moment, then said, "Oh, with Bronus. Of course not. Don't be silly. Let's go now so I can get cooking."

"You shouldn't be in the apartment alone," Helma tried, following Aunt Em, who was already heading for the exit.

Aunt Em waved her hand. "Ethel will be there," she said. "Stop worrying."

As Helma let Aunt Em into her apartment at the Bayside Arms, Aunt Em solemnly told her, "Tell your Ms. Moon I'm resigning from the VAPs. If I'm such a valuable older American, I want to be paid."

"I'll tell her," Helma promised just as seriously. "Don't open the door to anyone except Mrs. Whitney."

Aunt Em looked up at Helma, one corner of her mouth raised, and said nothing.

Then Helma drove to Saul's deli to meet Wayne Gallant. Tables sat outside on the sidewalk and Helma was glad not to spot the chief out front, but rather inside at a more private table, halfway back in the narrow restaurant. He raised his hand when he saw her and smiled. A glass of iced tea sat on the table in front of him.

"Sorry I'm late," she told him. "I had to take my aunt home."

"Five minutes," he said in mock seriousness. "I was debating whether to call the police."

"Fortunately it wouldn't be a long-distance call," Helma said as she sat down. She knotted her purse strap around the leg of her chair and asked, "Did you discover if Bronus has a record?"

"I did a quick check," he said. "He's from Pennsylvania, all right, working on his masters degree like he told you, attending summer quarter. Aside from a single speeding ticket three years ago, no record."

"Thank you," Helma told him. "What have you discovered about the murder?"

"All this before ordering?" the chief teased and motioned for a waiter.

"What can I get you guys?" the young waiter asked as he pulled a pad from his hip pocket.

"Excuse me," Helma said, "but I'm not a guy."

"Sorry, ma'am," he apologized. "What would you like?" He wore a ring in his nose which at one time would have offended Helma, but which now she barely noticed. And when Helma noticed she barely noticed, it made her strangely sad, as if the point of the ring had been stolen from the young man and so she gave him her order in a more tender fashion than she might normally.

"Has your aunt remembered any more about her plane trip or the purse snatcher?" the chief asked when the waiter had left their table.

"Nothing significant. Mostly, she's been recalling bits of her life from seventy years ago, incidents I never knew."

"A shock or an illness makes a person take stock of his or her life, I think," he commented.

Helma nodded and took a sip of water. "What have you learned about the dead man?" she asked, wondering how soon she'd have to divulge her phone conversation with Joseph Gobowski.

"Binder passed himself off as a detective now and then," Wayne Gallant told her, "finding lost boyfriends, debtors, a few divorce cases. Some old ads popped up in newspapers and magazines. 'Discreet inquiries,' that sort of thing. Knowing he had these kinds of contacts widens the scope." He absently removed a pen from his suit and began drawing squares on his napkin.

"Could Binder have been hired to track Aunt Em?" Helma leaned back. "No, that's impossible." She looked at the chief. "Isn't it?"

"All we know for sure is that he tried to steal your aunt's purse, she stabbed him, and he followed her here and was stabbed himself."

"With a telephone."

"Right."

"Of course," Helma said, touching his arm in excitement. "the killer could have carried a cellular phone on the airplane, undetected. He was on the same flight with Binder and Aunt Em, intending to kill Binder all along, but he didn't have a clear chance until our arrival in Bellehaven."

When Wayne Gallant's response didn't match Helma's eagerness, she asked, "You've already thought of this, haven't you?"

"It's good reasoning," he praised her. "We're checking the passenger list and so far everybody checks out." His piercing eyes zeroed in on Helma's. "Have you received any more flowers or anonymous gifts?"

"I'm not sure. Mrs. Whitney found a packet of cat treats being mauled by a stray cat on our landing. I threw it away."

He nodded. "Do you leave your outdoor light on all night?"

"Of course. Oh, by the way, today a man called the library and asked for Aunt Em, but when I took the call for her, he hung up."

He drummed his fingers on the table. "And your Aunt Em is alone at your apartment right now?"

"She said Mrs. Whitney was coming over. At least that's what she *said*."

"I'm sure she's fine." Wayne Gallant spoke in a reassuring voice. "But you might call to be sure or ask Ruth to visit with her until you get home from the library."

"Excuse me," Helma said, rising from her chair. "I'll do that right now."

The pay phone was at the back of Saul's near the restrooms. Helma turned her back to the men's door and dialed her own number.

"Of course I'm fine," Aunt Em said. "Ethel's right here." Helma heard only silence in the background. "I'm *fine*," Aunt Em repeated.

"Have a nice afternoon," Helma told her, resolving to go back to her apartment the instant she finished lunch with Wayne Gallant.

"Also, keep talking to your aunt about her flight here," Wayne Gallant said when she sat down, continuing their conversation. "Bring up details that might prod her memory: colors, sounds, clothes people wore, sights out the window. She's the key to this affair."

Their food was served: sliced turkey and butter on white bread for Helma, corned beef on rye, with all the condiments, for the chief.

Helma cut her sandwich into quarters before she asked the chief, "Is this why you asked me to lunch, to discuss the details of the murder?"

Wayne Gallant chewed, then swallowed his bite of sandwich before he said, "Partly. Also a personal matter."

Helma arranged the four quarters of her sandwich in a neat circle, edges pointed inward. Was this the moment he intended to tell her about his ex-wife? She folded her hands in her lap and waited.

"It's unexpected," he said. "An opportunity that's come out of the blue. I can't say it hasn't crossed my mind before but it's nothing I'd agree to without discussing it with you first."

"That's thoughtful of you," Helma said, and then catching what she suspected was a hint of sarcasm in her tone, she said, "It is. I appreciate it."

"Good. We've been friends for a long time, you and I, and I hope we've reached some kind of understanding. But . . . well, something's come up."

Helma felt her left eye begin to twitch. A buzz sounded in her ears as if her head were being enveloped by a raging cloud of wasps. She gripped her hands tighter to keep from waving her hand around her head. "And what is that?" she heard herself calmly ask.

"I've been offered a job in Arizona," Wayne Gallant told her.

"A job?" Helma said, her hearing and vision returning to normal. "You're talking about a job? That's good news."

Wayne Gallant frowned. A puzzled expression settled in his blue eyes. "You're pleased?"

"Yes. Well, I'm relieved. What's the position?"

"Chief of police," he told her, but now he appeared distracted, his concentration broken. "The city's larger than Bellehaven. A step up, higher pay."

"Congratulations."

He shoved his sandwich aside, still gazing at her, the frown frozen. "I didn't expect you to be so happy."

"It's just that I expected . . . well, did you apply for the position?"

"No, the city approached me. I have a week to decide. I'd been leaning against taking it until . . . recently." He glanced down at his watch. "I forgot I've got a meeting in a few minutes. Do you want to wrap up your sandwich and take it with you? I'll drive you back to the library."

"Thank you, but I have my car. You go ahead. I'll finish my lunch."

"I'll see you later, then," he said, rising and leaving his sandwich behind, only two bites taken from it. He gave her the briefest smile as he left the table and swiftly walked toward the door.

It wasn't until he was opening the door that Helma realized fully that chief of police Wayne Gallant had just told her he might leave Bellehaven, and that he believed she was *happy* about the possibility.

She leapt to her feet, her napkin fluttering to the floor. "Wait," she said but Helma Zukas wasn't in the habit of shouting and hadn't raised her voice, so she watched him stride through the door and down the sidewalk without ever being aware she'd called after him.

When Helma hurried home to her apartment, she found Mrs. Whitney with Aunt Em.

"I told you she was here," Aunt Em said. "We're going to cook up a storm." Boy Cat Zukas was draped across her lap, purring but watching Helma's every move. "Can you stop by the store for sour cream on your way home?"

Helma jotted "sour cream" on her day's list and asked, "Have there been any phone calls?"

Aunt Em shook her head. "But a man was here to sell you a vacuum cleaner."

"When?"

"Fifteen or twenty minutes ago."

"What did he look like?"

"How can you tell with a man who wears a beard?" Aunt Em said. "He wanted to come in and look at your carpets."

"I reminded him there was no soliciting allowed here," Mrs. Whitney told Helma. "There's a sign as big as a barn in front of the building."

"Was he tall, short, fat?" Helma asked.

"Tall," Aunt Em said.

"Short," said Mrs. Whitney.

"Brown hair," Aunt Em and Mrs. Whitney agreed.

"What kind of vacuum cleaners was he selling?"

"That's funny," Mrs. Whitney said. "He didn't have a vacuum cleaner with him."

"But he had a briefcase," Aunt Em said.

"I'll be home right after work. If you're here alone, Aunt Em, don't answer the door."

"Yes, yes," Aunt Em told her, shrugging her shoulders.

"I'll be here," Mrs. Whitney told Helma.

"Just don't forget the sour cream," Aunt Em reminded her.

Walter David was just pulling into the parking lot on his motorcycle, a bag of groceries in the basket where Moggy sometimes rode. He waved to Helma and she returned the wave, realizing he'd have been gone when the salesman rang her bell.

It was nearly closing time and Helma carried four books to the circulation desk to check out: two on memory loss, one on aging, and one on Arizona, when a woman standing in the health and weight loss section stepped forward and said, "Excuse me."

"May I help you?" Helma asked. The woman looked familiar, sleek, with close-cropped blonde hair, eyebrows plucked to swift arches like the inverted swoops on running shoes, lipstick a cool, clear pink, her slender body encased in white pants and an expensive cotton sweater.

"Yes, you certainly may help me," she said. Her eyes glittered and at first Helma thought she wore contacts. "Stay away from my husband."

"I beg your pardon?"

"Wayne Gallant."

"I believe the correct term is ex-husband."

"That's only a temporary situation," she said coolly, confidently touching her little finger to the corner of her mouth.

"Didn't we meet yesterday in Boardwalk Park?" Helma asked.

"Briefly."

Helma shifted the books in her arms. "Excuse me but if you don't have a library-related question, I have work to do."

"It's librarian related," the woman said, taking a perfumed step closer to Helma.

"Excuse me," Helma repeated, making a move to step around the woman.

"I still know people in this town," the woman said in a low voice. "I'll have your job."

"I doubt if you're qualified," Helma said and continued toward the circulation desk, hearing what sounded like a hiss from behind her.

## ❧ chapter twelve ❧

# DINNER FOR SIX

**H**elma was the last librarian to vacate the workroom at five o'clock. A manila envelope lay in the center of her desk with her name written in Ms. Moon's loopy handwriting. The envelope wasn't sealed and Helma untucked the flap and pulled out the enclosed sheets of paper.

"Bert and Lamb," the bold type on the cover sheet read. *"Understand the Space You Fill, Your Hue in the Earth's Rainbow."* Attached was the test: a rainbow-colored booklet of multiple-choice questions and a single answer sheet with the correlating circles to be blackened. *Use a number two pencil, please.*

The first question read, *I am happiest when*: and the choices were: *a) sitting by myself in a dark room, b) partying with friends, c) visiting my parents, d) snuggling with a pet.*

Helma returned the papers to the envelope and tucked it into her blue bag to take home where she could examine in a more leisurely manner just exactly what it was she had rejected.

On the way home she'd already driven past the entrance to Boardwalk Park, her thoughts a disturbing mix of murder, ex-wives, and Arizona when she remembered Aunt Em's sour cream. It was too far to her regular grocery store so she stopped at the closest one.

"Do you have your savings card?" the green-aproned cashier asked her.

"No," Helma told her.

The cashier rang up the sour cream and handed Helma the receipt, pointing to the bottom line. "See, this means you could have saved twenty cents if you had a card."

"No," Helma told her. "This means your store overcharged me twenty cents."

Even before she reached her apartment door, Helma sniffed the air. She tapped on the door to warn Aunt Em before she entered, thinking as she unlocked it that the spirits of long-gone aunts and uncles and grandparents should suddenly step from behind closed doors. Cousins, too. Surprise!

The air was rich with the odor of baking *kugelis,* that heady mixture of potatoes, eggs, onions, cream, and bacon, so prevalent when she was growing up that she'd rarely noticed it.

Aunt Em stood at the stove, aproned, her cheeks rosy, stirring a mixture in Helma's largest frying pan with a spatula: onions and bacon, the wicked topping that was spooned, along with sour cream, over the *kugelis* after it was baked and then fried. Arteries clogged just at the smell.

"Ah, here she is," Aunt Em said, waving the spatula at Helma.

Mrs. Whitney sat on the sofa braiding tiny wigs of colored yarn. Arrayed in front of her were bright skeins of yarn and six naked deodorizer cones.

"Helma," Mrs. Whitney said. "Your aunt and I are thinking of going into business making deodorizer cozies with holiday themes; don't you think that's a charming idea? Santa Clauses, Easter bunnies, little ghosts and goblins. Em thought we could even do a manger scene.''

''I'm sure you'll find a lot of customers,'' Helma said judiciously. ''Has it been quiet here this afternoon?''

''Like the tomb,'' Aunt Em said. Her eyes twinkled. ''Now there's an idea,'' she began. ''A Good Friday cozy.''

Mrs. Whitney giggled and Helma stared from one wrinkled face to the other, wondering which was influencing the other. Mrs. Whitney began rolling up her yarn wigs and placing them into a paisley bag. ''I'll let you two visit now. It's been a lovely afternoon, Em.''

''I'll help you, Mrs. Whitney,'' Helma offered, noticing Mrs. Whitney's cane leaning against the arm of the sofa; it was one of those days when her arthritis was ''knocking up.''

''Thank you, dear,'' Mrs. Whitney said as Helma carried her bag and a paper bag of deodorizers the few feet between their apartments. The newspapers had been tossed onto the landing and Helma picked up both hers and Mrs. Whitney's.

''Your aunt is a cheerful woman for everything she's been through,'' she said as she unlocked her door.

''The murder was a shock,'' Helma agreed.

''And two robberies.'' She shook her head.

''Actually, there was only one,'' Helma said, glancing at the newspaper's headlines: *Overweight group sues city for hefty amount over small council chamber chairs.* ''The purse snatcher was unsuccessful.''

''No, I mean at her home in Michigan,'' Mrs. Whitney said. ''Right in broad daylight while she was making raspberry preserves.''

Helma let the newspaper drop to her side. ''Aunt Em said that?''

Mrs. Whitney nodded. ''She said she didn't remember it very well because she had such a headache.''

''When?'' Helma asked. ''When was she robbed?''

''Why, just before she came here. Isn't that why you

brought her to Bellehaven? She said it was to keep her safe.'' Mrs. Whitney frowned. ''Oh dear. Am I telling you something you didn't already know? She didn't report the robbery?''

''There was some confusion around that time,'' Helma reassured her, ''and we weren't certain what happened. Thank you for telling me.''

''Well, it might not be quite true. You aunt gets confused sometimes, the poor dear. Oh, look, this must be that young man she was talking about. She said he was bringing his roommate.''

Three people strode across the parking lot toward the staircase. Bronus, Celine, and Douglas, chatting among themselves and walking in loose-limbed gaits as if they were on their way to a good time.

''Helma!'' Bronus arced his arm in a wave. Douglas smiled, flashing straight white teeth. Celine remained calmly beautiful, her posture flawless. The men bounded up the steps with Celine close behind.

If only Helma had ten minutes to question Aunt Em about the robbery in Michigan. Could it be true? *Two* robberies involving Aunt Em *plus* an attempted purse snatching? Not to mention the murder and all its implications.

''Do you think your Aunt Em will care if all three of us come?'' Bronus asked. ''I was going to call you to ask but your phone number's unlisted.''

''He's been raving about this legendary Lithuanian specialty,'' Douglas said. ''I won't stay long; I've got a hiking club meeting.''

''I'm sure Aunt Em will be delighted,'' Helma told all three of them. ''She's been cooking all afternoon.''

It was apparent that the meal of the evening consisted totally of slabs of *kugelis*. Aunt Em hurriedly pulled out plates and silverware and instructed Helma to set the table, all the time talking to Douglas and Bronus and Celine in a mixture of Lithuanian and English.

The doorbell rang as they were choosing where to sit at Helma's dining table. It was Ruth. "Am I too late?" she asked, pulling a bouquet of dahlias from behind her back. "Can I bribe my way in for a bite?" She held the flowers up and said to Helma, "Do not fear. I didn't find these on your doorstep; I bought them."

"Ah, Ruth," Aunt Em said. "Sit down. This is Bronus and Douglas and Celine."

Ruth's smile widened, her eyes gleamed. Both Bronus and Douglas met the first and toughest criteria necessary to inflame Ruth's interest: they were tall. Age had nothing to do with it. "Do you play basketball?" she asked both of them.

"So-so," Douglas told her. "I teach middle school in Spokane and I sub for the coach sometimes."

"When I get the chance," Bronus said. "Celine's really good." Celine blushed and shrugged. "Do you?" he asked Ruth.

"Yes," Ruth said although the only time Helma had ever seen Ruth on a basketball court, other than hanging around the players, was in high school when she was drafted to the girls' team due to her height but was quickly dropped because she ducked whenever the ball came her way. "Maybe we could find a couple of other players and have a three-on-three game."

Every frying pan in Helma's kitchen was being used for Aunt Em's concoctions. Grease sputtered, *kugelis* sizzled, frying onions turned translucent.

They sat around the table in silence while Aunt Em, who insisted that she didn't want help, served the platter of *kugelis*, a bowl of bacon and onions and another bowl of sour cream.

Aunt Em hovered, smiling in anticipation and watching their faces as they took their first bites. The *kugelis*, with its crispy outside and salty, mealy interior, was perfect. Helma skipped the bacon and onions and sour cream—it was important to cut *somewhere*—and savored the food.

"Fit for the gods," Ruth said.

"Bellissimo," Bronus told her.

"It's a lot better than it sounds," Douglas said, cutting off a bigger bite. He ate heartily, turning his fork upside down as he put each bite into his mouth.

"It's very good," Celine told her.

Aunt Em beamed and joined them, spreading a coat of sour cream over her portion like frosting. Bronus dabbed at his sour cream and said, "I'm embarrassed to admit I didn't realize that murder happened right here in your parking lot until Douglas pointed it out in the newspaper. Were you here when the body was found?"

"Oh yes," Aunt Em told them. "I stabbed him."

Douglas nearly choked on his food but Bronus nodded and politely asked, "To death?"

"No, earlier when he tried to snatch my purse at the airport. He was trying to steal something valuable."

"What was it?" Douglas asked.

"I don't know but he didn't get it."

"How do you know he didn't?" Ruth asked her.

"Then I'd be missing something, wouldn't I?" Aunt Em asked. "And I'm not missing a single thing."

"What about your money?" Helma asked.

"Money isn't a thing," Aunt Em insisted, "it's only a means."

"Tell my credit card company that," Ruth grumbled.

Helma wanted to continue this conversation in light of Mrs. Whitney's information but not in front of Bronus, Douglas, and Celine.

"Are you enjoying Bellehaven?" Helma asked Bronus, but his attention was on Douglas, who was saying, "So the purse snatcher followed you home from the airport and died for his trouble?''

Aunt Em nodded. "Crime doesn't pay. You could hear the police sirens all over town. My, there was a crowd."

"I went home to Spokane for the weekend," Douglas told her. "Missed all the excitement." He handed the bowl of sour cream to Bronus. "Did you hear them? You're on the same side of town."

For a moment, neither Bronus nor Celine answered, then Bronus shook his head. "Never heard a thing."

"But *who* killed . . ." Douglas began.

"Let's discuss something else," Helma cut in.

Douglas glanced around the table, stopping at Aunt Em. "Sorry," he said.

Celine said little; her eyes followed whoever was speaking while every other person in the room discovered their own eyes drawn to her. Helma found it curious; this sense of "presence" that the young woman projected. Although she rarely commented, there was no perception that she *wasn't* taking part in the conversation.

"I ran into Eve from the library on my way over," Ruth said, reaching for more bacon and onions. "I hear you're all taking personality tests."

"Not *all* of us," Helma told her.

"Have you seen the test?"

"I have a copy with me," Helma said, regretting it the instant she spoke. What she most wanted was for the evening to wind down and everyone to leave so she could question Aunt Em about the robbery in Michigan.

But now everyone's attention was focused on her, avid interest lighting their faces.

"Let's see it," Ruth said.

"A personality test," Bronus said. "This should be fun."

"It's not like the Myer-Briggs," Helma said, hoping to

dissuade them. "Instead of a rating, you're consigned to a color category."

Now she'd done it. Even Celine was intrigued. "How interesting," she spoke to prove it.

It took on a life of its own and before Helma knew how it had happened, everyone had moved to her living room with a pencil and a blank piece of paper while Ruth read off the questions and optional answers to hoots of laughter.

On her own paper, Helma drew boxes around diamonds inside circles while Ruth read off such questions as, *When I brush my teeth, I: a) leave the water running, b) rinse the sink out afterward, c) spit in the toilet, d) rinse with mouthwash immediately afterward.*

Following the last question about noseblowing in public places, Ruth said, "Okay, everybody, pass your papers in to me. What's this?" she asked, looking at Helma's meaningless doodles.

"I don't intend to take this test, even as a joke," Helma told her.

"Scared, huh?"

"Of course not."

"Can you get them graded for us?" Douglas asked. "I bet my color is Navy blue, something deep and masculine."

"I may be able to," Helma said, not at all sure.

Ruth evened the papers, grinning the whole time, and with a flourish, presented them to Helma. "These are a little gift for you, Helma. Just choose one and turn it in to the Moonbeam. Voila! Everyone's happy."

"Be warned," Bronus said. "If your director plans to reorganize based on these tests, you may end up emptying the trash."

*Now* the evening was finally winding down. Douglas glanced at his watch and stood. "I'd better get to my meeting." He took Aunt Em's hand, bending over it in a courtly manner. "That was a delicious experience, ma'am, and I thank you."

Aunt Em gazed at him, touching her own chin in the same spot as Douglas's cleft, a quizzical expression on her face, then she smiled and mused, "Isn't that curious?"

"Michael Douglas," he said, touching his chin.

"Deeper, like . . . Kirk Douglas," Aunt Em amended. "Come back again with Bronus."

"Thanks," he said. He surprised Helma by turning to her and saying, "I hope I see you again some time, Helma."

"She's at the library every day," Aunt Em reminded him.

Bronus and Celine also rose. "I have a paper to finish," Bronus said. "And Celine's getting ready for a summer stock play."

"What part will you play?" Aunt Em asked.

"Rosalind in *As You Like It*," Celine told her.

"You'll be perfect," Aunt Em assured her.

After the door closed behind them, Ruth sighed. "I'm a sucker for the tall ones," she said.

"And a few short ones, too, I'd guess," Aunt Em said.

"You're right." Ruth told her without any embarrassment. "What'll I do . . ." she began, then broke off, shaking her head as if erasing a thought.

"Sit down, Aunt Em," Helma said and motioned Aunt Em to the rocker. She sat down opposite her. "What happened in Michigan?" she asked. "Mrs. Whitney—Ethel—said you were robbed."

"What?" Ruth asked, dropping into the chair where Douglas had sat.

Aunt Em shook her head. "Isn't it funny. I can almost remember it, little bits and pieces. I was making raspberry preserves; it was a good year with all that rain in the springtime and then the sunshine . . ." Her voice faded away.

"The robber?" Helma gently asked. "Did he have a gun?"

"I don't think so. Who'd need to use a gun on an old lady like me?"

"What did he take?"

"I don't know. I had such a headache and I was in the yard when that nice June Zemke—remember her?—stopped and took me to the hospital." She shrugged apologetically. "I think I acted stupid."

"But no one knew a robber had been to your house?"

"*I* didn't remember it," Aunt Em said. "The house looked fine when Bruce took me home to pack."

"Excuse me," Helma said. "I'm calling Bruce."

"Ask him when my carving will be finished," Ruth told her. Bruce was a wood sculptor, the artistic one in Helma's family.

It was after eleven o'clock in Michigan and Bruce answered the phone. "This late I thought it would be you," he said. "Is Aunt Em giving you trouble?"

"Not at all," Helma told him. "But her memory's returning and she claims she was robbed before she was found walking in circles on her front lawn."

Bruce was silent, digesting this news. "What does she say was stolen?"

"She doesn't remember. Would you go over and look around?"

Again the silence. "The doctor said she shouldn't go home again, no matter how well she recovers," Bruce finally said. "She can't live alone."

"All right, I'll accept that for the moment but can you check her house and see what's missing?"

"Helma," Bruce said. "We couldn't leave her house empty. Everybody knows she's gone, and out there in the country like that. So we've been packing up her belongings."

Helma sighed. "You're saying that you wouldn't have any idea what's missing because you're taking the house apart while she's gone?"

"That's right. I'm sorry."

"Well, did the house look ransacked? Violated?"

"No, it was a little messier than usual but Aunt Em had been making some kind of fruit thing."

"Raspberry preserves," Helma told him.

"Right, but I didn't notice anything extraordinary."

"And now it's too late to bring in the police because the house is packed up."

"Almost packed up," Bruce conceded.

"One other thing," Helma said. "Do you know how much cash she had with her?"

"She started out with a bundle but I made her put it in the bank. I think she had about fifty dollars." Bruce cleared his throat. "I'm thinking of adding on a room to our house. I'm here every day so I could keep an eye on her."

Helma softened. Her brother and his wife had two sons, two jobs, and generous hearts. "Don't make any plans for a week," Helma told him. "Then let's all decide together."

Helma returned to the living room where Aunt Em and Ruth were speaking in easy voices, discussing alcoholic beverages. "I preferred straight rye," Aunt Em was saying. "You can hardly find it anymore." And when she saw Helma's face she said, "Bruce can't find anything missing, can he? Do you think I imagined it?"

"No, Aunt Em, I don't," Helma told her.

Because now it made sense. Peter Binder had attempted to rob Aunt Em in Michigan. She'd been making raspberry preserves, which Helma knew were heated beyond the boiling point. And she'd been discovered in her front yard holding a wooden spoon, a spoon she'd most likely been using to stir the boiling sugar and berry mixture. Aunt Em had defended herself with hot preserves, causing the burn that the chief had mentioned scarred the neck of Binder's body. Had he shoved her, hit her, or had he terrified her so badly it had caused her "brain incident"?

## ❧ chapter thirteen ❧

# TRAIN TALES

"**A**unt Em," Helma said, "Tell us again anything you can remember about the robbery in Michigan."

When Aunt Em appeared stymied, rocking her chair harder and absently massaging her left palm with the thumb of her other hand, Helma began for her. "You were making raspberry preserves . . ."

"He didn't knock," she finally said, her body going still. "He walked into my kitchen and he said . . ." She closed her eyes in concentration. "I don't remember if he said a single word."

"There was only one robber?"

"Only one."

"Are you sure?" Ruth asked.

"I only saw one robber," Aunt Em said, speaking distinctly as if she were explaining to a child.

Helma and Ruth exchanged glances. Aunt Em had *seen* only one robber. A second thief, perhaps the eventual murderer, could have been waiting in a getaway car, could still be waiting somewhere in Bellehaven, watching Aunt Em's every move.

"But you knew," Helma said, "even if he didn't speak,

that he was a robber. Did he wear a mask?''

''Maybe.''

''But he didn't have a gun?''

''I don't think so.''

''Could it have been the same man who tried to steal your purse at the airport?'' Helma asked.

''Did I hurt him?'' Aunt Em asked. ''With the wooden spoon?''

''Binder's burn,'' Ruth said, touching the side of her neck.

''If you did hurt him, it was because you were defending yourself,'' Helma assured her. ''It was an acceptable act, morally and legally.''

''I can't remember any more now,'' Aunt Em said, leaning back and turning her head to gaze out the window where the sky was turning to deep purples and pinks as the sun dropped behind the clouds. A broken line of boats, sail and motor, headed back toward the marina, most with their lights on.

''So whatever they were after,'' Ruth said, ''they believed she brought it to Bellehaven with her in her purse.''

''He,'' Helma corrected, nodding toward Aunt Em.

''Right,'' Ruth hastily agreed. ''He, him, I mean, not 'they.' Just one criminal, the dead one.'' She waved her hand toward the parking lot. ''Everybody's fine.''

Aunt Em smiled from Ruth to Helma. ''You don't need to protect me. I know there's a dastardly villain still loose in the city.'' She raised her hand to her heart. ''And I might be his quarry.''

''Or something he believes you have,'' Helma said. ''We've examined the purse twice. The only unusual item is the train ticket. What kind of trouble were you in, Aunt Em?'' she asked, ''that prompted Uncle Juozas to send you the ticket?''

''Love, of course,'' Aunt Em said. ''Love always gets

you into trouble. It clouds your head, especially when you are young." She gazed into the air between Helma and Ruth. "Marry a friend, that's my advice."

"In 1928," Helma said, remembering the date on the ticket, "you would have been eighteen years old."

"Very young," Aunt Em said, nodding. "I can't talk about it yet, not even now."

"What else, what else," Ruth mumbled. "What's of value? If he followed you, he thought you were carrying it with you."

Helma eyed Aunt Em critically, trying to see what the robber had seen. "Your jewelry?" she asked. "What about the amber necklace and earrings?"

Aunt Em touched the necklace at her throat. "I pawned them once, in Chicago," she said. "He only gave me a little money because he felt sorry for me. Five dollars, I think."

"How'd you get them back?" Ruth asked.

"A friend got them out of hock," Aunt Em told her.

"A man," Ruth said, more a statement than a question.

Aunt Em nodded, her eyes going soft. "For a Valentine's Day present he had them restrung so I could wear them all the time." She paused. "I always worried about losing them before that."

"May I see your necklace?" Helma asked.

For a moment Helma thought Aunt Em would refuse, but then she reached behind her neck and unclasped her necklace and gave it to Helma. "My fingers are not so clumsy today," she said.

Helma didn't know much about amber except what she'd seen relatives wearing and this looked like many of those necklaces: large beads of dark honey-colored amber, with some pieces clear and some opaque, or dotted with specks caught in pine resin millions of years ago. The best and clearest beads hung in the center of the string, the darkest close to the clasp.

"Any bugs in there that could be turned into dinosaurs?" Ruth asked, leaning forward to gaze at the necklace in Helma's hands.

"I don't see any insects at all," Helma said. No insects, nothing out of the ordinary that she could discern. And yes, the amber beads were strung on a heavy cord with a sturdy clasp.

"It's beautiful," Helma said as she refastened the necklace around Aunt Em's neck. "Do you know its original history?"

"One of your great-grandfathers carved the pieces of amber; that's why the beads are not quite perfect."

"When you left Chicago for Michigan," Helma asked, "how did you travel?"

"I went home with . . . a runner. Running with a runner," she said to herself as if she liked the way the words sounded.

Helma and Ruth watched Aunt Em fade in front of them, first her eyes going distant and then her head bending forward as she slipped into a doze. Suddenly, she jerked upright and stared at Helma and Ruth in wild surprise, as if for a moment she didn't recognize them.

"Aunt Em?" Helma asked quietly, touching her hand.

"Ah, I'm gathering. I'll go to bed now. I can't think anymore."

"Would you like some help?" Helma asked her.

"Of course not," Aunt Em snapped. "I'm not that old."

"Your Aunt Em has a past," Ruth said when they heard the door of the second bedroom click closed. "Who'd a thunk it?"

Boy Cat Zukas gave a strident yowl at the screened balcony door and Helma rose to let him in, forced to listen to two more impatient yowls before she slid open the door far enough for him to slip inside.

"I'll ask my mother," Helma told Ruth. Boy Cat Zukas

took a tentative step toward Ruth, then glanced up at Helma, hissed, and curled in his basket.

"When your Aunt Em was eighteen, your mother would have been a toddler. What can she know?"

"Those stories always survive in some form," Helma said.

"You're going to ask your mother for *gossip*? Tsk, tsk."

"Just information," Helma corrected. "That's all."

"And what did she mean when she said she went home with a runner? A drug runner?"

"Close," Helma said. "The country would have been in the midst of Prohibition. Alcohol was illegal and Chicago speakeasies procured their liquor from bootleggers in outlying areas where stills could be hidden."

"And somebody had to make deliveries?" Ruth asked. "Runners?"

"That's right. I believe they were sometimes called rum runners despite their cargo not always being rum."

Ruth whistled. "Wow, that must have been a great time."

Helma's mother picked up the phone on the first ring. "Does Emily remember we made up?" she asked as soon as she heard Helma's voice.

"Not yet, but she's beginning to recall other details so it probably won't be long," she told her mother hopefully. "She mentioned that she lived in Chicago as a young woman. Do you remember her then?"

"I wasn't even born yet," Lillian said, although Helma knew *that* wasn't true.

"What happened to her in Chicago?" Helma asked.

She heard her mother's breathing deepen, warming up to a good story. "Well," she said, stretching out the word the way she did before she related an especially juicy bit of information. "I was much too young, you understand, but the story I heard, not from Em, of course, but here and there, the family wasn't too keen on talking about it, was that as a girl Emily was a hot-headed troublemaker. She ran away from home when she was sixteen, ended up in Chicago, rip-roaring wild. Men, music, alcohol, living the fast life.''

''Aunt Em?'' Helma asked.

''The same.''

''What happened? What changed her?''

''She fell in with the wrong crowd and that scared her back home all right.''

''But Mother,'' Helma persisted. ''*What* scared her?''

''Who knows for sure? Love or love gone bad had something to do with it, according to your father but you know how he was; he'd cut off his arm before he'd speak a sour word against Emily. She could do no wrong, period. Womanhood personified.''

''Did you ever hear stories about bootlegging in Scoop River?'' Helma asked, feeling her mother about to launch into a deeper plumbing of Aunt Em's unwarranted status as the perfect sister.

Lillian laughed, successfully deflected. ''Of course. More than a few of our neighbors pulled their way up in the world by turning their crops into liquid. I heard about it: sudden new barns and houses, fast cars.''

''Were there runners who took the alcohol to market in those fast cars?''

''Yes,'' Lillian said warily. ''I heard that. But that was long ago. What kind of tale is Em trying to feed you? If it has anything to do with her brothers' pasts, don't believe it.''

''I heard her use the word, 'runner,' that's all,'' Helma told her.

''I only knew about runners after the fact,'' Lillian said too quickly, ''but I suppose they'd take out a back seat from a car and fill it with bottles of whiskey and off they'd go, sometimes with friends or family—small children even—sitting on top of the bottles to make it look legitimate to the police."

Helma made another quick calculation. "Was my father a runner before Prohibition ended?"

Lillian laughed, not a completely comfortable laugh. "Who knows what young men do before they learn responsibility? That was definitely before I came along."

"Then it was during Danute's time?" Helma asked, remembering Aunt Em's story about her father's first love. Across the room, Ruth, who was listening to every word, jumped up and frantically waved her arms and shook her head as if she were trying to flag down a driver barreling toward an oncoming train.

There was silence on the other end of the telephone. Helma pulled it away from her ear, then asked, "Mother?"

"She told you about that, didn't she?" Lillian finally demanded. "She just can't forget it, always bringing up the past, blabbing secrets like *she* has the right but nobody can talk about *her*. Well, I'll tell one of her secrets and you can ask her to explain it to you, go ahead, I dare you. In Chicago? Emily's lover died and it was her fault, she *killed* him. Tell her to stick that in her pipe and smoke it up the ying-yang."

And Helma's mother slammed down the receiver, fumbling it so it first clattered in Helma's ear, losing its impact.

Ruth watched Helma silently hang up the phone. "Hit a raw nerve, eh?" she asked, sitting down again.

"She didn't care to discuss Danute," Helma said.

"Never, *ever* bring up old lovers," Ruth said with unnecessary smugness, "even if they end up weighing five hundred pounds and growing hair all over their bodies. It shuts a conversation down real quick."

"But that happened at least a half century ago, and Mother *did* marry him, not Danute."

"Doesn't matter. So what else did she say?"

Helma wondered how much of her mother's claim about Aunt Em killing her lover was based on anger, or if any of it was true. Besides, Aunt Em had been so young. "She said Aunt Em's boyfriend died before Aunt Em returned to Michigan."

"Died?" Ruth asked. "Died how?"

"She didn't elaborate, but the story she heard was that Aunt Em ran away from the farm, went to Chicago, and lived a fast life."

"Then made a one-hundred-and-eighty-degree turn, came home, married the farmer next door, and lived an exemplary life for the next seventy years. Interesting, but that gets us nowhere. Thieves and murderers don't chase sweet farm wives thousands of miles across the country, let alone up that godawful freeway, to steal their purses and kill each other."

Helma rolled the placemats into long tubes, then unrolled them and stacked them one on top of the other, their edges matching. "Maybe the item he wanted wasn't in her purse."

"Then why try to steal it?"

"Do you remember in *The Searchers* how John Wayne was haunted because he didn't protect his brother's family from the Indian raid?"

"It wasn't his fault; the Indians lured him away. And what does John Wayne have to do with the problems of life and death in Bellehaven?"

Helma reached for the telephone. "Perhaps they weren't sure where the item was."

"They? Who's 'they'? The Indians? What am I missing here?"

"If one man tried to steal the suitcase while the other took the opportunity to snatch her purse," Helma said as she pressed numbers on her telephone, "one of them was bound to be successful, maybe both of them. And the worst that could happen is that we'd spot him trying to steal the suitcase and try to apprehend him, leaving Aunt Em vulnerable anyway.''

Ruth snapped her fingers. ''The guy who said he accidentally picked up her suitcase. Who are you calling?''

''Wayne Gallant. He has the airport surveillance tape.''

''Very good,'' Ruth said, giving Helma a thumbs-up sign.

The phone—Wayne Gallant's unlisted number—rang three times before an answering machine clicked and the chief's recorded voice began cheerfully speaking in her ear. Helma hung up. ''I'll call him in the morning.''

''He's probably with the ex,'' Ruth offered.

''Possibly,'' Helma responded.

''So what are you going to do about it?''

''I told you: call him in the morning.''

''No, about the ex?''

''Nothing,'' Helma said.

''No battle was ever won by sitting on your dufus.''

''I refuse to engage in any battle or war over a man,'' Helma told Ruth.

''Yeah, yeah, you already said that.'' She stood. ''So call me in the morning after you talk to the chief. I should see the videotape, too, since we were both chasing this guy down.''

''I will.''

''I'd help you with the dishes but I know I couldn't possibly wash them clean enough to meet your standards.''

That was true. Helma walked Ruth to the door and had just closed it behind her, about to turn the deadbolt, when Ruth knocked.

''Lookee here,'' Ruth said when Helma reopened the door, pointing downward.

In the center of her mat lay a single blood-red rose, its blossom crushed as if it had been trod upon.

## ❧ chapter fourteen ❧

# BY ANY OTHER NAME

"**D**on't touch it," Ruth warned, standing back from the rose as if it were explosive.

"I wasn't about to, at least not with my bare hands," Helma told her, retrieving a sealable clear plastic bag from the drawer that held wrapping supplies and donning a pair of rubber gloves from beneath her sink. Then she carefully nudged the damaged rose inside the bag. That completed, she sealed the bag and placed it in her refrigerator next to a bottle of low-fat Italian dressing.

"A blood-red rose is a bad omen. It means death or deflowering or something unsavory. A crushed rose has to be worse; total damnation, at least. Call the police," Ruth advised, gazing into Helma's refrigerator, then observing, "A person could starve to death on this stuff."

"He's not home," Helma reminded her as she closed the refrigerator door.

"Not him specifically, the police in general."

"And tell them to dust a rose left on my doormat for evidence? I'll wait until I can talk to the chief."

Ruth shrugged. "Yeah, they'd probably think you were a crank. So have them page him."

"Not tonight." Helma began stacking dishes by size in order to wash them.

Ruth threw up her hands. "You win, wait until morning to explain it to the chief of your dreams." She tipped her head. "Or maybe, with the ex-wife lapping at his heels I should say, 'in your dreams.'"

"I don't understand why you're distinguishing between the phrases, 'of your dreams' and 'in your dreams,'" Helma said.

"Put the emphasis on the word 'in,'" Ruth instructed. "In your dreams is like saying . . . *you* wish. Oh, never mind. But you're not paging him because you're scared he's out with her even as we speak, right? Terrified he'd come over with her in tow."

"I met her," Helma said.

Ruth leaned against the sink, her eyes brightening. "And how did you manage to do that?"

"She was in the library and introduced herself."

"Did she say, 'Hi, I'm here to renew my role as Mrs. Chief of Police, stay the hell out of my way'?"

"Not exactly in those words but yes, that was definitely the message."

"And you said?" Ruth prompted, making beckoning motions with her hands.

"I excused myself to pursue my library duties," Helma told her as she placed the silverware from dinner in her sink, all the handles pointing in the same direction.

"Is that all?"

"She mentioned something about wanting to be a librarian."

"So now she believes you're not in the game."

"I'm *not*," Helma reminded her again, wearily this time.

"But that could be to your advantage," Ruth went on, tapping her finger against her chin and ignoring Helma's protest. "She'll be off her guard when you go in for the kill."

"I'm sorry I brought it up," Helma told her. "We have more important matters to deal with right now."

"Yeah, death and robbery and a killer who's leaving nasty presents. Call me when the chief wants us to view this tape. I'll be up early. I have to finish the yellow squash."

Ruth's latest painting obsession was vegetables: defiant bright canvases that supposedly represented arrangements of elongated vegetables that unaccountably made some women giggle when they viewed them.

Before Helma went to bed, she stood by her window for a while, gazing out at the parking lot, alert for any unusual movement or sounds, her thoughts returning to the bruised rose in her refrigerator. Outside, the night was quiet, darkness softening whatever chose to lurk there.

She slept fitfully, dreaming of Aunt Em's wrinkled face atop a willowy girlish body, dancing in a Mexican bar Helma had seen in *The Searchers,* with a rose between her teeth.

The stealthy sounds of Aunt Em trying to quietly move about the kitchen woke her: the careful and slow opening and closing of cupboard doors, the sliding shuffle of slippered feet, all of it more alarming to a light sleeper than everyday movements.

It was only 5:45 but Helma rose, made her bed, and joined Aunt Em in the kitchen, in time to stop her from preparing a farmer's breakfast when all Helma longed for was a glass of orange juice and half a bowl of raisin bran.

"I'm phoning Wayne Gallant from the library this morning for an appointment to view more security videos from the airport. Would you mind looking at them again?"

"What for?"

"To see if we can identify the man who took your suitcase."

Aunt Em gasped, a slice of bread held over the toaster slot. "Somebody stole my suitcase?"

"No, but at the airport a man accidentally took it from the baggage claim. Would you look at the security tapes with us?"

"If it's early," Aunt Em told Helma as she dropped her bread in the toaster and opened the egg carton and took out two eggs, real eggs, not from the box of egg substitute Helma had bought specifically for Aunt Em's visit. "Bronus is showing me his college." She said it as if she were terribly sorry if plans had been made but she had a date.

"When did you plan this?" Helma asked.

"Last night. You were there. Oh, I think we talked in Lithuanian. And then in the afternoon Ethel and I are making deodorizer cozies. I have an idea for a flapper cozy."

"I thought you felt the deodorizer cozies were tacky," Helma said.

"Oh, I do, but I like Ethel and that's more important."

"Bronus is coming to the library to pick you up?" Helma asked.

She nodded, smiling. "I didn't want to forget it so I wrote it down."

"Aunt Em, you only met Bronus twenty-four hours ago. Before you go off alone with him, let's become better acquainted."

"He was here last night," Aunt Em said. Up went her chin; her eyes flashed.

Helma poured herself a glass of orange juice and suggested, "Call and invite him over tomorrow night." She tried to give Aunt Em a winning smile, recalling a book she'd found at the library last week for the distraught mother of a rebellious teenage girl.

Aunt Em huffed once and gave in. She dialed a number from a slip of paper in her pocket and spoke rapidly into the phone in Lithuanian, saying something apropos of nothing about a "fussy mother."

As they prepared to leave the apartment for the library, Aunt Em tucked a small square package neatly wrapped in aluminum foil into Helma's blue bag. "*Kugelis*," she said as if it were a peace offering, "for your lunch."

A silvery mist obscured the islands beyond the bay and hung across the tops of the trees, as if binding them together. It was a good sign; in an hour or two the mist would burn away and the day would turn sunny.

As soon as she removed her sweater and tucked her purse into her bottom desk drawer, Helma called Wayne Gallant.

"May I take a message?" the receptionist asked. "He's busy right now."

"Please inform him that it's a quasi-emergency," Helma instructed her.

A few moments later, the chief came on the phone, sounding distracted, as if he truly was busy. "What can I do for you?" he asked, abruptly so for Wayne Gallant. Helma wondered if someone was in his office with him.

"We'd like to view the airport videos again," she told him. "I suspect we saw the purse snatcher's accomplice, the man who may also be his murderer."

"And he would be on the tape?"

"I think so." She described the suitcase-mixup incident. "I didn't mention it before because it appeared to be an honest mistake. Now I'm wondering if it actually was an accident. How soon would it be convenient for us to come over?"

"Now's good. Ten, fifteen minutes?"

"I'll call Ruth," Helma said and told the chief good-bye, surprised when he only said, "All right," not even good-bye, before he hung up.

Ten minutes later, Harley Woodworth leaned across the book shelves. "That friend of yours is out front. Your aunt just let her in and Dutch is upset about that; it's *his* job to open the doors, you know." He gave Helma a frown of reproach. "Your aunt doesn't *look* sick."

"She's not." Helma rose and pushed in her chair. "She's elderly but she's quite healthy."

"Can you ask her what kind of vitamins she takes?" Harley asked as she left her cubicle. "Any special foods?"

"Feel free to ask her yourself," Helma told him. "I'm sure she'd love to discuss her health with you."

"Thanks, I will."

Helma entered the public area where the main overhead lights were still off and library pages busily reshelved books that had been returned after hours. She spotted Ms. Moon coming her way, a stack of manila envelopes pressed to her heart and a smile that dimpled both her round cheeks. Helma sidestepped through the biography section to avoid any possible Bert and Lamb conversation.

Ruth sat on a book truck in plain sight of the disgruntled patrons who still waited on the sidewalk for the library to open. Aunt Em stood beside her, absently turning the tip of her umbrella against the carpet, making a tiny crater in the nap. At the circulation counter, Dutch noisily sorted books, casting hot glances in their direction.

"Really?" Ruth was saying. "I always thought his pinks were unnaturally bright."

"Oh my, but his studio was a mess," Aunt Em said. "And cold. It was never warm enough for us girls. He should have painted us in fur coats instead."

"Excuse me," Helma said. "Wayne Gallant is ready for us to view the tape from the airport security camera. I can drive you, Aunt Em, if you're not up to walking."

"It's only across the street, isn't it? I can walk if we don't try to break any records."

They walked slowly, stopping every little while so Aunt Em could lean on her umbrella and catch her breath.

"Go on in," the receptionist told them when they entered the station, as if she'd been watching them cross the wide street and had time to puzzle out their mission. "Same room as last time."

Wayne Gallant was already running the tape, slouched in a chair in front of the monitor, staring at it. "This isn't good," he said, looking up as they entered.

"Don't tell me," Ruth guessed. "The camera was looking the other way during the suitcase-switching episode?"

"No, but we lost some of it when we examined the other scenes. Take a look."

They sat down while the chief adjusted the tape. "Ready?" he asked.

"Roll 'em," Aunt Em told him.

The tape began with a view of the turning carousel and the crowd of passengers waiting for their baggage.

"There's my suitcase," Aunt Em said. "The one with the flamingo on it."

A hand reached between two suited men talking beside the carousel and grabbed the suitcase. When the man was in plain sight two seconds later, only his back was visible, wearing a sports jacket, walking rapidly away from the carousel.

Then Helma's image came into view, rapidly following him, one arm outstretched. And then the image turned to static.

The chief clicked a button. "That's it," he said. "It's our fault; we accidentally erased the tape trying to zero in on the incident with the purse snatcher. I'll call the airport and ask them to send up the original. It'll be here this afternoon, or tomorrow morning at the latest." He rewound the images to the scene at the baggage carousel and replayed it. Aunt Em had lost interest, letting her head nod forward and her hands go lax on her lap.

Wayne Gallant played the scene twice more and said quietly so he wouldn't disturb Aunt Em, "At this point your description is more valuable to us than the surveillance tape.''

"There's the watch I noticed on his wrist when he gave the suitcase to Ruth," Helma told him, speaking softly and motioning to the black and white image.

"Can you describe it?" the chief asked.

"It was somewhat gaudy," Helma told him, "but probably expensive. I recall chunks of turquoise on either side of the watch face attached to the leather band."

"A Southwest flavor?"

"I'm not sure but I do associate turquoise with the Southwest."

"Turquoise," Aunt Em said, raising her head and blinking. "It was very popular years ago. Exotic."

"It's pretty blatant," Ruth said. "Probably one of a kind, hopefully anyway. But if *you* were trying to keep a low profile, would you wear something so flashy? Maybe the suitcase grabbing *was* a coincidence."

"It's the only real distinguishing characteristic I can recall," Helma said regretfully. "His beard and moustache disguised his face."

"They could have been fake," Ruth suggested.

Aunt Em daintily covered a yawn.

"Plus he wore glasses and a cap." Helma leaned back in her chair. "I admit I was more interested in retrieving Aunt Em's suitcase than in taking notes. If he hadn't given it up so willingly, I'd have been more observant."

"Did you see him return to the baggage carousel for the other suitcase?" Wayne Gallant asked.

"I didn't," Helma told him. "That's when we discovered Aunt Em was gone." She turned to Ruth. "Did you?"

Ruth shook her head.

"When can I have my hat pin back?" Aunt Em asked the chief.

"Once this case is wrapped up, I promise. All we can

do now is wait for the other tape to get here," the chief said. "I'll call you when it arrives."

Aunt Em shook her head. "I'm not coming next time. I didn't see this man so I'm useless to identify him. You call my niece instead. You can call her at home."

Wayne Gallant walked them down the hall and said good-bye, not singling out Helma and causing Ruth to glance sharply between the chief of police and her friend.

Fred, the elderly man Aunt Em had met the day before, was sitting in the newspaper section when they returned to the library, his thin hair freshly marked with comb tracks. He waved to Aunt Em and she wagged her fingers back at him.

"Later, dear," she told Helma, and headed toward the newspapers.

On her desk in the work room, Helma discovered a folder tucked beneath her telephone. She knew she hadn't left it in such an odd place; all her folders were alphabetically filed in her file cabinet, her desk top clean. On the edge that peeked from beneath the phone she could read the words "Top Secret," handwritten in red block print.

She warily lifted the telephone and withdrew the folder, rising from her chair to glance around the workroom. No one looked up in guilty corroboration, no one paid any attention to her at all. Top secret?

Her curiosity was too strong. She set the folder flat in the center of her desk, took a breath, and opened it.

First was a note printed on plain paper using the same word processing program that was available on all the library computers. It read:

"This is the key, should you decide to give in yet *not* give in," and it was signed, "A friend."

The next ten pages provided a breakdown to the answers on the Bert and Lamb personality test and how the respondent's scores placed him or her in the Bert and Lamb "Personality Color Wheel,'' from Hot Red through Pallid Beige.

Helma peered around the workroom again. This *was* top secret information. The pages had been photocopied from the original; someone had stolen this information from Ms. Moon's office. Helma should toss it into her trash immediately; it was illicitly gained, a punishable white collar crime. She held it over her trash basket but just then she spotted George Melville approaching her desk so instead she slipped the folder out of sight into her blue bag.

"Have you noticed what's going on next to you?" George asked in a low voice. He carried a cup of coffee in one hand and chocolate chip cookies piled four high on his palm. So much for his low cholesterol diet. He pointed his cookies toward Harley Woodworth's cubicle, his expression either humorous or appalled, Helma wasn't certain.

She rose from her chair just high enough to see Harley at his desk, poring over a booklet and a multiple numbered answer sheet she recognized as the Bert and Lamb personality test. He sat hunched in concentration, lips and finger moving at the same time, pencil poised.

"Our first comrade falls. The Moonbeam had him in her office for twenty minutes. *Closed door*," George added meaningfully, and continued toward his cataloging corner.

### ❧ chapter fifteen ❧

# PARENTAL ADVICE

"**H**elma, I must speak to you immediately," Helma's mother said into the telephone. "Now."

"Can you stop by after work?" Helma asked. "I just finished my lunch hour." She'd taken her cold *kugelis* to Saul's deli and asked the waitress to heat it on their grill, not in the microwave. It had been returned to her slightly smaller, delivered by the cook himself, humbly requesting the recipe. Helma had promised to ask Aunt Em if she'd share.

"I just finished my lunch hour, too," Lillian said briskly. "That's what we have to talk about."

"Your lunch?" Helma asked.

"Don't be funny. I insist you meet me on the bench by the crab apple tree on the library lawn. I'll be there in five minutes."

"But, Mother," Helma began.

"No buts about it," Lillian said and hung up the phone.

Helma hadn't heard her mother so forceful with her since she was a child and she hung up, puzzled.

"Here's that new book you wanted on Prohibition," George Melville said, setting a book with the unmistakable likeness of Al Capone gracing its cover on Helma's desk.

170

"Hot times. I kind of wished I'd lived back then."

"It was a lawless period in our history," Helma reminded him.

"Must have been great. This isn't cataloged yet so give it back to me when you're finished."

"Thank you, George," Helma told him, picking up the unread book, holding it close to her face to smell the odor of new print before flipping to the volume's final pages and judging its worthiness by the length and breadth of its index. There it was: "Runners, rum." She herself would have simply indexed the term as "Rum runners." This alone was sufficient to make the book suspect but she found it rich with black and white photographs from 1920 to 1933, the years of Prohibition, replete with criminals, dance hall scenes, and temperance marches.

"It seems like your aunt would be a better source for stories about Prohibition," George said. "She lived through it, didn't she?"

"She's reticent about some of the details," Helma told him. "I thought she'd enjoy reading about it."

"Foggy on names and dates, you mean?" George asked.

"That's right."

George stroked his beard and nodded toward Ms. Moon's office. "Did the Moonbeam tell you she'd take the Bert and Lamb test for anyone who refuses to do it him or herself?"

"She did. Have you taken it?"

George shook his head. "I might let her do it for me. I'd like to see if her idea of my perversions jibe with my own."

Helma glanced out the window of the workroom and spotted her mother crossing the library lawn and approaching the wooden bench near the crab apple tree, her step firm and her face resolute. She wore a new dress, a size smaller and years younger than her usual style.

George followed her glance. "They say if you want to know what a woman will look like in twenty years, look at her mother." He grinned at Helma. "I'd say you have a good future."

"Excuse me," Helma said. "I have to meet her for a few minutes in the present."

"I'll cover for you," George called after her.

Lillian sat on the bench, her back straight, both hands on top of her purse, which sat squarely on her lap. She watched Helma approach, her mouth a tight line, no hint of a smile. Helma braced herself for a continuing saga of her quarrel with Aunt Em.

"Sit down," Lillian said, patting the seat beside her. Helma brushed off the seat with a tissue and sat.

"Now you know how I hate to interfere in your life," Helma's mother began. "What you do is your own business, I don't believe in foisting my opinions on my children like some women do, but . . ." She took a deep breath. "I just met Rebecca Martin at Sam and Ella's for lunch. You remember her; she's the one with only one kidney."

"I don't remember her, Mother," Helma said. "Why do you need to speak to me?"

"Well, we weren't the only ones in the restaurant."

"Probably not," Helma agreed. Sam and Ella's was a popular lunchtime dining spot.

"What I mean is, your chief was there, with his ex-wife."

"That's his business, Mother," Helma said, "not mine." She made an impatient move, preparing to rise. "Is that the urgent news you had to share with me?"

"I want to tell you about Danute."

"Mother . . ." Helma made a gesture toward the library.

"Wilhelmina Cecilia," Lillian said, exaggerating each

syllable the way she used to when Helma was six. "Please sit still when I'm talking to you."

"All right, Mother," Helma agreed, leaning back against the bench, momentarily experiencing that old feeling of *being* six. "Tell me about Danute."

"That's better," Lillian said, fidgeting on the bench like a reluctant student being forced to recite. She cleared her throat and moved her purse from her lap to the bench beside her. A seagull landed on the library lawn and Lillian waited until it folded its wings before she began speaking.

"Danute was one of those women, like your friend Ruth, only more refined. And shorter. And more beautiful." She tipped her head, remembering. "Blonde. Maybe not so loud."

"Mother," Helma pointed out. "That doesn't sound like Ruth at all."

"But with that same spark. Bold." She took a deep breath. "Your father was crazy blind over her; he hardly noticed me. I was younger and not . . . beautiful—or exciting. When Danute ran off with that marble layer, your father and I became friends." She shook her head. "He mourned for her. A year went by, then two." Lillian went silent, her eyes closing for long moments.

"And then Danute came back," Helma supplied.

Lillian nodded. "To be specific, she came back for *him*. The marble layer turned out to be a drunk and a womanizer and she was oh so sorry; couldn't he please forgive her? Your father was confused. She'd broken his heart and he was a proud man, like everybody in that family. Your Aunt Em encouraged him to take Danute back, to give her another chance."

"Why would she," Helma asked, "if Danute had hurt him so much? He was her favorite brother."

"Because that's what your Uncle Juozas did for her. Emily ran off to Chicago and Juozas waited for almost three years. He had a one-track devotion and he took her back; he helped her hide.''

"Hide from whom?'' Helma asked. "You said she killed someone in Chicago.''

"I said that in anger,'' Lillian said, not looking at Helma but at a young mother pushing a stroller past. "I don't know the story, only that he was supposedly her lover and he died and it was partly Em's fault.''

"And Uncle Juozas knew the details?''

Lillian nodded. "And didn't care, from what little your father said. Because she ended up with a happily-ever-after marriage herself. I suppose Emily identified with Danute and believed your father should give her another chance. She pushed him toward Danute.''

"But he didn't take her back,'' Helma pointed out. "He chose to stay with you instead.''

"We'd been close, good friends, pals,'' Lillian continued, "but we'd never discussed love. Neither of us knew how the other *really* felt.'' Lillian's voice slowed, grew softer, and Helma leaned forward to hear.

"He began spending more time with Danute and less with me and it was obvious she was going to win him back. Everybody said so, trying to prepare me.''

"What happened?''

Lillian turned and looked intently into Helma's eyes. "If I would have minded my own business I *know* he would have returned to Danute. But I decided to tell him how I truly felt. If he turned his back I'd be humiliated but at least I'd have been honest. Otherwise I'd always regret not having done *something*. So I took the chance.'' She laughed, startling the seagull, which rose from the lawn and flapped away with a single cry. "It turned out he hadn't believed I loved him; he thought I only wanted to be good friends.''

"And so you had your own happily-ever-after marriage."

"Hardly. But it was fun." She smiled and patted
Helma's hand. "Don't be a coward, Helma. Tell him."

Helma didn't ask who her mother meant by "him."

"That's all the wisdom I have, dear," Lillian said, picking up her purse and rising from the bench. "You can go
back to work now." And she began walking up the sidewalk toward the parked cars.

"Mother," Helma called after her.

Lillian didn't turn around but she said over her shoulder,
"If you're going to tell me thank you, don't until you talk
to him and see how it turns out." She waved and hurried
toward her car.

"I found a rose on my doormat last night," Helma told
the chief ten minutes later from the telephone on her desk.
"I forgot to tell you about it this morning."

"No note?" he asked. "Just a rose?"

"Just a rose." And when he was silent she added, "Long
stem, slightly crushed as if it had been stepped on."

"What did you do with it?"

"It's in the refrigerator. Do you want to examine it?"

"I'll send someone by to pick it up." And when Helma
was silent he asked, "Will that work?"

"If they come by after five."

"All right. That's what we'll do then."

The deodorizer cozies covered Mrs. Whitney's coffee table: cone pilgrims, clowns, Santa Clauses, ballerinas and
Bo-Peeps, nuns and friars, kangaroos, rabbits, and two
skunks.

"You didn't make all of these today, did you?" Helma
asked.

"Oh no," Mrs. Whitney told her. "I was just showing

Emily my collection. Would you like to choose one for your bathroom, dear?''

Helma tried to imagine one of the costumed deodorizers in her bathroom. ''I'll wait to see if you have any left after your sale,'' Helma told her. ''I wouldn't want to deplete your inventory.''

''That's thoughtful of you,'' Mrs. Whitney said.

''Diplomatic, you mean,'' Aunt Em murmured.

''I need to return to my apartment,'' Helma told them. ''Someone is stopping by.''

''Your policeman?'' Aunt Em asked eagerly. She and Mrs. Whitney exchanged glances.

''Not today,'' Helma told them.

''I may as well go with you,'' Aunt Em told her. ''It's been fun, Ethel.''

''I'll see you tomorrow,'' Mrs. Whitney told her with a wave.

Helma's mat was clear of any anonymous gifts but she could hear her telephone ringing as she unlocked the door. Helma never rushed to answer the telephone but Aunt Em hurried inside as soon as the door was unlocked and picked up the receiver.

''Hello?'' she said, and then frowned and hung up. ''Dial tone,'' she said. ''You should buy an answering machine.''

''That's what I've been told,'' Helma told Aunt Em as she removed her sweater. ''If it's important, people always call back.''

''I have one,'' Aunt Em said. ''I could show you how they work.''

Before she could take the boneless skinless chicken breasts she intended to broil for dinner from the refrigerator, Helma's doorbell chimed. So instead of chicken, she removed the plastic-encased rose from her refrigerator and carried it to the door.

Her mind was so set on seeing a policeman, it took her

a second to recognize the smiling man who stood on the landing.

"It's Douglas," he supplied. "Bronus's friend from last night? Is your Aunt Em here?"

"Of course. I'm sorry. Hello, Douglas. I was expecting . . ."

He grinned, deepening the cleft in his chin and pointed to the rose in her hand. "You were expecting someone more interesting."

From behind Helma, Aunt Em said, "Douglas! You found it," saving Helma from having to answer.

Then Helma noticed Douglas carried Aunt Em's red umbrella. "Here you are, ma'am. You left it in Bronus's car."

"I thought it was gone forever. Would you like to come in? Helma has some nice wine in her refrigerator."

"No thanks. I've got an evening class. I'll see you later." And he gave a jaunty wave and trotted toward the stairs.

After Helma closed the door, Aunt Em said, "Now don't look at me like that. They're nice boys."

"I thought you spent the morning in the children's room at the library," Helma said.

"That's where *you* wanted me to spend it."

"You should have told me."

Aunt Em snapped and unsnapped the strap of her umbrella. "I had a nice morning and here I am, safe and sound."

"What did you do?" Helma asked.

"Looked at the college. I saw Bronus's house. We talked mostly."

"What about?"

Aunt Em shrugged. "This and that," and she closed her mouth tight.

Helma's doorbell rang again and this time it was Officer Sidney Lehman. "I was instructed to pick up one long-stem red rose,'' he told Helma with as much seriousness as if he'd come to view the body.

"Can you take fingerprints from a rose stem?" Helma asked him as he carefully handled the rose in its plastic bag.

"You'd be surprised sometimes," he told her.

"I'd like to be this time," Helma said.

After dinner, Helma remembered the Prohibition book. "I brought you something to read," she told Aunt Em. "It's a new book."

When she removed the book from her blue bag, the "top secret" folder holding the key to the Bert and Lamb test came with it and Helma set it on the table. Aunt Em was drawn like a magnet to the book.

She touched the cover photograph of Al Capone. "He'd only allow pictures of the right side of his face," she said. She touched her left cheek. "Because of the scars."

"Did you ever meet him?" Helma asked.

"No, I only heard about him."

"Please, take it and read it. Would you like to go to the park tonight? There will be free music."

"Mmm? No thank you. I'd rather read this. There are pictures." She turned a page. "Oh. I had a dress like this, almost exactly. It was the color of an October maple leaf."

She settled into a corner of the sofa beneath the reading lamp, avidly turning the book's pages and murmuring over the photographs.

Helma sat at her table, the key to the Bert and Lamb test in front of her. It wouldn't hurt just to read the descriptions of the colors the developers had assigned to each personality. Within five minutes it was obvious that "Cool Blue" and "Serene Green" were the colors of choice: "well-rounded, centered, a credit to any organization," read the plaudits, the only difference being one was more "inner directed" than the other.

Right here in Helma's hands were the answers that would assure that her personality test scores equaled either of the most desirable colors. She wondered who had left the top secret folder on her desk. George Melville was the obvious choice but she doubted he would have been so secretive, more likely he would have blatantly posted the key on the staff bulletin board.

She set the Bert and Lamb papers aside and glanced over at Aunt Em. The Prohibition book lay open on her lap and Aunt Em's head was bowed over it, resting to one side. Helma heard a tiny snore and rose to wake Aunt Em; she'd have a crick in her neck from sleeping like that.

She approached Aunt Em carefully, trying not to startle her, and began to gently slip the book from her lap when she realized the page was damp. Aunt Em's face shone in the reading lamp's beam of light and moisture glistened in the wrinkles of her cheeks.

She inspected the open book more closely. One page was text and the other a large black and white photograph.

In the photograph, six men lay dead, one slumped against a chair, the others sprawled on the floor next to a bullet-riddled brick wall. Blood pooled out from the bodies, death froze each face. Beneath the photograph, the caption read, "Six of the seven members of Bugs Moran's gang gunned down in the St. Valentine's Day Massacre, February 14, 1929."

The page was dampened by Aunt Em's tears.

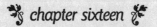

# chapter sixteen

# ANOTHER LATE NIGHT

**"T**ell me about the men in this picture, Aunt Em," Helma asked softly. She'd sat down on the sofa beside Aunt Em and begun speaking in a voice that at first was only a whisper, gradually raising the level until Aunt Em woke up without realizing she'd been asleep.

Aunt Em clasped her hands together on her lap, holding them tight as if to restrain herself from touching the page. "They're all dead," she said in a flat voice. "I didn't know about it for hours afterward, not until the middle of the afternoon. Acting like it was a normal day. You'd think you'd *feel* it somehow, but you don't. Then Lukas came banging on the door and told me I had to get out, that I wasn't safe." She closed her eyes and Helma waited, not moving.

"Lukas was his best friend. I knew they did some work for Bugs but I didn't know he could get killed for it." She bit her lip. "Well, maybe I did. They were just boys it seems like now, with their promises to each other and all their silly boyish names. Boys playing with money—and lives, it turned out. It was my fault he went to the garage." She tapped the photograph in the book without looking at it.

"How could it be your fault?" Helma asked.

"He wasn't going to go; he said the others could handle it, he wanted to stay with me. But Lukas said there was big money tied up in the deal and everything had been going so well so I told him to go." Aunt Em shook her head. "For the money. I was greedy for the money."

"That doesn't make it your fault," Helma told her. "If . . ."

But Aunt Em waved a hand, dismissing Helma's words. "That's not all," she said. She closed her eyes tight and scrunched her face, lowering her head once the way people did sometimes when they'd committed an act they couldn't believe.

"There was a phone call before he left. An anonymous call warning him not to go to the garage." She rocked her upper body. "I didn't tell him." She raised her head and looked at Helma, her eyes as young and grieving as if she were still eighteen. "And so he died."

Helma took Aunt Em's hand in her own and said, "I'm sorry."

They sat that way for a long time until Aunt Em touched the amber necklace at her throat. "He gave this to me that morning, for Valentine's Day. That's why I wear it."

"Your mother didn't give it to you?" Helma asked. That had been the story she'd heard all her life. Passed down through the women in the family.

"Oh yes. But I pawned it, remember when I told you? I had no money for a while, before . . . I thought I'd never see it again. And then he bought it back for me. Someday I'll give it to you, when I'm dead. And now it will mean more to you, because you know its secret."

"Who was he?" Helma asked. "Which one?"

Aunt Em shook her head and closed the book. "I've never said his name since that day, never once." She touched her heart as if it were burned there. "I didn't want to put anyone else in danger. Not my family. And not Juozas.''

"Uncle Juozas knew?"

Aunt Em shook her head again. "Not all of it. He only knew there could be trouble. He saw more clearly, what do you call it, the bigger picture. Now, with all your computers it's hard for you to believe, but then, a person could appear and disappear; it wasn't so easy to trace your past—or your future.''

"So you disappeared from Chicago?"

"Like a puff of smoke," Aunt Em said with a slight smile.

"Then you didn't use your real name in Chicago?"

"At least I was smart enough not to do that. But I'd changed my name so I could disappear from *Michigan* so your grandfather couldn't bring me back. I never thought I'd need to disappear back *into* Michigan. No one knew my other name but Juozas.'' She sighed. "In a way, I've tried to pay for what I did. My life since then has been the hardest penance of all: I became good.'' She smiled. "A life sentence of penance,'' she said, savoring the words.

"What happened to Lukas? Why wasn't he killed?"

"His car broke down. He arrived at the garage too late. After that day, I never saw him again.''

"Do you think he tried to find you?"

"He said he would but everyone, even Lukas, thought I was from Massachusetts. I'd visited the Lithuanian cousins in Worcester once so I knew enough about it to fool them. It was better that way. I didn't take anything from Chicago back to Michigan with me except Lukas's old suitcase and the things I'd taken from home when I ran away, that's all.''

"And everyone in Michigan was happy to see you, like the prodigal daughter?"

"No," Aunt Em said dreamily, "like Natalie Wood in

*The Searchers*, when John Wayne brings her home from the Indians. At last she's home and her relatives are thrilled but you know that deep in her heart she'll never truly be happy and that they'll never truly accept her.''

Helma sat beside Aunt Em for a long while, their shoulders touching. Then she asked, "May I look at your suitcase? Maybe what's so valuable is the suitcase itself.''

"Go ahead," Aunt Em told her. "I'm going to get ready for bed.''

In Aunt Em's bedroom, the empty suitcase sat on the floor of the closet, all the mementos now in drawers and on top of the bureau. Helma examined the old leather case from the inside out, running her hands over the lining, even ripping away a corner of it to peek beneath the faded green silk. She inspected the clasps and hinges and the flamingo decal with its peeling feet.

After going over it twice more, Helma sat back and stared at it, disappointed. It was clearly nothing more than a battered old suitcase.

Aunt Em entered the bedroom carrying the Prohibition book in both hands. "I'm going to read this until I feel like sleeping," she said. "Not all my memories are bad, just the way it ended.''

Helma returned the suitcase to the closet, pausing to straighten Aunt Em's new clothes on their hangers. "I'll be up for a while if you feel like talking.''

"*Myliu tave*," Aunt Em said. I love you.

"*Mylieu tave*," Helma told her.

Helma knew she'd be awake for a long time this night. In the 1920's, Aunt Em was involved with a member of the Bugs Moran gang? And Lukas, who she'd called her "best friend," and also her dead lover's best friend was a gangster, too. No wonder Helma hadn't found Lukas's name listed in social security files or on the Internet; he probably hadn't used his given name any more than Aunt Em had.

She glanced at the clock; the library was already closed. Her personal reference collection was too meager to provide more than a few general lines on the St. Valentine's Day Massacre. A gangland murder; Al Capone's henchmen probably responsible. No one ever brought to trial.

Helma's phone rang and she jumped for it, afraid it would disturb Aunt Em. "Hello?"

The line went dead. Startled, Helma slammed down the receiver, her mind still filled with gangsters and massacres. Then, remembering the two other phone calls she'd received when the caller had hung up, she hesitantly lifted the receiver, listening to the dial tone. She pushed down the receiver buttons, counted to five, and then lifted her finger to hear the dial tone again before she dialed *69.

The mechanical operator came on and gave her the telephone number of her last caller, which she jotted down and after that, Helma pressed the number one, which dialed the number. It rang four times.

"Yeah?" a man's voice said. Brisk.

"I believe you just dialed my telephone number," Helma told him. "May I ask why?"

"You're wrong on that one, lady," the man said. "This is a pay phone. It rang; I picked it up and that's the whole ball of wax."

"Did you see the last person who used the phone?"

"What do you think I am, a detective? I was walking by and like I said, it rang and here I am."

"Where are you?" Helma asked, grabbing her pencil.

"I don't know," he said peevishly. "Downtown, a block from Jerry's Bar." He paused, then said in a warmer voice, "Hey, you doing anything tonight? Want to come down and have a drink? I got stood up."

"Thank you, but I don't believe so. Good luck."

"Yeah, same to you," he said and hung up.

The only reason Helma could think of for anyone to call from a pay phone and then hang up—wasting a quarter—was if the caller was afraid of being traced. Helma's number was unlisted but she knew it was available to any astute user of the Internet.

Unless it was a wrong number, this call was a call that was intended for her. Why? Checking to see if she was home? Or if Aunt Em was alone? She jotted down the probable address beneath the pay phone's number and the time, intending to give it to Chief Gallant.

The Bert and Lamb personality test key lay in front of her and she absently leafed through it, trying to soothe her troubled thoughts. Often, if she redirected her attention her mind continued to puzzle out a problem until it was solved.

Red Hot, Spicy Orange, Jolly Gold. The types sounded more like foodstuffs than personalities.

She glanced over at her coffee table where the Bert and Lamb tests her guests had taken just the night before still sat in a neat pile.

There were five tests on the table, no names on them, only two columns of letters: the answers. She didn't know which paper belonged to which person except she recognized Aunt Em's penmanship from years of correspondence and she could almost guess which was Ruth's.

So she scored Aunt Em's test first and wasn't surprised to find Aunt Em rated high in the Spicy Orange category. She continued on, finding that the paper she suspected was Ruth's rated a Red Hot. Beyond those, there was an Ice White, a Serene Green, and lastly a Bad Black.

Helma turned to the booklet and read about Bad Black. "Shame on you," the description chastised. "You haven't answered this test very honestly. Please try again later."

Which guest hadn't answered honestly: Douglas, Bronus, or Celine? Did Bad Black dislike tests as much as Helma did and so purposely fudged his or her test? Or was Bad Black afraid the test might reveal his or her true personality?

Helma stayed up, thinking, until Aunt Em's light turned off, which wasn't until after midnight, and when she woke up in the morning her eyes had a scratchy, swollen feel.

"What time are you going to Ethel's?" she asked Aunt Em.

"At nine." Aunt Em's eyes narrowed. "Don't you stay home from work just to be sure I get from here to there safely. I can sit alone for forty-five minutes. I'll drink coffee and pet the cat."

Boy Cat Zukas sat in his basket but Helma knew that he'd been sitting under Aunt Em's chair only moments before she entered the kitchen—the dish of egg bits was still there to prove it—and he'd probably have the run of the house after she left.

"You're treating me like a child," Aunt Em said in a bristly voice.

"I'm sorry," Helma told her, glancing at the telephone. "I worry."

Aunt Em softened, patting Helma's hand. "And I'm grateful, Wilhelmina, truly."

The chief phoned Helma at the library at nine o'clock, before she had time to research the St. Valentine's Day Massacre. "I've got the rest of the film from the airport. Can you drop by this morning and take a look at it?"

"Certainly. I'll call Ruth."

"Actually, she's already here. She wanted to explain how she'd found the rose on your doormat."

"I'm sure that was interesting," Helma said, wondering how Ruth could embellish glancing down and seeing a rose lying on the doormat.

\* \* \*

Ruth sat in the room with the video screen, drinking a Diet Coke and chatting with Officer 087.

"Ma'am," he said, rising when he saw Helma, his smile freezing.

"C'mon kids," Ruth said lazily. "Make up."

"This is not an incident to discuss in idle conversation," Helma said. "It's a matter for the courts."

"You said 'courts,' " Ruth said. "Plural, as if you're going to fight this traffic ticket beyond our fair city's judicial system."

"I may," Helma said.

"Excuse me," 087 said. He touched an invisible cap and left the room.

"You scared the little guy," Ruth told Helma. "He's not so bad if you don't challenge his integrity."

"His integrity isn't in question, just his judgment."

"So split hairs."

"Wayne Gallant said you dropped in to explain how you found the rose," Helma said as she sat in the chair next to Ruth.

"I'm just trying to oil the gears is all, keep your image in his forebrain."

"I'm perfectly . . ."

"Cheese it," Ruth interrupted. "Here come the cops."

Wayne Gallant entered the room, carrying a file folder, which he raised, calling their attention to it. "Sorry I kept you waiting. I was picking up the analysis of the man who took the suitcase. They're doing some computer enhancements in the lab."

"Is he a fake?" Ruth asked.

"First, let's watch the complete tape." He flicked a button and the film began where the first one had: with the hand reaching for Aunt Em's suitcase. Then it continued on, showing the man walking away, followed immediately by Helma, then Ruth. He turned, appearing startled, then apologetic, immediately handing over the suitcase to Ruth.

"He's just a hairy guy," Ruth commented, half singing it.

"Is the beard and moustache a disguise?" Helma asked.

"We believe so. Also, his jacket shoulders may be padded, making him appear larger than he actually is."

"Could it be a woman?" Ruth asked.

"It would have to be a very clever one."

"I believe that's the kind of person we're dealing with," Helma said. "A clever murderer."

On the screen, the man walked casually out of camera range.

"So he didn't meet up with that elderly couple he pointed to," Ruth said.

"He didn't return to the carousel for the correct suitcase," Helma pointed out, "so there was probably no connection to that couple."

The chief agreed. He played the video again. "Does he look familiar to either of you?"

"If I picture a beardless, skinnier guy, maybe even hairless, without glasses, he could be a lot of different men," Ruth commented, and Helma agreed.

"Jack in the lab analyzed his image," Wayne Gallant said. "The man we're looking at is probably six feet to six foot, two, maybe smaller built than he appears, under thirty-five. As I said, the beard and moustache are likely fakes. We don't have any good closeups of his face but Jack's coming up with a couple of beardless images."

"What about hair color?" Helma gazed at the black and white image. "I recall dark brown."

"Too easily altered to say for certain. Have you gleaned any other information from your aunt?"

"Only that she was in Chicago during the Prohibition days and may have known a few crime figures."

"Did she say who?" Ruth asked.

"No, she didn't," Helma said. It was the truth; Aunt Em *hadn't* named names. "She was only a teenager at the time."

"Do you believe her past is connected to the robbery attempt and the murder?" the chief asked.

"It's the only oddity in Aunt Em's life, a secret she's kept for almost seventy years," Helma said. "Maybe we've been wrong looking for a valuable item she *has*; what's of interest to these felons may be something she *knows*."

"Like where they stashed the loot," Ruth suggested.

"As you said, that was seventy years ago," Wayne Gallant said. "Most everyone connected is probably dead."

"But the information could have been passed on," Helma said. "Men have lost their lives searching for treasures of which they've only heard rumors."

"Binder being a case in point," Ruth said.

"Aunt Em must inadvertently know or possess a clue to whatever these men desperately want," Helma said.

The chief rubbed his chin, then made several rapid notes in his notebook. "Can you bring your aunt in today for a long chat and a look at an enhanced image of the suitcase snatcher? Maybe in an hour? I have a quick piece of business to attend to out of town."

"Yes," Helma agreed. "She's at Mrs. Whitney's. I'd also like to discover who's leaving gifts at my door. Or who called and hung up when I answered."

"When did that happen?" Wayne Gallant asked.

"It's happened three times in the past two days but last night I had the call traced," Helma said. She handed him the time and number. "Here are the particulars. I used star-six-nine."

"Thanks," he said, taking the slip of paper.

"You guys should try using star-six-nine to trace a call," Ruth told the chief. "It would sure be cheaper than all that equipment you see on TV."

"We did find partial fingerprints on the rose stem, by the way," Wayne Gallant said. "We're still trying to match them. But don't get your hopes up; they probably belong to the florist."

"All we have to do is uncover that guy," Ruth said, pointing to the frozen frame of the suitcase snatcher, "and bingo, case solved."

"Okay," the chief said, rising and slapping his folder against his palm. "I'll see you and your aunt in about an hour, then."

There were times when holding a private conversation in the midst of a crowd was far more private than in a restaurant booth or over the telephone, so as Wayne Gallant walked them through the lobby, where a line of people stood in front of the receptionist's desk, a man and a woman argued about a rent check and two toddlers stared at each other and cried, Helma turned to Ruth and said, "Go ahead. I have business to discuss."

"Gotcha," Ruth said cheerfully, winking.

So Helma and Wayne Gallant stood facing each other as the darker side of Bellehaven was preoccupied around them.

"Business?" the chief asked.

"Personal business," Helma told him. She cleared her throat and stood so straight she felt her ankle bones pushing one against the other. "About your job offer in Arizona."

He bent lower, closer. "You've been thinking about it?"

"Yes."

The quarreling man and woman raised their voices. "I have never bounced a check in my entire life," the woman shouted. "Not once. I am not that kind of woman."

"Quiet down," a man's voice shouted back.

"And?" the chief asked.

"My opinion is that you should consider the offer very

carefully,'' Helma said. "I mean, whether the position is to your benefit or not.''

"What do you think?''

"I'm not aware of any advantage Arizona has over Washington state but I could do a search for you at the library.''

"No, I mean what do *you* think?''

Helma tried to swallow but her mouth was too dry. "I think, that is, I believe, that you should reconsider. Your departure would be a great and irreplaceable loss—to Bellehaven . . .'' The toddlers screeched and Helma added, "and to myself.''

"If I were to take this position in Arizona,'' he said, rocking on his heels, "I was hoping you might accompany me.''

"As?'' Helma asked, the word issuing forth in a croak.

"As . . .'' Wayne Gallant's face flamed red. "As my . . .'' He sidestepped as one of the toddlers raced past him, took a breath, and said, "As my librarian.''

## 🌱 chapter seventeen 🌱

# BELATED NEWS

"**Y**our aunt was supposed to be here at nine o'clock to work on the Halloween cozies," Mrs. Whitney told Helma over the telephone, "but she didn't show up and there's no answer at your apartment door or on the telephone. Do you think something's happened?"

"I'll be right there, Mrs. Whitney," Helma told her. "It won't take more than ten minutes."

Helma grabbed her purse from the bottom drawer of her desk and left the library without informing anyone. If the stoplights were in her favor on Main Street it took her seven and a half minutes to drive from the library to the Bayside Arms. If they were against her, ten minutes. Today they were not in her favor.

Mrs. Whitney stood on the landing outside her apartment, her hands to her mouth, watching Helma hurry toward the building. Helma held her keys in her hand as she rushed up the outside staircase, but when she tried to insert the proper one in the lock, she was surprised to discover her hands were trembling.

"Let me, dear," Mrs. Whitney said, placing one of her hands over Helma's and gently taking the keys from her.

When the door was unlocked, Mrs. Whitney blocked

Helma's entrance. "You wait out here." She smiled sadly at Helma. "I've done this before."

"No," Helma told her. "I have to do it," and she stepped inside, her breathing sounding too loud in her silent apartment.

There was no one in the kitchen or living room. "Aunt Em?" Helma called.

"Emily?" Mrs. Whitney asked, standing behind Helma.

They both waited, straining to hear a reply. Aunt Em had left the shades up and every piece of furniture in Helma's apartment seemed overly bright, sharply ominous. There were no signs of disorder or violence.

She peered down the hallway toward her bedroom. "Aunt Em?" Helma called again, this time in a loud whisper.

"Wait, Helma," Mrs. Whitney said. She stood beside the kitchen counter holding a piece of yellow notepaper, smiling. "She's all right. She left you a note."

Helma took the note, releasing her breath in a rush. It was Aunt Em's handwriting. Helma recognized the tightly spaced letters with the old-fashioned loops and swirls.

Helma read the note, feeling a mixture of relief and irritation. "I've gone out with Bronus," it read. "Back by suppertime."

"A man will make a woman forget her promise to her girlfriends every time," Mrs. Whitney said, shaking her head.

"She didn't mention Bronus to me this morning," Helma said, "only that she was spending the morning with you."

"Maybe she was afraid you'd discourage her."

"But she's behaving as if I were trying to run her life," Helma said.

Mrs. Whitney raised her eyebrows. "Well, dear, you are very . . . concerned for her."

"She's been ill," Helma said.

"Not really," Mrs. Whitney contradicted. "And she *is* used to running her own life." Mrs. Whitney patted Helma's shoulder. "She'll be fine. You tell her to give me a call when she gets home."

Helma closed her door and slowly walked through her apartment, checking each room, still not completely convinced Aunt Em's note was legitimate, searching for signs of disruption. What if the note had been coerced?

A cup sat in the sink, one chair was askew at the dining table, and one of Aunt Em's movie magazines lay on the sofa, open to an article on Harrison Ford.

In Aunt Em's room, her bed was unmade. Helma absently began to make it as she gazed around the room, noting only Aunt Em's usual carelessness: the drawer of the bedside table ajar, a candy wrapper that missed the trash basket, a belt over a chair.

As she fluffed the pillow, her hand bumped a hard and cool object. She jerked back in surprise, then lifted the pillow off the bed. Coiled beneath it lay Aunt Em's amber necklace. This was the first time Helma had known Aunt Em not to wear the necklace. Always, when she was awake, the amber beads circled her neck.

Helma picked up the light beads and let them slip across her fingers. Why had Aunt Em left them behind, beneath her pillow as if she'd hidden them? They weren't valuable, Aunt Em had claimed. Helma wondered how she knew that; whether she'd ever had them appraised.

She reached over to close the drawer of the bedside table and caught sight of the scissored photo Aunt Em had shown her of Lukas. It rested on top of the drawer's jumbled contents.

She pulled it out, touching her finger to the cut edge where the other man had been excised. Had he been the mysterious lover, shot to death on Valentine's Day almost seventy years ago?

Helma touched the disembodied arm, then traced her finger across Aunt Em's shoulder to Lukas's arm so casually draped across her shoulders.

Helma's finger stopped. She turned on the lamp and bent closer over the photo.

The snapshot was grainy and taken from a distance, but a large watch circled Lukas's wrist. Stones appeared to decorate the band. If only the photo were in color so she could see if the stones were turquoise. Yet even in monochrome, the watch in this photo looked remarkably like the watch on the black and white surveillance tape.

She studied Lukas's face, imagining him seventy years older. Had she seen him in the library? On the street? But the man at the airport had been under thirty-five, the chief had said.

Helma slipped the photo into her purse to give to Wayne Gallant so it could be enhanced, the same as the surveillance tape.

Helma carried the necklace to her own bedroom and found a velvet-covered box that held a faux pearl necklace her nephews had sent her for Christmas. She removed the pearls and replaced them with the amber necklace. Then she carried it to her car and drove downtown to the owner of the only jewelry store whose name she recognized as being the holder of a library card.

She circled the block twice before she found a parking place near the small shop that sat a block off the main street.

The gray-haired man sitting behind the counter in Stephen Boyce's Fine Jewelry was reading a library book titled *Diamonds in the Rough*. He glanced up at Helma and smiled, showing a gap between his teeth. "Can I help you?" he asked. Then he frowned, snapped his fingers and said, "Library, right?"

"Correct," Helma told him.

He touched his library book. "Not overdue."

"That's not why I'm here," Helma assured him. "Are you Mr. Boyce?"

"The one and only."

"I'd like you to examine this necklace and appraise its value." She set the velvet-covered box on the glass-topped counter.

He licked his lips before opening the box, as if anticipating something delicious, then nodded, touching the beads with his fingertip. "Amber," he said.

"Do you do much work with amber?" Helma asked.

"Not much, but it's interesting stuff, millions of years old. Mysterious, catches the imagination. Movies, cloning dinosaurs, ancient mosquitoes. Sap running down a tree. Zap! Unobservant and slow-moving bug trapped for eternity." He spoke rapid fire in maddeningly incomplete sentences as he gently removed the necklace and set it on a felt pad.

"Old all right," he continued, dispassionate as if he were performing an autopsy. "Hand cut by an amateur. Restrung, nice clasp. Large beads of graduated size but not matching to either side of the main bead. Reddish color, various grades of transparency." He turned the beads one by one. "Hmm."

"Are they valuable?" Helma asked.

"Depends." He switched on a light over the counter and put a glass to his eye. "Amber's not uncommon. I'm no expert. I read." He tapped the library book. "Anyone or anything. Learning all the time. Used to have a photographic memory when I was a kid; now the mental ink fades sometimes." He laughed shortly and picked up the necklace, examining the largest bead in the center.

"Baltic amber," he said. "Pick it up on the beaches after a good storm. You get plant hairs from oak buds in Baltic

amber. Star shaped. No other amber has that.'' He continued examining each bead, saying between his *mm-hmms*,
''Ever heard of the Amber Room? Built in the seventeen
hundreds for some mucky muck in Russia. Worth hundreds
of millions. Dollars. Well, the whole room disappeared during World War Two. Think about *that*.''

''Then these beads aren't exceptionally valuable?''

''I wouldn't say so. A curiosity maybe, because of the
cut. Value's increasing all the time, though, like everything
on this earth we're using up. A lot of fakes out there.''
He'd worked his way almost to the clasp. ''Are you trying
to sell them?''

''No. I'm just curious.''

''This is odd,'' the jeweler said in a distracted voice,
holding the necklace closer to his face.

''Did you find an insect?''

He was too absorbed to answer, making grunts and humming sounds in his throat as he examined the amber beads,
pulling them closer to his face and the lamp light. ''I have
to get a better glass,'' he said. ''Right back.'' He left Helma
alone in the shop as he stepped through a curtain to the
rear.

She waited, gazing for a while at a display of crystals,
and then she picked up the blue jeweler's cloth from the
counter and dusted off the pieces.

The jeweler returned with a piece of battered equipment
that resembled a lighted microscope. He ignored Helma,
setting it up on the counter and fussing with the focus.

''Do you know the necklace's history? Has it been altered at all?''

''My aunt's worn it since the nineteen twenties when it
was restrung. No other modifications have been made that
I'm aware of.''

''You ever seen tortoiseshell?'' he asked.

''Actual or the plastic?''

"Actual. Been around forever. Take layers from the hawksbill turtle's shell, heat them up, and mold them into shapes, beads, buttons."

"You're saying this isn't amber; it's tortoiseshell?"

"No. There's also celluloid," he went on. "Been around since the eighteen hundreds, cheaper than tortoiseshell, it can be made to mimic tortoiseshell, or amber."

"Then these beads are celluloid?" Helma asked.

"No." He counted the beads on the necklace, moving his lips as he did. "Thirty-seven beads, thirty-one straight amber, six altered." Three on either side of the clasp where they wouldn't be noticed. Darker. Lower grade amber.

"Why were they altered? To enlarge them?"

"Not exactly. Take a look."

Helma peered through his microscope, blinking at first in the bright light until she brought the bead into focus. "What am I looking for?" she asked.

"Keep examining the bead, you'll see it."

She stared, first seeing only the amber-colored bead, cloudy, its facets throwing off different degrees of light, then as her eyes adjusted, she looked *into* the bead until she saw the cord that ran through its center and on either side of that two shapes were visible, both the same, one slightly smaller than the other, yet both only shadows.

Helma leaned back and blinked, readjusting her vision. "Six of the beads are like this?"

He nodded, lowering his face to the microscope again.

"What is it? What are the shadows?"

"Have to cut the beads open to be sure. Light a match to them, maybe. Amber smells like pine if you apply heat, and if it's celluloid, it's flammable big time. First used it to make cue balls but they'd explode in a hot game. Ha ha. Joke."

"No thank you. Please just venture a guess."

"Gems. A hole was drilled into the amber beads, the gems inserted, then filled with a celluloid resin and sanded smooth. Forgers do the same thing with insects. Lizards used to be popular, poor little fellas. Some of those guys are so good an expert has trouble detecting the fake. This one isn't as clever.''

"Please," Helma said. "What kind of gems?"

"Diamonds."

"Diamonds!"

"Yep. Well, I'd want to cut one open. But that's what I'd say. Diamonds. What do you think of that?"

Helma was too startled to respond. Aunt Em's necklace had been restrung by a man who died in a gangland murder, a man who'd probably been in many nefarious dealings, whose life had been built around subterfuge and shady transactions. He'd given the necklace to Aunt Em, restrung, so she could wear it always. He'd given it to her and then he'd died and she'd disappeared, a fortune innocently hanging around her neck for seventy years.

Until now.

"So what do you think?" the jeweler was asking her.

"I beg your pardon?"

"If I send this to Seattle? Have it examined by the pros. Get a certificate."

"I'll take it with me. Thank you, though. You've answered several questions."

"That's all I have: questions. There's a story behind those beads. Take care of them. Big bucks there."

"I will," Helma said as she tenderly replaced the necklace in the velvet box. "Thank you again."

"Sure. I'll stop by the library to see what you decided to do with it."

"I'll look forward to seeing you," Helma told him, holding the velvet box tightly in her hand as she left the store.

A yellow parking ticket flapped on Helma's windshield. "Oh Faulkner," she murmured as she tore it off and stuffed it in her purse.

Aunt Em had said she'd gone out with Bronus. Out where? She knew where he lived; Aunt Em had pointed it out on their way to the library the day before; a Victorian house near the college that had disintegrated into student housing, bicycles on the porch, a broken railing, the only landscaping overgrown rhododendrons.

Helma drove toward the college, the amber necklace in her purse on the seat next to her, touching her leg. She wouldn't let it out of her sight again.

No cars were parked in front of the fading Victorian, no bicycles leaned against the porch railings, and the front door was closed in the warm day.

Helma got out anyway and walked up the sidewalk to the porch. Barking sounded from inside the house, growing in intensity the closer her approach, turning frantic as she knocked on the smudged and scratched door.

She knocked three times, counting to twenty-five between each series of three knocks. No one answered; even the dog finally quieted, receding deeper into the house with a few growls to remind her he was still on the job.

Bronus's house was only five blocks from Ruth's and next she drove there. Max, Ruth's gray cat, sat in an open window. Its front paws were hanging over the sill and its rear was still inside, resting, Helma knew, on Ruth's kitchen counter.

She rarely visited Ruth's house, which was chaotic in the best of times: the single bedroom turned into a studio, the living room serving as the bedroom, and every other possession crammed into the kitchen, so disorienting to Helma that she felt like the floors were askew.

The door was open, revealing Ruth standing in front of her stove, barefoot, toasting a marshmallow on a fork over a flaming gas burner.

"Come on in," she said when she saw Helma.

"Lunch?" Helma asked, nodding toward the marshmallow and taking a single step inside.

"Breakfast."

"I believe it's on fire."

"Just the way I like 'em," Ruth said, turning the fork so the flames blackened the marshmallow evenly. "What's up? It must be serious for you to show up *here* unannounced."

"Aunt Em's gone off with Bronus and she left her amber necklace behind."

"Well, golly gee, call the police," Ruth said, biting the flaky black marshmallow.

"I intend to. Did she happen to tell you where they were going?"

"Nope. Never mentioned it." Ruth turned off the burner. "Let her have a little room, Helma. You hover over her like she's some kind of misguided teenager."

"This is different."

"How? She has a date and you don't?"

"That isn't fair."

"You're right; it isn't. Sorry." Marshmallow ash clung to her lips. "All you have to do is whistle, you know and he'd come running. You know how to whistle, don't you? You just purse your . . ."

"Ruth, this is serious," Helma interrupted.

"So quit jerking around and tell me what's up."

"When I found her amber necklace I took it to a jeweler and six of the beads have been altered . . ."

"Yeah?" Ruth asked, her interest piqued.

"They were drilled out, gems were inserted in the spacings, and then a celluloid resin poured into the holes, sealing them inside."

"Gems?"

"The jeweler says they're diamonds."

That fact *did* strike Ruth silent. She let her marshmallow

fork clatter to the countertop and Max her cat turned from his perch in the window and hissed. Finally, Ruth speculated, "The guy who murdered Binder knew about the diamonds. That's why they were after her."

"I don't believe Aunt Em is aware the diamonds exist," Helma added.

"She's with Bronus? Where?"

"That's what I'm attempting to discover. No one's home at his house. I'd hoped you knew. We have to find her."

"You think Bronus is the suitcase snatcher? He's tall."

"I don't know, but he's been very attentive to her since she arrived," Helma told her. "May I use your telephone to call the police?"

"You have to ask? Go ahead."

If Helma hadn't already known where Ruth kept her telephone, she wouldn't have found it. It sat on the seat of a chair beside her kitchen table, a damp bath towel draped over it.

Wayne Gallant wasn't in. "Surely you can radio him," Helma said. "Or page him."

"I'll try. What message shall I give him?"

"If you contact him within the next ten minutes, ask him to call Ruth Winthrop's house; after that, the library."

Across from her, Ruth raised her eyebrows, mouthing "the library?"

"Is this an emergency?" the receptionist asked.

"Yes, it is," Helma assured her. "Your cooperation is appreciated."

Ruth had pulled sandals from beneath her sink and sat on the floor strapping them onto her feet. "Where did the diamonds come from? Definitely not the old country, I'm guessing."

"When Aunt Em lived in Chicago during the twenties, she may have been deeply involved with the criminal element."

"So you hinted in the chief of police's chambers yesterday. What do you mean 'deeply'? Are we talking 'intimate,' like some gangster's lover? Was she or wasn't she?''

Helma considered the question. Aunt Em's story went against all Helma had ever believed about her favorite aunt: her generous and genteel life, her diplomacy and discretion. But not for a moment had she doubted Aunt Em's words as she'd silently wept over the photo of the St. Valentine's Day Massacre. Aunt Em had been young, a runaway teenager actually. Her perceived culpability in his death had changed her life forever.

"She was," Helma finally said. "Her lover had the necklace restrung for her. He was involved with a mob and I suspect that's when the beads were altered. But he died shortly afterward."

"He obviously told somebody about the diamonds. They were loot from a heist, I bet. Why wait seventy years to go looking for them?"

"Aunt Em disappeared and she hadn't used her real name in Chicago. It may have taken seventy years to find her."

"I bet they found her on the Internet. Our shoe sizes are on the Internet. Some punk—maybe her charming Bronus—put in the phrase 'diamonds and amber' and up popped your aunt's name."

Helma glanced at her watch. Nine minutes had passed. Obviously the chief wasn't about to call. For the briefest moment she tarried over the memory of her conversation with Wayne Gallant in the police station waiting room. Arizona?

"What are you smiling about?" Ruth demanded. "I thought we were looking danger up the nose."

"A conversation is all. I'm going to the library via the parks."

"I'm coming with you," Ruth said. "You look out one side of the car and I'll look out the other."

Bellehaven was renowned for its plentiful parks. Helma chose those with distinguishing features: edging the water, waterfalls, exceptional sculptures, wondering where else Bronus might have taken Aunt Em, dreading the answer.

"Bleaker and bleaker," Ruth said as she waved to a group of boys playing touch football on a grassy field in Center Park. "Why stop at the library?"

"I told Chief Gallant to phone me there," Helma told her. "Besides, I left without explaining the situation."

"You've kissed the guy, right?"

"That's personal," Helma told her.

"Okay, I'll take that as a yes. So why don't you call him Wayne? W-A-Y-N-E. 'Chief Gallant,' geesh." She gazed out the window. "Do you think I could lose five pounds by next week?"

"You don't need to lose five pounds."

"Five inches off my height is more like it. This guy's two inches shorter than I am."

No messages from Wayne Gallant awaited Helma at the library. Ms. Moon sat in her office and when she spotted Helma through her open door she beckoned to her. Papers were spread across her desk and Helma recognized the answer sheet of the Bert and Lamb test.

"How do you feel about aromatherapy?" Ms. Moon asked.

"I have no opinion."

Ms. Moon bit her lip. "That's a 'd' then," she said, darkening a circle with her pencil.

"Helma does believe in chemotherapy, though," Ruth interjected.

"Oh, hello Ruth," Ms. Moon said, her enthusiasm waning. "I saw your new show last month. You do use . . . interesting color combinations."

"I strive to meld the complexities of my aura with those of the universe," Ruth told her in apparent seriousness.

"The result isn't always harmonious. Is that what you mean?"

"Yes, certainly."

"Excuse me," Helma broke in, "but an unforeseen emergency has arisen. I'm forced to be absent from work the remainder of the day."

"If you truly listen to the world," Ms. Moon said, squaring her shoulders and raising her chin, "you'll discover that there are very few unforeseen emergencies. Signs always proceed them. You may as well have taken off the entire week like you'd originally planned."

"Excuse me, Helma," Pamela, one of the pages said, standing in the doorway of Ms. Moon's office, "there's a man here to see you."

"Thank you," Helma told her. At last, Wayne Gallant had received her message.

## ❧ chapter eighteen ❦

# A LONG WALK

It wasn't Wayne Gallant waiting for Helma in the public area of the library; it was Bronus Muszkaviczas. Helma glanced to the right at the book stacks, to the left at the periodical area, and ahead of herself at the clutch of computers. "Where's Aunt Em?"

" 'Fess up," Ruth, who'd followed close on Helma's heels from the workroom, added. "What have you done to her?"

"Nothing, I . . ."

"The chief of police will be here in a few moments," Helma said. "He'll want to ask you a few questions."

"Although," Ruth interrupted, placing one hand on her hip and frowning, "I suppose if you'd done something wicked to Helma's aunt, you wouldn't rush right over to brag about it to her, would you?"

"Why would I hurt your aunt?" Bronus asked, taking a step back from the two women and nervously brushing his blond hair off his forehead. Helma noticed his watch: an inexpensive digital Timex. She was surprised; she would have expected Bronus to prefer analog.

"I just came to get a sweater for her," Bronus finished.

"Where is she?" Helma asked again.

"At Saul's Deli."

"You left her there alone?"

"No, she's with Douglas. They're waiting for me. She said you'd have a sweater she could borrow."

"Douglas," Helma repeated.

"Yes, with Douglas. She's fine. *Do* you have a sweater?"

"Douglas, your roommate?"

"He's not my roommate. I met him up at the college."

"But the first night you brought him to meet Aunt Em," Helma protested, "when she made the *kugelis*, you introduced him as your roommate."

He frowned. "No, Celine's my roommate." He snapped his fingers. "I'm sorry. I was probably speaking to your aunt in Lithuanian."

That was true; he had been. Helma had been expecting Bronus's roommate and from the gist of his Lithuanian conversation, when she thought she'd heard a word similar to roommate, that's exactly what she'd surmised: that Douglas was his roommate, not Celine.

"Why does Aunt Em need a sweater? Where are you taking her?"

"To the old coal dock. She wanted to walk out on it; she said it reminded her of a breakwall or something in Michigan."

"The breakwall in Pere that extends into Lake Michigan," Helma said. "There's a lighthouse on it. We must find them immediately."

"We don't have to *find* them," Bronus said. "They're at Saul's Deli."

The coal dock was north of Bellehaven, long abandoned. It stretched into the bay and since the road had been bulldozed closed years earlier, visits by the public were discouraged, although not prohibited. The surrounding land was uninhabited, remote, its ownership tied up in old court cases. "Excuse me while I make a phone call," Helma told Bronus.

Helma left them and returned to her desk, pretending she didn't see long-faced Harley Woodworth raising his hand like a student trying to catch her attention. She debated, then quickly tapped out the police station's office number rather than 911. "This is Miss Helma Zukas from the library. Has the chief of police responded to his messages?"

"Not yet, ma'am."

"When he does, please tell him to proceed immediately to the old coal dock."

"Is it still an emergency?"

"Now more than ever," Helma told her.

She grabbed the extra sweater she kept folded on a bookshelf beside her desk and a clean notebook.

Harley Woodworth stood beside her cubicle, twisting a rubber band in his hands. "Helma, I have to explain something before you're told by the . . ."

"I'm sorry, but I'm in a hurry, Harley."

"But this is important," Harley continued. "I'm the one . . ."

"Later," she told him and hurried from the workroom to the public area where Ruth and Bronus stood chatting as if this weren't a matter of life or death.

"Will you please tell me what this is about?" Bronus asked as they hurried to Helma's car. "Douglas wouldn't hurt your aunt."

"If Douglas isn't your roommate," Helma asked, "then who is he?"

"I met him on campus. We hit it off, that's all."

"When did you meet him?" Helma asked as she unlocked the rear door for him. "At the beginning of summer quarter?"

"No, just a few days ago, the same day I met your aunt. Why? What's Douglas done?"

"You'd be surprised," Ruth told him.

"He said he was a teacher," Helma said as they pulled out of the library parking lot, "but did he tell you what he taught?"

"History. American history, I guess because he was writing a paper on Prohibition. An uncle or his father or somebody was involved."

"In Chicago?" Ruth asked. "Please don't say it was Chicago."

"I'm rusty in the history department," Bronus confessed. "Is that where Al Capone hung out?"

"Bingo," Ruth said, lightly slapping her forehead. "Grandma and the Big Bad Wolf."

"Didn't the wolf eat the grandmother?" Bronus asked.

"It depends on which version you read," Helma said, glancing at him in the rearview mirror. "In Grimm, the wood cutter slices open the wolf with his ax and releases the grandmother and Little Red Riding Hood unharmed. In the more sanitized version the woodcutter saves both of them before the wolf can do any damage."

"Right now I prefer the sanitized version," Ruth said, craning her neck to see inside Saul's Deli as Helma braked out front.

Saul's Deli held six people, none of which were Douglas or Aunt Em. Helma didn't even turn off her engine.

"We were sitting right in the window next to that fern," Bronus said as he rolled down his window, clearly puzzled. "Maybe they went to the restroom."

"Both of them?" Ruth asked. "Even the table's been cleaned off."

"Let me go ask," Bronus told them, opening his door. "Something's wrong."

"I agree," Helma said.

They watched Bronus run inside, speak to a waiter, and then raise his hands in frustration. Helma put her Buick in gear, pressed her foot to the gas pedal and pulled away, the rear tires squealing.

"Stop," Ruth shouted. "Are you crazy?" She turned and looked behind them at Saul's. "What about Bronus?"

"We don't know a thing about him, not really," Helma told her, glancing in her rearview mirror and seeing Bronus dash out of Saul's onto the sidewalk, his arms waving. "He could be a partner in this with Douglas, trying to divert us, just like at the airport. He could be Bad Black."

"Who the hell is Bad Black?"

"I graded the personality tests everyone took the other night. Bad Black is the color designation given to a participant who answers the questions dishonestly."

"Yeah? What color was I? Oh, never mind. How do they figure out a Bad Black?"

"There are probably correlating questions built into the test that highlight irregularities."

"Bad Black," Ruth repeated, glancing over her shoulder once more. "But Bronus could be telling the truth, too, you know. Where are you going, to the police?"

"We're going to the coal dock," Helma said, turning north at the corner. "That's where they'll be."

"That's crazy. If Douglas is Bad Black, he wouldn't have told Bronus where he was *really* going. That was just a ploy. They could be anywhere. Maybe he took her out of the country, to Canada."

"No," Helma disagreed. "If Bronus is telling the truth, then so was Douglas. This way, if there's an 'accident' he can appear innocent."

Ruth leaned forward into the seat. "You're saying we're trying to play the sanitized version of the woodcutter here and stop the wolf—or big Bad Black."

"That would be an accurate analogy," Helma agreed. Taking one hand from the steering wheel, Helma unsnapped her purse and reached inside. "Look at the watch on this man's wrist," she said, handing Ruth the cut snapshot from Aunt Em's past.

"Where'd you get this?" Ruth asked, squinting at the picture. "Who got cut out?" Ruth studied the photo, then screeched so loudly Helma jumped. "Em! This little dollie is your Aunt Em!"

"That's right. Check the intact man's wrist," Helma reminded her.

"What about it?"

Helma stopped at a red light, tapping her finger on the steering wheel. "See his watch?"

"Kinda. It looks clunky."

"To me it appears to be identical to the watch worn by the man who took Aunt Em's suitcase at the airport."

"It does?" Ruth tipped the snapshot closer to her window. "Couldn't prove it by me. Didn't this guy know he was supposed to look at the camera? I can tell you one thing, though, *he* did not nab the bag. He'd be a hundred years old by now."

"At least ninety, I expect," Helma told her. "That's Aunt Em's friend, Lukas."

"A mobster," Ruth breathed in awe. "You think Douglas or Bronus got ahold of this watch? It's connected to the diamonds? Like a treasure map?"

"It may be," Helma said, passing a car waiting to make a left turn, first glancing in her mirror to be sure there wasn't a motorcycle policeman behind her.

They drove north, close to the shore of Washington Bay, pushing the speed limit. The tide was in and the water was calm, with a breeze that lightly puffed the sails of a boat heading toward the mouth of the bay.

A concrete barrier blocked the old road to the coal dock but to either side of the barrier, vehicles had worn tracks around it. Helma turned off the main road, following the rougher tracks to the right.

"Ouch," Ruth cried as her head bumped against her window. "Why didn't you take the other track? It was better."

"Because it was on the left," Helma told her.

The roadway was paved but heaved and broken from disuse, giving the impression of desolation and abandonment. Weeds struggled up through the cracks. A rabbit dashed across the road in front of them but Helma didn't brake. Ruth screamed.

"You almost hit it," she told Helma.

"I knew he'd make it," Helma told her. "Wild animals aren't hit by vehicles as often as you'd think."

"Then at least slow down, would you?"

Helma raised her foot slightly from the gas pedal. "Every second counts."

"What do you think Douglas would do, push an old lady into the drink?"

When Helma didn't answer, Ruth said, "Okay, go a little faster if you want to. I guess I can hang on."

The road suddenly ended in a bulldozed ridge of dirt stretching from shoulder to shoulder.

Helma slammed on her brakes and the Buick shimmied, slid sideways, then screeched to a stop inches from the barrier. Helma unbuckled her seatbelt and jumped out, inspecting the foot trail that led over the ridge and down to the coal dock. One car was parked in the rough open area which, judging from the beer bottles and fast-food wrappers, was a popular spot for teenage parties. The car was a rental, a white Ford.

"We'll walk from here," Helma said, leaning back into the car for her purse. Ruth still sat in the passenger seat, her seatbelt buckled and hands braced against the dashboard.

"What's wrong?" Helma asked. "We have to hurry."

"I thought it was all over," Ruth said.

"When?"

"Saints protect us," Ruth said in an exaggerated Irish accent, shaking out her hands and then unbuckling her belt. "What do you need that for?" she asked, nodding to Helma's purse.

"Aunt Em's necklace is in it."

"Damn. I was hoping you'd packed something more practical, like a nice shiny little pistol."

Once they climbed the bulldozed ridge, the view opened up before them: high grasses sloping down to the tide flats; here and there across the expanse lay broken and rusted machinery, abandoned where it had faltered years ago. A wind blew ashore, not strong but steady, rippling the grasses and blowing Helma's hair back from her face.

The coal dock extended far out into the bay, an angled structure, over the shallow flats to the deeper waters so long-ago ships could dock against it and be loaded with coal. At its terminus sat a boarded-up building, a hole in its roof discernible from shore.

Two figures were visible in the distance beneath them, just stepping onto the dock. It was obvious who they were: Aunt Em's sturdy shape, the red of her umbrella, and next to her, tall Douglas, his dark hair gleaming. They walked slowly side by side and Helma didn't see any sign that Douglas was forcing her along the dock. He appeared to be a solicitous young man ushering along an elderly relative.

"Call them," Helma told Ruth.

"Why me?"

"Because you have a louder voice than I do."

"Well, thanks," Ruth said, but she cupped her hands around her mouth and shouted, "Douglas! Emily!"

Neither figure turned and Ruth placed her little fingers between her teeth and gave such a shrill whistle that Helma felt it in the bones behind her ears.

"They can't hear you," Helma told Ruth. "The wind and water are against us. We'll have to go after them," and she started down the scooped trail of loose sand that led to the dock.

"Maybe it's better he didn't hear us," Ruth said as she followed Helma. "If Douglas *is* Bad Black, hearing us shouting at him wouldn't exactly convince him to walk Aunt Em sedately back to shore."

"I think it would have," Helma disagreed. "Whatever he's up to, he doesn't want witnesses. If he heard us, the whole incident would turn out to be a big misunderstanding."

"Maybe it still will," Ruth said. She was puffing, one hand against her side, already tired, even with her longer legs.

By the time they reached the dock, Aunt Em and Douglas were two-thirds of the way to the end. Aunt Em appeared to be slowing down, leaning heavily on her umbrella. Douglas held his hand to her elbow.

"Shall I shout again?" Ruth asked. "They could probably hear us this time."

"No. Don't startle them." Helma kept her eyes on Aunt Em and Douglas, pretending not to see the narrowness of the dock, the way the water lapped against it, always in motion, back and forth, back and forth, as if the dock itself were swaying.

"What's she waiting for?" Ruth asked. "This is the moment for her to swing her umbrella and knock him flat."

"She wouldn't have a chance," Helma said, hoping Aunt Em wouldn't think to defend herself.

The first fifty yards of the old dock was built of concrete and beyond that, of heavy creosoted timbers.

Helma took a deep breath as they stepped from concrete to wood. It *looked* solid. Within five feet, the vibration of their steps alerted Douglas; he spun around, his hand still on Aunt Em's arm. He and Aunt Em stood still, side by side, at first a smile visible on Douglas's face and then, as they drew closer, a narrowing of his eyes as he judged their expressions and forthright approach.

Helma stopped ten feet from Douglas and Aunt Em, Ruth a step behind her. They all stood silently regarding one another, the water slapping gently against the pilings beneath them, the wind ruffling their clothes and hair. Beyond the dock, the water stretched away to the islands.

"Are you having a pleasant stroll?" Helma asked Douglas, who kept his hand on Aunt Em's arm, just lightly above her elbow.

"We're enjoying the day," Douglas said calmly, his expression gaining confidence. "Care to join us? We're walking to the end of the dock and back."

"Are you all right, Aunt Em?" Helma asked.

"Certainly I'm all right." Aunt Em stood taller, straightening her shoulders as if offended Helma might have thought otherwise. "But it took you long enough to get here." Her voice was raspy, sounding out of breath.

They all looked at Aunt Em. Confusion played across Douglas's face. He leaned down to gaze into her face, then took an uncertain step back, his hand still on her arm.

"You were expecting us?" Ruth asked.

"Of course. To figure out what he was up to," Aunt Em said, nodding to Douglas. "I knew you two were smart girls."

"I think he wants your necklace," Helma told her.

With no expression of surprise, Aunt Em slowly nodded her head. "A long time ago, I was told to always wear that necklace—unless somebody started asking questions about it; then I should hide it."

"Do you know why?" Helma asked.

Aunt Em shook her head. "But I have a feeling he does,

since he was the one who asked the questions." Again she nodded to Douglas.

"But why, Aunt Em. If you were suspicious of him, why on earth did you come out here *alone* with him?"

"Because I want to know who you are," Aunt Em said, turning to Douglas and gazing at him with a sorrowful expression. "The night you came to Helma's apartment with Bronus, I realized who you reminded me of." She touched her chin. "The cleft, and your eyes. It's so obvious."

"He's Bad Black," Ruth said.

"I don't know what either of you are talking about," Douglas said. But Helma noticed how he swallowed, his eyes shifting from her and Ruth to a strand of seaweed floating in the water.

"You lied on the personality test," she informed him.

"Well, there's a serious crime for you." He looked at the three stern-faced women and Helma saw the instant when he realized it was futile to deny or pretend.

"Where's the necklace?" Douglas demanded. He reached a hand toward Aunt Em's neck but she pulled her collar aside herself, exposing her bare throat.

"Then you have it," Douglas said to Helma. "Otherwise you wouldn't know it was valuable."

"It's in a safe place and you'll never get your hands on it," Helma said.

Douglas's grip tightened on Aunt Em's arm and she winced. "Maybe. What's in your purse?"

"I always carry a purse," Helma told him.

"For her lipstick and things," Ruth said. "You know how we girls are."

"Let's see it." He took a step closer to the edge of the dock, pushing Aunt Em ahead of him.

"Release Aunt Em first," Helma told him.

"Are you Lukas's grandson?" Aunt Em calmly asked,

not even glancing at the edge of the dock only a few inches beyond her foot.

Douglas's lips tightened but he didn't answer and Aunt Em said, "I know you're related. The resemblance is too strong. But you can't be a very *close* relative because Lukas never would have stooped as low as this. He was a good man. He helped me when I was desperate."

Douglas's face reddened. A muscle ticked beneath his eye and he turned to Aunt Em, looming over her. "I *know* that. My mother *knew* that. We had to live with your memory all our lives. A phantom in the house."

"You're too young to be his son," Aunt Em said, staring up into his face.

"My mother was twenty-five years younger than he was. Thirty years younger than you, not that it mattered. You were forever a girl in his mind."

"He *told* you about me?"

Douglas spat the words out, his voice rising so loud that if a boat had been nearby it might have sailed closer to investigate. Long-held rage and resentment was apparent in every syllable. "We only heard bits and pieces until he got senile, enough to make me hate your hold on him. When he started losing his mind, it didn't take much prodding for the story to come out, the whole sordid story. How you were a kid but a gangster's mistress, about the necklace you were always supposed to wear. My father didn't go to the garage on Valentine's morning—didn't you ever wonder if his car *really* did break down? And then he warned you to get out of town."

"I never saw him again."

Douglas gave a harsh laugh. "Oh, he tried to find you. But you'd given him a false name and claimed you were from Massachusetts. You left your apartment but you forgot a book and he swiped it: a little keepsake. Sweet. *The Water Babies*. Only a kid would be reading that book, except when *I* was a kid he wouldn't let me touch it. Your name on the first page was blocked out but I had a hunch so I had it chemically uncovered.''

''And then you hired Peter Binder to find her,'' Helma said.

''Why should I? I could track her down myself on the Internet. It wasn't hard to figure out. I already had your name, her actual maiden name. Zukas, remember?''

''The Internet,'' Ruth said smugly. ''Didn't I tell you?''

''So you and Binder *weren't* partners,'' Helma guessed and saw assent in Douglas's face, in the way he curled his lip at the mention of Binder's name, as if Binder were a contemptible idiot. ''You hired Peter Binder to rob Aunt Em in Michigan,'' Helma went on. ''You told him it would be a simple job: just steal a seemingly ordinary necklace from an old lady. It should have been easy but Aunt Em hit him with boiling raspberry preserves.''

''Ooh, must have stung,'' Ruth said, rubbing her neck and taking a small step in the same direction Douglas was pushing Aunt Em.

''Then what happened?'' Helma asked, aware of Ruth's intent and trying to distract Douglas. ''Was Binder overly curious about the necklace? I'm guessing that it was a surprise to you when he followed you to Bellehaven, wasn't it? Was he trying to cut in on the caper?'' Helma held Douglas's eyes, aware of how small Aunt Em appeared next to him, how fragile.

''Caper?'' Douglas said, frowning.

''The plot, the loot, the treasure,'' Helma explained.

''Oh.''

''Did Lukas have a watch with pieces of turquoise on the band?'' Helma asked Aunt Em.

''The watch,'' Aunt Em said. ''Weren't we talking about a watch with that nice chief of police? Turquoise, oh yes.

It was gaudy but Lukas loved to show it off. It was in the picture I showed you.''

"Father to son," Ruth said. "So you're not only Bad Black and a murderer, but the suitcase thief, too."

"And you ransacked my apartment," Helma added.

"Not at all like Lukas," Aunt Em said sadly. "He never would have threatened a woman. It's a blessing he didn't live to see this. His own son."

"Stop talking like he was a saint," Douglas told her. "He was a cheap gangster."

"Did you ever stop to think that maybe in that world, he *was* a saint?" Aunt Em reprimanded.

"No," Douglas said abruptly.

"You realized Binder had followed you and Aunt Em to Seattle," Helma went on, "and so you gave him the task of stealing Aunt Em's purse at the airport while you went after her suitcase. When that was unsuccessful, you killed Binder in front of my apartment as a diversion so *you* could finish the job. You wanted to be rid of him, anyway."

"Whew, pretty hard core," Ruth said. She was an arm's reach from Aunt Em.

"Lukas couldn't forget me?" Aunt Em asked.

"You were the girl of his dreams," Douglas said sarcastically.

"He loved me? I didn't know that." She tsk-tsked and patted Douglas's arm. "You poor boy. And your mother, too. I'm so sorry I was the bane of your lives. You must have been miserable."

"Well, he's dead now; the diamonds are small compensation."

"I don't have any diamonds," Aunt Em said, "but if I did, I'd certainly give them to you. That's such a sad, sad story." Just the slightest smile played around her lips. "Lukas was a haunted man."

"You do have the diamonds," Douglas told her. He glanced sharply at Ruth, who took a casual step back. "I guess your loving niece here forgot to mention them. My father knew all about them; his best friend told him how he'd hidden them inside the amber beads, up near the clasp so they wouldn't be noticed. It's funny nobody bothered to tell you, isn't it?''

"Not really," Aunt Em said. "There were a lot of things they kept from me."

He pushed Aunt Em another step closer to the water and said to Helma, "I've been watching you; you wouldn't have risked coming out here unprepared. Hand them over."

"Not until you release her," Helma told him.

He pushed Aunt Em again and one of her feet momentarily swung out over the water. "I'll do it," he threatened. "I mean it."

"God, Helma," Ruth said in a low voice, "that water's so cold. It could kill her before we pulled her out."

Aunt Em didn't hear her but Douglas did. "That's right. Now give me the necklace."

"I will, but first, plant Aunt Em's feet firmly on the dock and let go of her."

"Give it to him, Wilhelmina," Aunt Em said. "I've had the responsibility of it long enough. It's only sad memories. He can have it with my blessings."

Helma pulled the velvet-covered box from her purse and held it out to Douglas.

"Take it out of the box," Douglas ordered.

She did, holding it so the necklace draped across her palm, each bead glowing, even those she knew now were altered.

"That had better be the right necklace," he said.

"It is," Helma and Aunt Em said simultaneously.

Helma handed the necklace slowly across the expanse to Douglas, while just as slowly, his eyes never leaving Helma's hand, he released Aunt Em, pushing her forward. The amber gleamed from within itself in the midday sun, reddish gold drops of light dangling between Helma and Douglas. Helma held her breath, trying to watch Douglas's outreaching hand and Aunt Em at the same time.

As Douglas's fingers touched the necklace, just as Helma released it from her fingers, Aunt Em swung her umbrella and struck Douglas full on the wrist. She grunted with the force of her swing. For an instant, the amber necklace hung suspended, defying gravity. Then it flew through the air in a flash of gold and landed with a splash in Washington Bay. Seagulls flew up from somewhere, screeching.

"Why you . . ." Douglas cried, reaching for Aunt Em.

But Ruth bent low and with an inarticulate shout, rammed into Douglas, butting him with her head and knocking him sprawling to the boards of the dock. Helma desperately lunged for Aunt Em, but at that very moment Aunt Em fell face forward, the length of her body balanced on the edge of the dock, seconds and inches from falling into the bay.

"Aunt Em," Helma cried, trying to reach her but Ruth and Douglas were in her way. "Aunt Em," she cried again. "Don't move."

There was no answer. Aunt Em's head hung over the water.

Finally, she climbed over Douglas, who now lay prone with Ruth pushing a comb into his back and threatening, "I mean it, one smart move and I'll pull the trigger."

Helma dropped to her knees beside Aunt Em and gripped her shoulder, her heart pounding. Was it a stroke?

"Wait," Aunt Em said in a muffled voice. "I've almost got it."

And then Helma peered over the edge of the dock where Aunt Em was fishing for the necklace with the handle of her umbrella. "Amber, *real* amber, floats in salt water," she told Helma, "although this is sinking fast."

"That's because there's more to some of the beads than

amber," Helma told her, taking the umbrella from her and snagging the sinking necklace. She carefully pulled it out of the water and gave it to Aunt Em, who kissed it once before she sat with it cradled in both her hands. "There really are diamonds?"

"Yes," Helma told her. "They were sealed in long ago, probably when your . . . lover had the necklace restrung. Do you know where they came from?"

Aunt Em shook her head, drying the beads on her skirt. "They changed money into 'merchandise' sometimes."

"I thought you wanted Douglas to have the necklace," Helma said.

"Never," she said simply. "It's mine. It's been mine for over seventy years."

"Look who's coming," Ruth said, nodding towards shore.

"Your goose is cooked now," Aunt Em told Douglas.

There was no mistaking the shoulder-swaying walk of Wayne Gallant. Beside him strode Bronus and they were just setting foot on the coal dock.

Helma stood and waved.

"Then Douglas *didn't* plan for Binder to be on the same flight as him and Aunt Em?" Helma asked.

Wayne Gallant had removed his jacket and spread it over a corner of an unfathomable hulk of machinery rusting in the tall grass. Helma sat on it, facing the water and the coal dock, breathing in the rich salty odor of the sea. The chief hunkered in front of her, twisting a strand of grass between his fingers. His hair was fluffed by the breezes.

"No," he said. "Douglas thought he and Binder were finished. He didn't count on Binder being so curious—or as avaricious as himself."

"Douglas isn't a teacher from Spokane, is he?" Helma asked.

Wayne Gallant shook his head. "He's from Florida, but

I think we'll discover he's been on the road the past month or so tracking down your aunt.''

When the wind turned, Helma heard snatches of Lithuanian as Aunt Em dramatically shared her experience on the dock with Bronus, with interjections in English from Ruth. An ambulance had arrived but Aunt Em had refused to ride in it to the hospital although she *had* allowed two of the EMTs to carry her from the coal dock to the end of the trail where Helma's car and the police cars were parked.

"And when Aunt Em stabbed Binder with her hat pin," Helma surmised, "he was doubly determined to be part of Douglas's plan. Douglas was desperate to get rid of Binder before he did something stupid like walk up to my apartment, knock on the door, and demand the necklace."

"That makes sense," Wayne Gallant agreed. "Douglas had other plans."

"Douglas couldn't restrain Binder with words, though," Helma said. "That's probably what they were quarreling about in the parking lot that night. But Douglas *was* prepared: his cellular phone weapon took forethought.''

"Premeditation," the chief said and looked away. Helma shuddered, wondering who Douglas had had in mind when he fashioned his weapon.

"The reason Aunt Em was so preoccupied with the past," Helma said, "is because Binder opened up all those memories when he tried to rob her in Michigan. That crime reminded her of the criminal life she'd known in Chicago. She'd buried her history for seventy years." She looked at Wayne Gallant. "She said her life has been a penance since Chicago."

"That's a tough punishment," he said. "Maybe she'll be able to let it go now." He looked at Helma and grinned. He raised his eyebrows. "Do you really know how to whistle?"

"Whistle?" Helma repeated. "I can't . . ." She gazed

into his twinkling eyes. "Well, maybe. If I had a blade of grass."

He passed his hand over a tuft of long grass and chose one blade from its center. "Will this do?"

Helma caught the end of the blade between her two thumbs, surprised that her fingers formed the complicated stance without effort, holding the blade taut. "My brother taught me," she said. "I wasn't very old. I don't know . . ."

"Go ahead," he urged her.

Helma held her hands close to her mouth, smelling the grass's sweet fragrance. Then she took a deep breath, pursed her lips, and blew against her thumbs, her cheeks filling.

A high, sweet note filled the air, floating across the sloped land like birdsong. The note held until the blade of grass broke before Helma's breath ran out. She removed her hands from her mouth and flexed them, dropping the broken blade. She smiled. "That was good, wasn't it?" Helma asked Wayne Gallant.

"That was excellent. Congratulations." He grinned at her and rose. "I guess I'd better get back to the office and tend to business."

Helma stood, too, removing his jacket from the machine and brushing it off. She could see Ruth, Aunt Em, and Bronus sitting on the ridge near the cars, all three facing the water as if they were simply enjoying the day. Puffy clouds hung along the horizon but the sun was warm, the breeze cool. Sweet and sour, Helma thought for no reason.

"About Arizona," the chief said as he reached for his jacket.

"Yes?" she said, standing very still, the jacket held between them.

"I've decided." In the folds of the jacket, his hand touched hers. "I'm staying in Bellehaven."

"I'm glad," she told him, taking a small step closer.

## ❧ chapter nineteen ❧

# ONE MONTH LATER . . .

**"T**oo bad you had to be in court," George Melville told Helma as she opened her umbrella and set it on the floor with the others to dry. "The project's canceled and the Moonbeam's in a snit. Every single test scored a big bad Bad Black."

"But how could that be?" Helma asked him, unbuttoning her coat.

George looked both ways in the workroom, then in exaggeration over both shoulders. "Tell me," he said in a low voice, "did you find a folder titled 'top secret' on your desk? With an anonymous note attached?"

"It sounds familiar," Helma told him. "Did you?"

"Me and every other Jake and Jill in this joint. I think it was an inside job."

"But who's responsible?" Helma had new respect for the astuteness of the Bert and Lamb test developers. She'd allowed Ms. Moon to take the test for her as she'd threatened to and the verdict had legitimately been Bad Black.

"Who cares? Administration by personality color has been derailed, that's all that counts." His grin faded. "We're safe until the next wave of ideas rolls over her."

He followed Helma to her cubicle, which was unusual

for George. Helma stepped inside her square of space and stopped.

There on her desk sat a rectangular, single-layer cake, frosted with white frosting and decorated with a face peering out through thick chocolate jail bars, gripped by little pink frosting hands.

Helma stared at it in surprise, then looked up to see most of the library staff gathered around her cubicle wearing pointy hats, each and every one of them black.

"Thank you," Helma told them. "I think."

"How did you plead?" Eve asked.

"It was Officer 087's word against mine," Helma told her.

Eve gasped. "Do you have to go to *jail* over a red light? I don't know if I've ever heard of a librarian, not a *real* librarian, going to jail."

"It was a yellow light, not red," Helma corrected.

"There has to be somebody," George said. "I'll look it up after we eat."

"Not jail," Helma explained, reaching for the knife that sat beside the cake and making the first cut, preserving the jailed figure in the center. "I've been sentenced to fifty hours of community service at the mission. I've always been curious about its operation."

Helma gave the first piece of cake to Harley Woodworth, who'd been surprisingly meek since the police had matched the partial fingerprint lifted from the rose on her doormat to a set Harley had requested the police take two years earlier in a preemptive strike against potential kidnappers.

"I can't figure out what came over me," Harley had apologized to her, confessing also to the daisies and snapdragons. Helma didn't understand either, but she was surprised to discover that when he withdrew into humbled silence, she actually missed Harley's gloomy observations which had, by comparison, improved the tenor of her own days.

Now she tried to be conscious of Harley but so far her acts of courtesy had only made him more tongue-tied. He'd denied any knowledge of the hang-up phone calls Helma had received, and so had Douglas, although Helma had doubted his denial, suspecting that Douglas had been trying to catch Aunt Em alone in Helma's apartment. Since the calls had been made from a pay phone, she'd never know. Ruth had blamed Wayne Gallant's ex-wife, who'd left town a week after Douglas's arrest, "back to her cave," Ruth had claimed.

"Am I too late?" a voice asked.

It was Ruth, bearing the gift of a black and white striped t-shirt. "Here you are. This is to wear during your sentence. It oughta endear you immediately to some of those guys that hang out at the mission."

"Is Aunt Em with you?" Helma asked, cutting Ruth a piece of cake.

"Your mother took her and Mrs. Whitney over to the complex to measure for curtains."

The two women planned to share a two-bedroom apartment in Helma's mother's complex, one floor below Lillian, if they could ever agree on their furnishings. They'd failed so far to find a cat "exactly like Boy Cat Zukas," although both Helma and Bronus had driven them to the Humane Society and down the back alleys of downtown Bellehaven.

"Can you cut me another piece?" Ruth asked. "Paul's waiting out front. If he doesn't want it, I'll eat it."

Helma did, covering it with a napkin. It had been three weeks and Paul from Minnesota was still in Bellehaven. Ruth reluctantly glowed, complaining every time she saw Helma that, "it simply can't and won't work. No way."

Helma had stopped commenting, although she did still politely listen.

When the festivities had ended and Helma had removed all the cake detritus and washed off her desk top, her telephone rang.

"I just heard about the community service hours," Wayne Gallant said. "You're going to work at the mission?"

"That's correct," Helma told him.

"I don't think it's . . . I mean, well, if you need the money to pay the fine, I can . . ."

"I have the money," Helma interrupted. "I'm not paying the fine because I did nothing wrong. The city can punish me but they won't profit from it. It's a matter of principle."

"The mission, eh?"

"Yes, I'm looking forward to making a difference." Helma wasn't sure but she thought she heard a chuckle on the other end of the phone.

"When do you begin?" he asked.

"Tomorrow evening."

"All right then, Miss Zukas," he said. "May I invite a condemned woman out for a last meal?" He paused. "Just the two of us. At my apartment?"

"I'd be delighted," Helma told him.